Crash Philosophy

First Collision

Mature Content

The stories within this anthology are created as works of fiction. Some of them contain mature content and deal with intense emotional, psychological, and occasionally physical situations. All stories handle the content with the utmost care, kindness, and discretion. However, due to the sensitive nature of some of these stories, readers may choose to skip them due to personal triggers or preferences.

The stories that deal with sensitive and emotional issues will be identified with an asterisk (*) in the table of contents and before each story in the main text. The sensitive topics that these stories address are: loss of a child, sexual abuse, and suicidal depression. If any of these subjects are mentally or emotionally triggering for the reader it is advised that these stories should not be read.

If you are triggered and need support, please reach out to the following groups for assistance:

Suicide Prevention Lifeline: 1-800-273-8255
RAINN National Sexual Abuse Line: 1-800-656-4673

Nerdy Things Publishing and all authors and contributors support and advocate for mental health services. If you are in need of services, please seek support from a mental health care professional.

Crash Philosophy: First Collision

Table of Contents

Introduction................. i

Choose by Setting
Location One: Apocalyptic Wasteland

Location Two: Evil Laboratory

Location Three: Human Mind

Location Four: The Ocean

Location Five: The Triassic

Choose by Character

Character One: Alien

Character Two: Clown

Character Three: Imaginary Friend

Character Four: Kaiju

Character Five: Robot Assassin

Introduction

If you checked the back cover, or the table of contents, and asked yourself, "What the hell is going on with this anthology?" Allow me to explain. Several years ago, I wanted to do an anthology about dinosaurs. But, in trying to think of a way to make the anthology unique, it wasn't clicking. I couldn't think of a way to create an anthology that excited me enough to take on the immense challenge of recruiting authors, getting covers designed, and everything that goes into the process. So I sat on the idea. Then it came to me: let's put the dinosaurs in unusual settings! Places you'd never expect to find them. From there, I felt a desire for more. The desire to make this an expanding universe that could grow and empower the reader with choices. That desire is what became *Crash Philosophy*: the ability to choose your character and setting, then get a unique story combination.

With so many authors writing for these combinations, you should jump around! No one should read this book from cover to cover. Jump around, try different possibilities, live the varying tones from different authors. If you like a specific author, hop to their other stories. The experience of *Crash Philosophy* can be different based on how you choose your combinations. As you read, some stories even have connective tissue. You may discover a connected reading experience.

Also, when I mentioned an expanding universe, it wasn't a cool selling point that sounded like a solid marketing hook. It's real and you have a voice in how it expands! Head to CrashPhilosophy.com to vote on the next character and setting that will be introduced in future installments! That's right, we'll add new characters and settings and give you, our readers, the chance to decide what they'll be. With each new addition, the old will interact with the new. Previous characters will step into the new settings and existing settings will be introduced to the new characters. *Crash Philosophy* will keep going as long as readers enjoy the fictional possibilities in front of them.

If you enjoy a particular story, find that author. Most of these writers have published works and social channels. Think of this not just as a reading experience, but a chance to fall in love with new writing.

Thank you sincerely for purchasing *Crash Philosophy* and look for more installments that will expand this literary universe.

Thomas A. Fowler

"Affirmation" by Thomas A. Fowler
An Alien in an Apocalyptic Wasteland

Tan clouds swelled through the skies, filled with sand in a constant storm that covered the sun and suffocated all signs of vegetation. The skeletons of a functional society decayed, remnants of thriving life stripped to naked nothingness.

Two aliens stood in a dry desert. They flinched as their long, gray toes touched the sand. Using their metallic operating consoles, attached to their arms, they activated light armor to cover their feet. They wanted to know the sensation of sand, but the heat caused a painful experience they hadn't ever felt. One shook his boot, getting the stray grains of sand out of his boot. The duo scanned the horizon, using their one, elongated eye to look from left to right, searching for any sign of life. They pulled up monitors. Simon, the taller of the two, used his webbed fingers to review his data.

"This is Earth?" Simon asked.

He stopped, looking at his readouts, covering his face with goggles to avoid fragments of sand from pelting his eye or from entering his wide-open mouth that gaped at the found destruction.

"Where's the life?" Nick asked.

"I told you humans would fuck it up," Simon kicked at the soil.

"There were minor life readings, thought it was because of the distance," Nick looked up.

He searched for a bird, a bug, any sign of biological creatures, even one clinging to life would mean a successful mission, but it seemed that project fail was the only outcome. The Earth's cracked surface trapped the shell of a small centipede's corpse. The earth had split from arid turmoil. With no moisture to keep the soil together, what used to be loam shattered into broken chunks of dust. Nick pulled the centipede corpse out, placing it in a jar.

"Well, tell Home Base we can check back in a few million years?" Simon suggested. "See what comes out of this god damned mess?"

"Yep, give evolution time to reset, hope the next round of inhabitants aren't complete shits," Nick said.

"Cool, let's ditch this turd hole," said Simon. "This party died a while back."

Simon and Nick's ship left the once fertile planet behind, searching for something better.

"Mirage Proximity" by M.M. Ralph
Clown in an Apocalyptic Wasteland

I'm not going to make it.

It's a bleak thought and one I've always tried to keep at bay. You have to. When dust is all that remains of the world that was, the key to staying alive isn't about supplies and resources like you'd think. It's not about what you can find or how you can use it while fighting off who's trying to use you. It's motion and keeping your thoughts light so it's one less heavy thing to carry.

There's no shortage of things to worry on or despair over, but last time I checked, none of that will make finding water or shelter any easier. My aunt used to say something like that, but I don't remember. It's been too many years since I've seen her. The true memories and the daydreams of what I wish have too long mixed together and I don't know which is which.

But I know what I see in front of me is no daydream, no trick of the light or mirage of the heat.

My mouth is hanging open. I can feel the dry, desert air starting to creep down my throat. I know I'm lingering too long, that I shouldn't waste time, but I can't help it.

I've never seen a clown before.

I've heard of them, sure, even saw a picture in a book once. But like the dinosaurs, giant green forests of trees, and even that book, they don't exist anymore. Extinct, I think the word is.

I look around. I see no tracks, aside from the road and those are at least a day old.

I lean closer, not wanting to close any more of the 4 feet between me and... I think it's a "him." I'd seen the mass of rainbow from a distance. I thought it was a blanket lost by the road. I see his chest move, a gentle rising and falling, and I can smell gasoline from where I stand. I feel like a fool. I got too close before I realized what I was doing. I let my guard down at the sight of so much color and I signed my own death warrant.

I know I need to go. I've been in one place too long. Scanning the horizon for any flashes of light or shadows buys me a little time. My instincts are warring against my curiosity, but this thought hits me deep.

I'm not going to make it.

It's like lightning to my brain but I can feel it in the pit of my stomach. As soon as I realized I was seeing a clown, a piece of forgotten time right in my path, I knew I had a shelf life. I had done my damnedest in the face of impossible odds that had taken everyone I knew from me, but I am extinct and out of place in this world— living on borrowed time.

The clown is a harbinger. I know it. I feel it. I freeze despite the desert warmth. I rub my arms to shake the chill.

"Stop the Tuna!" The clown sits up so violently fast that I stumble back a few steps, tripping on the ruts of the road.

My weapon is raised before my ass hits the ground.

He sees me. I should shoot. I have a good angle, I'm propped up on my elbow and my hand is steady. I should shoot— but I don't.

"Who the hell are you?" he says.

"No," I breathe. "Who the hell are you?"

"Where are we?" He asks.

He looks around. He actually took his eyes off of me to look around. I've never seen anyone do that before.

"What are you doing, stop!" I'm almost yelling at him.

"What?" He says.

"I have a loaded weapon pointed at your head." I sit up a little more. "You don't just look away from someone who has a loaded weapon pointed at your head."

"Ah, so I'm out West, where civilization comes to die. Well, that's just great." He starts to get up.

I shift my weight and kick his legs out from underneath him.

"Don't do that," I tell him as he lands hard, a small puff of dust rising up from his large impact.

"What are you doing?" He groans.

"Stay down," I tell him. I haven't taken my weapon off him.

"Look, kid," He stops and finally takes a good look at me. "Jesus, how old are you anyway?"

"Not your business." I don't take my eyes from his but something shifts, more than just repositioning his weight. He's done something with his hands, I don't dare look. His pockets, I never checked to see if he had any or what was in them. I didn't want to get close enough. Again, the thought comes.

I'm not going to make it. This mass of rainbow stripes has done me in.

"Are you with The Tuna?" He asks.

I don't react. I don't move.

He leans forward. "I said, are you with the..."

"No." I cut him off. "Never."

"Ok, that's the first good news I've had all day." From the corner of my eye, I see his hand move. Before I can say or do anything, he raises it to his face. Water sprays from the center of a big, yellow, plastic flower into his mouth.

I can feel my mouth hanging open again.

"You want some?" He holds it out to me.

I am frozen, a statue of shock and disbelief.

"Kid, you can lighten up. I'm not going to hurt you." He smiles.

"Are you real?" I hear myself say. "A real clown?"

He reaches up and presses his red nose in response. Beep. Beep.

I find I'm smiling. The sound is clear, louder than I thought it would be, and bright. There is brightness to the sound that I hadn't expected.

I also didn't expect him to start laughing but he does. He's laughing. It's been so long since I've heard anyone laugh.

"Your eyes are huge!" He laughs. "You should see. You look so surprised."

After a few moments, his laughter becomes unsettling. I look around. Now I've really been out in the open too long.

"Stop that. Too much noise," I tell him. I put my weapon away and get to my feet.

I look past him to see if there is anything else; anything else that might be where the gasoline smell is coming from.

"Looking for this?" He holds up a small, plastic handle with a circle on the end. In the circle is what looks like clear resin.

"What is it?" I ask.

He taps on the circle and the sound is even clearer and brighter than his nose. "Glass." I breathe.

"Yes, it is. And," He puts the glass in front of his mouth and moves it back and forth.

I stare at him, watching his mouth get larger the farther away he holds the glass.

He cocks his head sideways at me. "Barely even a smile?" He asks. "You're a tough critic. A magnifying glass, they call it. It can be useful, but it's also worth a pretty penny. All glass is." He holds it out to me.

"I've never seen it whole before. Out here, if you can find it at all, it's cracked and broken. Just shards, not thick like this." I step toward him to take the glass. My nose confirms my suspicions. "Why do you smell like gasoline?" I ask him.

"The guys who left me out here, they covered me in the stuff and left me with that. They were hoping…" He stops. "Well, I won't tell you what they were hoping I'd do. It's not a very family friendly story. Suffice to say, I need to get out of these clothes and I need to get back to Metal City."

"Because of Tuna?" I ask.

"The Tuna." He says. "It's a group of… well we had a difference of opinion and I need to get back and straighten it out. But first, I need to clean up."

"I can only help you with one of those things. And I can only help you if you give me the glass." I tell him. The value of the glass is not lost on me despite the danger I know in. This can keep me fed and safe for a long time.

"You're the one holding it, ain't ya? It's yours." He tells me.

"Ok, we need to move now. Got to get away from the road." I look around again. "It's too exposed out here."

He takes a step toward me. My weapon is out before his second foot lands.

"What are you doing?" I say.

His hands are up. "You're a jumpy critter, aren't you? There's a lizard on your pack. I was going to…"

"Don't." I tell him. "Don't touch me. Ever."

"I…" He starts.

"Ever," I bark. I quickly un-shoulder my pack. There is a lizard there. I usher it off with a wave of the canteen.

"How long have you been on your own?" He asks me.

"Not your business." I tell him, rolling my shoulders as I prepare to put the pack back on.

"It's not, you're right," He says. "But you're helping me and I'm grate…"

"It's not help," I tell him. "You're paying me. It's not helping if you're paid." I start walking.

"That's not true. Who told you that?" He catches up with me in a few strides. He's big, tall, but also well fed. If he looked less flashy, he might be good protection.

"What?" I quicken my pace.

"You can get paid and still be helping," He says.

"That's not how the world works," I tell him.

"And just how much of the world does a kid in the West know?" He jokes.

"More than you'd think." It's almost a whisper but it's enough for him to hear.

"Tell you what? Let's change it," He says.

"What?" I look at him.

"The world. Let's change it. Let's say you can get paid and be helping at the same time. Let's say it can be both." He looks at me waiting for my response.

I say nothing but keep on walking.

"Ok then," He says, catching up again. "We agree. We're changing the world."

I try to keep from smiling but I can't help it. Everything about today feels different. And then it hits me. He is a harbinger.

I'm not going to make it.

I'd forgotten something my aunt used to say. She used to say that adaptability is how nature survives. I've seen wind change the landscape and I've seen lizards change their skin. Already today I've done at least 7 things I promised myself I'd never do again. When I let the idea settle in and stop trying to keep the thought from my mind, the complete thought comes to me.

I'm not going to make it, not as I am.

I need to change my skin, like the lizards. I need to adapt. When the next thing comes along, I'll adapt to that too.

I'm walking with a clown and a magnifying glass is in my pocket. The day looks nothing like it did when it first started, but my thoughts are lighter than they've ever been. Right now, they weigh nothing at all.

"What's your name?" He asks me.

"Shell," I tell him. It's not my name. It was the shape on the building where I lived with my aunt. I always liked the sound of it, bright and clear.

"Ok, Shell," He says. "It's a whole new world. Lead the way."

"Blessed" by Scott Beckman
Imaginary Friend in an Apocalyptic Wasteland

"You know," Olivia said between laborious breaths. "You could carry the pail once in a while." She walked with it between her knees. The water inside sloshed to and fro with each step, and regularly spilled over the edge to splatter the thirsty ground.

"That's not why I'm here," Blaine said in his typical, disaffected tone. He always walked two steps behind Olivia, never before her. She could feel his eyes on her without looking. He never looked away. Not ever.

They passed the Assaria city limits sign. It still read "Population 665" even though Olivia and Blaine had been its entire population for a long time. There was nobody but Olivia who could change the sign, and she didn't have a mind to.

A loose screen door banged in the wind somewhere in the trailer park to the left; to the right, rusted farming equipment sat like skeletal remains poking up from the dead earth. In the distance, the red brick building that had once been the Assaria Lutheran Church beckoned them home. It was not God's grace that had seen the church through the cataclysm that had leveled the surrounding homes; it had been Olivia's magic.

She set the pail by the front door of the church and took a moment to catch her breath. "I swear it gets farther and farther each day. One of these times, it'll take from sunup to sundown just to fetch the water. There won't be any time left to drink it."

"One of these days."

With only a mote of effort, Olivia felt for the latent energy in all that surrounded her and then, focusing, she zeroed in on the latent energy in the water itself. She used a bit to heat the water until it boiled with such fervor that the pail trembled. "You thirsty?"

"No."

"Fine, me neither. We'll let it cool on its own. No need to use magic where you don't have to. That's a lesson Feichiera taught me, a long time ago."

"I know."

Feichiera had been one of the first to discover magic. She had literally written the book on the subject and had spent much of her life spreading its teachings. Most wizards were students of Feichiera's to some degree, but Olivia had been close enough to call the woman a friend. The calamity that had led up to the war had separated them and Olivia did not know if Feichiera lived or if she had joined the billions of others who had died the day that magic ravaged the surface of the earth with a ferocity, and rage, and terror that made Revelations seem like a children's story by comparison.

A small, dark shape crossed the gray skies far in the distance. Olivia squinted. "What is that, do you think? A hawk?"

"Maybe it is."

Olivia watched a moment longer. "It is. I'm sure of it." The hawk circled away, then dipped down toward the ground. Olivia lifted the hem of her skirt and took the steps to the church's front door. "I think we'd better get ready for company."

She put her own tea recipe— an assortment of Kansas grasses— into four teacups and brought them out to the front porch on a platter. With her magic, she lifted fist-sized globes of water from the pail and slipped them into the teacups to mix with the tea. A blink set the water boiling again.

Olivia settled back in her chair to wait for her guests to arrive. Blaine leaned against the doorframe, arms crossed. Olivia flashed him a smile which he did not return. "Why do you look so dour?" she asked. "We haven't had company in years. You should be excited for the chance to scowl at someone else for a change."

"There's a reason we haven't had company in so long."

Olivia's memories stirred and for a moment, the dead yellow fields that stretched out to all horizons appeared vibrant and green as they had once been. Then the vision was gone.

The strangers entered the Assaria city limits from the east. There were three of them, all in rugged leather garb with heavy backpacks. Two were armed; the woman at the head of the trio had a sword on her back and one of the men behind her carried a bow. The other man had his hands together at his waists, hidden in their sleeves. They approached the church directly.

Olivia smiled and waved. "Hello, and welcome to Assaria, travelers."

The trio stopped a few paces from the porch. They stared, silent. Olivia pointed to the hawk on the archer's shoulder. "I saw your friend there and thought you might be coming. What would you say to a cup of tea? I've just made it so it's nice and hot."

The woman with the sword came forward and the men followed suit. Olivia grinned as they took cups, but when the unarmed man extended his hand for his and a hairless black spider fell from his sleeve on to the porch rail, Olivia's smile faded. "Who are you?" Her voice trembled and she saw in their faces that they heard her fear.

"I'm Gladia," the woman with the sword said. "These are Arco and Velhax."

"I'm Olivia, and this is Blaine. We've been living here since before…well, you know what before. You're our first visitors."

"You're Olivia Stavish, then." Gladia said, setting her cup down on the tray.

"Yes."

"We met once, you and me."

Olivia raised an eyebrow. "Did we? I'm sorry that I don't recall."

"It's all well and good. It was a long time ago. You were still a teacher of magic back then. I was a student in New York, but you came to speak at an event. I couldn't wait to see you. It cost me a hundred dollars for a ticket. A hundred dollars I didn't have at the time, but I borrowed it from my grandmother. I just had to go. You lectured for an

13

hour on magaspa and when you were done, I made up my mind that I would pursue that very discipline."

"So you're a magaspada, then?" Olivia forced a smile. "How grand."

"It was a practical decision, too," Gladia said. The men behind her had not sipped their tea. They only stared at Olivia. "In that time, we were very sought after. All the big companies had to have at least one magaspada in the room for every business dealing. To know the thoughts of those across the table. To influence them."

"Ah, yes. What a terrible shame we didn't know the price we would pay."

"Yes." Gladia smiled. "What a shame."

There was a moment of silence. Blaine cleared his throat and Olivia cast him an admonishing glance. "Why don't you fetch some of the corn I shucked last night? I'm sure our guests are hungry from the road." Blaine frowned but then disappeared inside.

Gladia nodded to the empty doorway. "Who is that, then?"

"Blaine? He's been my companion since the war." Olivia remembered meeting him, the first day after the world shook and the winds blew and all Assaria's citizens were killed by magic— or worse. "I hadn't known him before, but I'm so glad for him. It would be terribly difficult to live this kind of life on my own."

"Yes, I suppose it would be." Gladia took a breath. "Do you know that we can't see him?"

Olivia gripped the arms of her chair white-knuckle tight. She did know, but there was much that Olivia knew that she was so unprepared to face that she had become adept at avoiding them. "What brings you, eh? You've surely come a very long way, and I can't imagine you just wanted to check up on little old me." She tried to turn her grimace into a smile and hoped it worked.

Gladia nodded thoughtfully. "Actually, we did come looking for you. The war destroyed nearly everything, but there are some of us on the East Coast who are trying to rebuild."

"You want me to join you." Olivia shook her head. "I won't do it."

"No, you misunderstand. We haven't come to ask you to join us. You see, we know that it was you who cast the spell that leveled the Midwest and murdered all its citizens. It was war, and we all did terrible things to protect ourselves, but now it has fallen on me to ensure that the civilization we build on the ashes of the last will be allowed to thrive. How can we rebuild it knowing that there are those, like you, with the power to bring it all crashing down again?"

Olivia saw the trio with new eyes; their weapons and their magic. "So it is like that."

The archer dropped his teacup and the other man tossed his casually over his shoulder. Their eyes remained focused on Olivia, as if waiting for her to do something. Gladia reached back for her sword. "I'm sorry, Mrs. Stavish, but there's no other way."

"You won't let me beg? Let me plead for my life? I've been out here for years. I'm not hurting anybody. I won't get in your way."

The sword sang as it slid from its sheath. "There is no other way," Gladia said.

Olivia drew upon the latent energy in the surrounding fields and commanded it to immolate the trio, but the spell faltered. At first, Olivia feared it was Blaine who had stolen the energy from her but, in truth, the strangers had done so and their will proved stronger than hers. Gladia took a step closer and Olivia desperately called upon her own energy, the only source that nobody could take away, but Gladia broke into her mind with magaspada— the same magic Olivia had once taught— and refused to let her. Olivia pushed back and for a brief, elated moment, she knew she was stronger, but then an arrow pierced her shoulder and her mind cracked open, laying itself bare and vulnerable before Gladia's psychic assault.

The final blow came from the third man, who appeared before Olivia with two, long knives in his hands. He thrust them into her abdomen and leaned in close. Spiders crawled about inside his collar and hood. He grinned a wicked grin, then tore the blades out.

Olivia crumbled to the porch floor. More and more of her life left her with each breath. She reached out for someone to hold on to, terrified that she might die alone with the three assassins. In the fields, the ghosts of Assaria's 664 citizens watched and waited. Olivia cried out to them but they did not come. The pain ebbed and flowed, blinding and darkening, and the ghosts turned their backs on Olivia. None would guide her through the world she had made them citizens of. None would show her the mercy she had not shown them.

Blaine took Olivia's outstretched hand and knelt beside her. He looked back with eyes very much like her own.

"I'm dying," she told him. The words did not calm her. They brought on warm tears.

15

"Yes," Blaine said. The features of his face swam with change as each Assarian ghost moved inside him. "You're dying. You come at last to your judgment."

"I would take it all back if I could." She had said these words before. They rang hollow even in her own ears.

"You fear receipt of the gift you gave to countless others," Blaine said. "Embrace it instead. Your pain dies with you. Your suffering ends now."

"Will I have peace?"

"No. There is nothing at all after death." The world darkened until Blaine's shifting face was all Olivia could see. "But nothing is more than you deserve and you are, therefore, blessed."

"Below the Surface" by A.L. Kessler
Kaiju in an Apocalyptic Wasteland

The wind still stirred up the fallen ash off the ground, even five years after the volcano had erupted and took out a third of the world's population. The number of humans continued to drop drastically through starvation and mysterious deaths. Those who survived did so with careful tactics, constantly moving, going back to the nomadic lifestyle, and gathering food and water where they could. Technology disappeared except for main cities, which were disappearing fast, left as sitting ducks to the monsters. The Kaiju.

Named by the Japanese, these strange monsters took over once the ash sky blocked out the sun. Some thought them to be demons that lay in waiting in the pits of the Yellowstone volcano. Some people believed that they were creatures created by chemicals in the air, water, and earth. Others simply didn't care what they were, but knew they needed to be avoided.

I straightened my gas mask as I walked over the gray rock of hardened ash. My caravan of people was two miles back, just outside the old city limit sign. This city was one of the first to go. Its inhabitants were killed almost instantly in the week-long eruption. Below the dusty surface lay bodies of humans and animals, all trapped in the horror of trying to escape too late.

A modern-day Pompeii.

Our goal was to reach the sight of the eruption to see how the Kaiju were being summoned or created. This town, though, was where I had grown up. I'd been on vacation with a friend when the volcano blew. I'd been lucky. My family? Not so much. My mother had been on sight, researching, studying the numbers, the tremors, the signs, to try and warn the rest of the world. It'd all been in vain though. No one believed that the supervolcano would erupt. My father had been home with my brother. I'd swallowed my grief and dedicated my life to studying the Kaiju. There was nothing I could do about the force of nature, but the monsters...they could be killed. They could be stopped.

"Feeling nostalgic, Katie?" My friend's voice sounded almost mechanical in the gas mask as she climbed up on a rock next to me.

I glanced at her. She'd chosen to shave her head at some point during our journey. Easier to maintain, less dust and grime, less sweat, but it didn't take away from her feminine-shaped jaw and her slightly slanted eyes set in olive skin.

"Imagining the rolling hills and green mountains, is all. Any plant life trying to grow back is being choked to death with the water shortage and the ashy atmosphere." I shoved my hands into the pockets of my ragged jeans. "Hailey, this is the first time I've been back."

"The government forbids people from crossing over into this area." She nudged me with her shoulder. "Guess it's a good thing they keep all their men away from here."

I snorted and walked down the sloped land. A 'Welcome' sign hung from a twisted and melted metal rod, the other rod nowhere to be seen and the words long gone. Only my memory told me it was the welcome sign. We'd come this far in cars, but the ash in the air still held too much debris for the engine air filters. From here on, it'd be backpacking up to Wyoming. I adjusted the pack on my back and looked north. When the volcano erupted, the crater took out most of Wyoming and some of Northern Colorado. Denver had disappeared into sunken ground, while the rest of the state was covered in ash. All we needed to do was find the edge of that destruction.

"Suicidal research project." Hailey linked her arm with me and started to skip. "We're off to see the monsters, the wonderful monsters of all," She sang at the top of her lungs, her gas mask distorting the sound.

I tried not to roll my eyes. She was right, of course. The trip was suicidal, but the only way we were going to learn how to defeat the Kaiju was by learning where they came from and how they came into our world.

I'd seen images on the news when the volcano first erupted. No one had expected the crater to be so large, but no one really believed that the supervolcano was actually going to erupt. The edge of the highway disappeared into the hole. The giant, gaping canyon spread over the horizon, not giving us a glimpse of anything on the other side.

"So we're here. Now what?" Hailey dropped her bag near the edge and held her arms out. "All of Denver gone. Not a monster in sight. Do you ever get the feeling that the Kaiju are just a myth? A scary story told to keep our minds occupied with something other than the end of the world?"

"Don't be so dramatic. It's not the end of the world." Except, it would be. The Kaiju were killing off what was left of the human population, volcanic ash still polluted the air with no signs of stopping, starvation killed those who were strong enough to survive everything else. As if on cue, my stomach rumbled. "I doubt the Kaiju are a myth."

Something moved in the fog. My heart skipped a beat. We hadn't seen anything living on the way up here, not a plant, or an animal, not even a cockroach. I grabbed Hailey's arm and motioned to the darkened figure. "Through the fog they came."

"Creatures of ash and fire," She muttered.

"Kaiju." I took a step back as the shadow started to take a humanoid shape.

"With glowing eyes of hell-fire." Hailey grabbed her bag, turned, and ran back down the dusted highway.

I waited, just another moment. The fog started to part and the figure emerged from the fog, walking in the air, even with the cliff of the highway, as if there wasn't ground missing below. Human in shape, but with black, cracked skin with angry orange and yellow burning below; the creature could only be described as a strange monster. Not the typical Kaiju of Japanese culture, but strange nonetheless.

The creature reached a hand out towards me. My chest became heavy as my lungs refused to draw in air. My limbs tingled at the sensation of oxygen being cut off from my brain. I met the glowing eyes set in the almost skull-like face. The hand it reached out stopped short before the creature disappeared back into the fog.

I gasped, sucking in air as I finally remembered how to breathe. I put a hand to my aching chest, drawing in a few deep breaths through the filter of the gas mask. The creature was gone. It was no myth. The Kaiju were real and they were terrifying.

"Katie?" Hailey's voice cut through the terror in my mind.

I turned around to see her wide eyes. "You left me here."

"I was saving my ass. We weren't sent here with any weapons to defend ourselves against them." She waved at the cliff widely.

I nodded. "But it ran off. Something scared it."

"Maybe it was you." There was a slight joke to her voice.

"I doubt that." But something had scared it away. "Let's go make camp." I turned away from the edge. Wind whispered around me, seemingly trying to draw me back to the cliff.

My steps hesitated until Hailey looked back at me. "The gasses are getting to your head. Come on. I want to get set up before dark."

The only difference between day and night was gray and black. Normally, we'd hole up in an old house, but nothing here resembled an old house. I hiked my bag farther onto my back and followed her down the road. The wind kicked up behind us and I swore that I heard voices coming from the caldera. I shook my head. Just the wind.

A mile down the road we found a flat spot to pitch our tents. We removed our gas masks and replaced them with medical gauze masks to give us a break from the tightness of the gas masks. I pulled out my notebook and leaned back so the light of the gas lantern would shine on the page. The light was contained in a glass top, with a cotton wick soaked in kerosene. We only used it sparingly so we didn't have to carry much with us. The two of us had become dependent on the little light during the day. Sleep at sundown, wake at sunrise.

"Making notes already? We've barely gotten a look at the caldera." Hailey yawned and stretched. "We'll start fresh in the morning when we have more time to explore it. I think we'll head down into it first, then start exploring the rim?"

"Rim first, I don't want to go in it until we figure out if there's any activity left in it. Including the Kaiju." I made a quick sketch of what I'd seen. "People say that this is their resting place."

"Yet they show up all over the world." Hailey shook her head. "I really think it's just a scary story. Remember when the world went crazy about clowns showing up? And how it turned out to be a bunch of bullshit spread by fake news?"

That had gotten out of hand, a lot of people had thought it was a publicity stunt. "I don't think that's the case. We don't have fake media anymore. Hell, we don't have media any more. Gone are the days of social connection over the internet. Back to snail-mail that may or may not make it to the cities." I shook my head.

"Word of mouth? Things can get mixed up." She leaned back against her sack.

I shook my head. "Why are you so insistent that they don't exist?"

"Why are you so insistent that they do?" She closed her eyes. "Don't forget to turn out the lamp. I'm going to sleep."

It was her way of telling me the conversation was over. I finished my thoughts in my notebook and put it back in my bag before extinguishing the lamp. I rolled over on my side and closed my eyes.

Something rustled outside the tent and I jumped to my feet. I glanced at Hailey who was still sound asleep. I reached for my gas mask as the noise continued. I removed my gauze mask and put the gas mask on. I unzipped the tent and snuck through the opening before zipping up the canvas door as soon as I was out.

I stood still, waiting. A shuffle came from my left and I turned. I didn't know what I was expecting to be there. Nor did I know what I was going to do if I found a Kaiju or another human there. Nothing moved in the darkness. The wind howled around me, shaking the tent. Maybe it had been the wind. The rustle of fabric could have woken me. But I hadn't heard the wind.

My heart pounded in my chest and sweat beaded on my palms. That same choking feeling from before seized my lungs even with the gas mask on. Dust and ash kicked up around me, creating a white and gray fog in the dark of the night. A screeching sound pierced through the wind, making me cringe. I touched my ears to make sure they weren't bleeding from the insane pitch.

The sound of a zipper came from behind me and Hailey stepped up next to me. "What the hell?"

"Kaiju." I muttered. My eyes scanned over the area, looking for the creatures.

"That sounds like human screaming, not monster." She stood close enough that our shoulders touched.

I could feel her tension through her arm. Ready to run if need be. Her fight or flight instinct was heightened. As researchers, we didn't have anything in the way of weapons. Getting your hands on a firearm was nearly impossible now, and more traditional weapons had basically disappeared.

The noise and wind died down just as quickly as it appeared. I unclenched my hands and looked around the campsite.

"Vents." Hailey broke the silence after a minute. "Heat escaping from underground."

It wasn't out of the realm of possibilities, but that didn't explain the wind. I gave a shaky nod. "Yeah, just nature playing with our heads." We turned back to the tent, but I hesitated slightly.

"Come on, Katie. You can't do anything tonight."

She was right. There was nothing that the night had to offer me; a misstep at the caldera could mean death. Best to do it when we had more light.

We packed up the next morning. Hailey pulled her bag on and looked towards the caldera. "So, we walk the rim? That'll take us what?"

"Depends on how fast we walk, but a few days at the least. We don't have to walk it all, just enough to collect data. I want to take a detour though."

"What? Why? We only have enough supplies for a two-week trip and the nearest city is a two day walk."

"Just a couple miles. My house was close to here." I motioned down the crumbling off ramp. "My mom kept all her research in a lock box."

Hailey raised a brow. "There's at least three feet of ash here."

"It was fireproof." So I hoped. My mom took her research seriously. She pounded in my head that you not only back up your computer files, but you back them up onsite, offsite, and in hard copy— just in case technology died. "And if we can get it, it might give us an idea of what we're dealing with."

Hailey sighed. "Okay, just a couple miles?"

I nodded. "Five miles off the highway."

"That's more than a couple." She groaned.

"If we walk quickly, it'll take use two hours at most. Come on." I started down the ramp, being careful as I climbed over chunks of concrete. "Think of all we can learn if the research survived."

"And if it didn't?"

"My dad had a nuclear fallout bunker. We might be able to get some more supplies."

She gaped at me. "What was wrong with your family?"

"Nothing. They just believed in preparing for the worst. Dad was military; he built the bunker after 9/11. Mom studied volcanos for a living...she believed in preparing for, well...an apocalypse caused by Yellowstone."

Hailey followed me down the road. "And yet all of them were killed."

It sounded harsh, but I knew she didn't mean it that way. "They were killed because they weren't home when it happened."

"How do you know that?"

"Because when I was out visiting you, they went with my mother to Yellowstone. She went up to study the activity that was going on. No one at the site could have survived." Leaving me an orphan at the age of nineteen.

She nodded. "Talk about a passion for a job. Your mother must have really loved it if she was willing to risk her life."

"Yeah, she was obsessed." I chuckled and stopped at the bottom of the off-ramp. Hardened ash had taken over the terrain of the city. What once was a lively city road that led to hotels and subdivisions now lay in gray and black ash, creating a cast of the city. Volcanic rain had continuously wet down the ash and then it dried with the new particles on top.

We hiked through the city making small talk. Hailey hadn't been to Denver before, not when it was a glorious city. She'd ask me questions as we passed something that caught her attention. At one point, we could see the ruins of the stadium and amusement park. We walked down the hill that led into my neighborhood. Most of the houses had collapsed under the weight of ash and debris. My house, though, stood strong with three feet of ash rock at the base.

"Now that's a miracle. Had they been home..."

"They might have survived, but not without the right breathing equipment."

"But your dad was a Prepper, he would have had the gas masks in the bunker." Hailey motioned to the house. "What if..."

"No, they weren't home. Don't try and get my hopes up. Yes, he had the gas masks. But the car is gone, if they had been home and tried to leave, the car wouldn't have made it far."

"No lava paths down here..." Hailey looked around. "I thought the lava took out the city."

"No, the blast and the rain of ash did. The lava flowed away from the city, most of it in the caldera made from the blast and out the side vents."

"Meaning?"

"Meaning we may see some on our way around the caldera, but this part of the city was taken out by ash and debris." Which was good for us, no chance of accidentally stepping into a lava stream under the ash. I walked up and tested the door. Locked. Of course it was locked. I hadn't held on to my key over the last five years, either.

Hailey laughed and I looked back to find her hands on her hips. "What?"

"The windows are busted out. Just climb in."

I looked at the big, bay window. Gone was the glass and the shards that were left on the window were melted into harmless curves. "Well then..." I shook my head and climbed through. Hailey followed. The furniture had a fine dusting of ash on it. The television screen had melted from the heat, long forgotten. We'd watched game shows as a family there.

My heart ached at the empty couch. Hailey put a hand on my shoulder. "Remember what we're here for."

"Research." I nodded and pressed forward. My mom's office was at the back of the house. The further into the house we got, the less ash had settled. It'd been nothing short of a miracle that the lava hadn't come to this side of the highway, that the ash hadn't collapsed the house, and that my mom's office was virtually untouched.

I walked over to the closet and grabbed the lock box off the top shelf. I set it on the ground and dusted it off.

"Amazing that it survived the heat."

"Well, it is fireproof," I muttered and flipped the latches to open it. I held my breath as I raised the lid. What if nothing had survived? I didn't think lock boxes were volcano tested.

Inside lay a notebook with colorful tabs sticking out the side. I let out a relieved sigh. A tape recorder with some mini tapes sat in the box next to the notebook. My mother was diligent about her notes and for once, instead of being annoyed with her organization, I was ecstatic.

"Looks like you've got a lot to go through." Hailey motioned around. "This is fairly secure, why don't we set up camp here?"

"It's an hour away from the caldera."

"So was our last spot." She pointed out. "We have shelter here, in case it rains. The house is still solid. Very little damage from the rain and the ash."

Almost like it had been protected. "Okay, deal. Let's check the bunker and see if we have anything useable down there."

"Do you think there's food down there that would have lasted this long?"

"MREs don't expire. They're gross, but they'll do in a pinch." I closed up the lock box and stuck it in my bag. "Today we study, tomorrow we go back to the caldera and collect data."

"You sound so hopeful."

"My mom predicted that Yellowstone was going to erupt, it just happened earlier than she was prepared for. If there's something that can help us save mankind, it's in her notes."

"I don't think there's a lot we can do against the aftermath of the eruption to save mankind. Your mother's job was to predict the disaster, not figure out how to survive it." Hailey walked out of the room.

I tucked the notebook and tape recorder in my bag before following her out. She stopped in the hall, waiting for me to lead. I headed to the back of the house where the converted garage served as the entrance to the underground bunker.

"Your dad was worried about nuclear fallout, or something else?"

"He was worried about everything." I chuckled and went over to the door. I pulled up the large, silver handle and yanked the heavy door open. The stairwell leading down gave no hint of light or life below. I pulled out my flashlight and clicked it on. The beam bounced off the walls, wobbling with every step that I took into the bunker. I resisted the urge to call out to see if someone was down there.

I stepped into a wide room with Hailey at my back. My beam landed on empty shelves and turned over boxes.

"Pillaged?" She asked softly.

I shook my head. "Hard to say." I turned around, making sure that the light shined on every corner of the room. Black words had been painted on the wall.

"We were right all along, Katie."

My heart dropped. It was a message for me, but there was no telling who left it or what they meant. I tried to contain my worry. Had my dad or brother left the message? Did that mean they survived?

"What does it mean?" Hailey walked towards it.

I licked my lips. "There was a theory out there that my mom was convinced was crazy, but my dad, older brother, and I always thought it'd make a great ghost story."

"Do you think that's what it's talking about?"

"I don't know who left this message. It could be travelers like us just trying to spook people who might be seeking shelter." I turned to leave the bunker. "I like to think that if they survived, they would have tried to contact me somehow— before the world went to complete shit."

She nodded and headed up the stairs. I glanced back at the words and shook my head. There was no way that our scary story was what was going on.

Hailey sat on the floor and leaned against the wall. "Let's get a look at that research. Maybe it'll give us an idea of where we can start with our own."

I sat in front of her, opened the lock box, and pulled out the notebook. I flipped through it. "This is everything that we know. She predicted the earthquakes that came before the eruption. She knew what the damage was going to be."

Hailey pulled the box close to her and pulled out a small paper that had stuck to the bottom. "What's this?"

I looked up in time to see her eyes widen. "What?"

"Who's JA?"

"That's my brother's initials, why?"

She turned the paper around. The black and red sketch stood out against the paper. I knew exactly what I was looking at. "Kaiju."

Hailey nodded. "Your brother had seen them before."

"No, that's the creature we dreamed lived in the volcanos. My mother told us it was just our overactive imaginations. John and I grew up thinking she was right, but we always entertained the idea that they lived in the volcanos. When we moved from Yellowstone to here, the dreams stopped."

She shook her head. "So, you and your brother knew the Kaiju existed before the volcano erupted. That's insane. Why didn't you know what you were looking at when we saw it at the caldera?"

"I never put my visions of it down on paper. I didn't know John did. There was this...odd sense of déjà vu, but that was it." I flipped to the back of the notebook. "Looks like mom took notes on mine and John's dreams, too."

Hailey snorted. "So she did believe you. Maybe she saw them too and just didn't want to admit to it." She motioned to the tape recorder. "I haven't seen one of those in at least ten years."

"Mom wasn't much for digital technology." I opened up the battery compartment to make sure the batteries hadn't corroded or exploded. "Here's hoping they kept their charge."

I pressed the play button.

"March 30th, 2030." My heart ached at hearing my mother's voice for the first time in years. "Yellowstone National Park. Research trip number thirty. John has started to dream of demons again, so I brought him with me. In the middle of the night, I found him standing near Old

Faithful, and in the mist of the steam and rising waters, I saw what he'd described to me so many times. Just a blurred version of what he drew for me, but I'll never forget those burning eyes. I feel that all the research and preparations for the eruption of the Yellowstone supervolcano may be in vain, as no one can prepare our world for demons."

"That was a month before the volcano erupted." Hailey shook her head. "Demons?"

I ignored her and dug through some more of the notes, looking for ones that were close to that date. I found a few from the week after. "Looks like my mother found an old myth."

"How old?"

"Dating back to ancient Rome. In Pompeii." I muttered and read through the notes.

"I call bullshit on this." She shook her head. "I say we continue with the theory that the Kaiju are hallucinations caused by the gases in the atmosphere."

I glanced up from my mom's notes on the myth. "That's a pretty good theory, but you haven't mentioned it before."

"Yeah, it's on another loose piece of paper in here." She held it up. "It's dated in January of 2030."

I took the paper from her and read through it. "It would make sense why the demons appear more near a volcano than they do further away."

"And why they are all around the world. What's the myth say?"

I put the paper back in the lock box. "That the demons were locked away under the surface of the earth and they escaped through the volcano to terrorize and destroy the world. They were locked away to prevent the end of humankind."

"Who locked them away?"

"The gods, with the help of the seers." I closed the notebook. "It's just a myth."

Hailey nodded. "Let's hike back to the volcano and see what we can during the daylight. We'll head back here for the night and then tomorrow we'll head down into the caldera."

"I want to walk some more of the perimeter first."

"Okay, you're the lead on this project. I just came along to get out of the city and have an adventure." She held her hands up in surrender. "I didn't actually expect to see any Kaiju."

And yet, I had. "Research trip be damned." I laughed. "Let's figure this out."

"Deal."

"They say that the souls of the damned are locked away under the surface of the earth," John's voice echoed in the empty classroom. "I've dreamt about it. It's in the mythology of Pompeii."

"There's no research to prove that myth exists," My mother's annoyed voice came next.

I stood out in the hall, leaning against the door, listening in on the argument. I remembered the day well. John and I had decided it was time to tell our mom about the dreams.

"Your father should never play into your silly fantasies. He put you up to this, didn't he?" She chuckled. "Look, John, if there was a myth about creatures living in the volcanos, I would know about it. Now, get your sister and let's head home. I have finals to grade."

John made a huffing noise that told me he was irritated. "Katie has seen them too."

"Katie is much more level-headed than you or your father and knows that they are just dreams." She started towards the door and I bolted down the hall...which wasn't how it happened in reality.

The tiles of the floor started to melt into streaming lines of red and orange lava, the black cooling surface bubbled and disappeared into the fiery substance. I screamed as the tiles under me disappeared and I fell into a blinding pool of magma.

I had expected pain, but none came. Kaiju moved through the magma, untouched by the burning substance. The liquid moved and flowed around them, almost welcoming them. The world pulled back and I could see the extensive tunnels and flows of magma through the earth. Everything was connected either by massive pits or narrow halls, allowing the Kaiju to travel. The science was all wrong.

"Hello, Seer."

I jerked out of my sleep at the words. The sun barely peaked over the horizon, casting a gray light over the ground. I rubbed my eyes and got out of my sleeping bag. Just dreams, just like my mother had said— except the Kaiju were real, they were living in the earth and now coming out...because whatever magic that had locked them away was gone now.

"Sleep well?" John's voice caught me off guard and Hailey jumped out of her sleeping bag.

I looked at his shabby blonde hair and yellow beard. I threw my arms around him. Questions flooded through me and my brain refused to sort through them all.

His strong arms wrapped around me. "You're alive," he whispered.

"Me? I was away from the blast. How the hell did you survive?" I hit him in the chest. "Why didn't you come try and find me? Dad? Mom?" I spoke a mile a minute. "Have you seen the Kaiju?"

"I've been traveling around the world. I left at the first signs of the eruption. Dad went to be with mom." He shook his head and closed his eyes for a moment of silence. "Yes, I've seen the Kaiju. They're all over the place. The demons are going to destroy the world and make it theirs."

Hailey raised a brow. "And how do you know this? Have you talked to one of them? These...illusions?"

"She's not a believer?"

"She thinks they are ghost stories to scare us." I shook my head. "But she brings up a good question."

"Like I said, I've been traveling. Volcanos are erupting all over. That's why the Kaiju are appearing everywhere. They are creating their own entry into the world."

"They use the chambers of magma to travel." Just like it had been in the dream. "The constant eruptions explain why the situation hasn't improved over the last few years. We're way past the predicted affected time."

I paced the room for a moment. "You can come with us to the caldera."

He shook his head. "I'm not getting that close; the demons will drag you to their hell."

"There's no other way to figure out how to stop them." I put my hands on my hips. "You've clearly studied them more than I have."

"And do you plan on stopping them single-handedly?" He shook his head. "Pack up and head back to your assigned city. Secure all the resources you can, water, food, clothing— things are only going to get worse."

"I plan on turning in my research to the mayor of our city so that they can work with the military or something to take out the Kaiju."

He shook his head. "There's nothing they can do against an enemy like that." He put a hand on my shoulder. "I'll head back with you two to make sure you get there safe."

"We're not heading back." Hailey stepped up next to me. "We came this far, we're not walking back across that wasteland without some type of answers."

John turned his gaze to Hailey. "Says the non-believer. Do you think they would have sent you out here to investigate if they didn't exist?"

"It was actually a volunteer mission." I stepped between the two of them. "We came out here to collect data. To see how the environment was faring and see if there was a cause for these monsters to be showing up."

"Then you've lost your mind. Go back. The myth says they can't be stopped." John ran his hand through his hair. "I'd like to see you live through the rest of this apocalypse."

I snorted. "If they can't be stopped, then what's the reason for going back? Eventually, they'll catch up." I spun on my heels and started cleaning up my stuff. "Hailey and I are going out there. You can come with us, or you can stand here and pout."

He rolled his eyes. "I'm not letting you go out there alone."

"You do realize that I'm not a child, right? That you haven't seen me in five years?" I tied my sleeping back to the top of my hiking bag.

"I know that, Katie, but the volcano isn't a place to just run around for research. You aren't equipped to deal with the Kaiju."

I headed out of the house. "You're not going to dissuade me right now."

He let out an exasperated sigh and started trekking along with Hailey and me.

Hailey stopped at the broken edge of the highway and looked over the caldera. "Here we are. Where are the monsters?"

I set my bag down and looked at John. "See, no scary monsters right now."

"You have the key words, 'right now.'" He motioned to the sky. "Sun's still up, give it till closer to dusk."

I'd seen the one Kaiju the night before. I didn't doubt they were there, but I had time to collect some samples before the sun went down. "So, if you've been alive this whole time and dad was with mom, what's with the message in the shelter?"

"I think mom and dad came back for something before going to Yellowstone. Though I don't know why you were the one he left the message to. I was the one who told mom about the myth."

I nodded. "But I was the one who kept talking to dad about it. I didn't talk to mom about it because I knew she wouldn't believe us."

"So dad wanted to let you know that we were all right. That you weren't crazy like mom thought I was."

"That's what I assume." Something moved in the distance and I swallowed, trying not to panic. "Let's go down a few feet. I want a soil sample from further in."

Hailey glanced over her shoulder at me. "I thought we were sticking to the rim today."

"Changed my mind." I walked past her and started to make my way sideways down the steep slope. "You coming?"

"Katie!" John's voice echoed after me. "Katie, you can't go down there."

I ignored him and kept my focus in front of me so I didn't go tumbling down. Hailey caught up to me. "Your brother is joining us."

"Don't really care at this point." We reached an odd plateau and stopped for a moment. "John says there's no way to stop them, but mom's notes sounded like there was a chance."

"So if there's a chance, do you think we're going to find the answers here?" Hailey motioned to the dusty air surrounding us.

"Maybe. I don't know."

John slid down next to me. "No, we'll find the answer in mom's notes. She must have come back and put her research back in the lockbox. I didn't even think of checking for it."

"You just assumed that she took it all with her? With how meticulous she kept her files and her backups? You should have known better."

John shrugged. "Yeah, maybe, but I also wasn't looking for research."

"Except you were. You went all around the world during the apocalypse and brought back knowledge of the other volcanos erupting." I shook my head. "Don't try to kid yourself."

"Yep, that sounds like research to me," Hailey chimed in, "but I think we have more important issues on our plate right now." Her sing-song voice turned into something that sounded a bit more frightened.

John and I turned to look out into the caldera. Glowing eyes of hell-fire stared at us. Twenty pairs in the particle-filled air. My heart skipped a beat as I tried to figure out what to do. Climbing back up quickly wasn't an option because of the steep incline. The figures moved closer. Instinct kicked in and I stepped in front of Hailey and John. I didn't have anything to fight with. I had no plan of defense, but the move felt right. It gave me a sense of calm in the panic of fight or flee.

The creatures hesitated, stopping just short of the ledge; closer than the last Kaiju I had encountered. With a group this large, I could feel the heat beating against my skin in waves. Their black, cracked skin seemed more like scales than actual flesh. Though, unlike the first time, I could still breathe. There was no sense of them attacking us.

I stared at them. The one closest to us let out a screech and they all faded back into the gray. Hailey grabbed my shoulder and spun me around to face her. Her wide eyes searched my face and she cupped her hands over my cheeks.

"My God, they are afraid of you!" She sounded half petrified and half amazed. "But why?"

John let out a loud sigh and motioned to the top of the caldera. "Let's get back up there and I'll explain."

"Explain what?" I snapped.

"That you're a seer."

After carefully watching our footing, we reached the top. John started walking away from the caldera without speaking to either Hailey or me. I stomped after him. "Aren't you going to tell me what the hell you meant?"

"I want to see mom's notes first. Did she leave anything else?"

"Recordings, but those are all old. Seers are things of legends and bedtime tales. You don't really think that I'm one, do you?"

Hailey laughed. "And I thought I was the disbeliever."

"You just saw twenty Kaiju, you can't seriously say that they don't exist," John snapped. "Wake up, woman, monsters are real. So are seers, Katie, and you're one of them."

We followed him back to the house. Hailey threw her bag down and put her hands on her hips. "Don't you call me 'woman' in that tone again."

"John, we all know that the Kaiju are real, but even if seers were real, there aren't any left." I put my bag down. "I think you've inhaled too many fumes." I pulled off my gas mask and replaced it with the gauze mask.

He shook his head. "Okay, how about this? Let's listen to some of mom's more recent recordings and hear what she says about it. If she has handwritten notes, then she's bound to have recorded ones as well."

"Why don't you just tell us about them? If you know about the seer, then you must know how this is going to help us."

John looked away. His gaze darted around the room, landing on everything but me. "You're right. I do. Only a seer can lock the Kaiju away."

"Seers don't typically have magic, do they?" Hailey crossed her arms. "You sound like you're spouting a lot of bullshit."

John sat down and looked up at us. "It's true, typically seers don't have magic, in a traditional sense. But, some do and that's what allows them to see the future or the past. It's what will allow Katie to lock them away."

"If you knew I could lock them away again, why did you try to get me to go back to the city?" I sat down and leaned against my bag. "You should want to help me get rid of them." Though I wasn't exactly sure how I was going to do it, I had some hope in my heart that we could end this and help heal the world.

John put his head on his knees. "Because it requires a sacrifice. The original seer killed their child as a sacrifice. I didn't want to put you through that."

"But what is one life to save many?" Hailey stated. "I don't know about you, but I'd gladly kill one person to save the world."

I could see her point, but I looked at the two people in front of me. I'd already grieved my brother once and didn't want to repeat the grief, and Hailey had been my rock through everything.

John looked up at me. "I was going to try and do it. I'll be the sacrifice."

"What?" I screeched. "You're going to volunteer for me to kill you?" Premature tears stung the corner of my eyes. "What do you mean you were going to try?"

"Remember, we both had dreams about the Kaiju. We both had dreams about the volcano erupting before the predictions. I show the signs of being a seer as well."

"But?" Hailey prompted.

"But, the Kaiju don't react to me like they do Katie. Which means that I'm not the one who can do this."

I shook my head. "I don't want you giving up your life. I don't understand where you're getting all this information."

"My dreams and piecing it together from the research I collected over the last five years. Look, Katie, you've already grieved me. Hailey will be there to pull you through it again. You want to stop the Kaiju, this is how you do it."

I took a few deep breaths, trying to sort through the emotions running through my head. "How do I do this, though? Did you find that in your research?"

"You let the Kaiju know that you're sending them back to where they belong. We climb down to the bottom of the caldera and you give me to them. The magic should happen from there."

That wasn't a very solid plan. "I don't know..."

"Either you do it, or you return back to your city and I try it myself." He looked at me. I knew that cold look in his eyes. It was a look of determination. There was no getting away from this.

"Fine." And as I said the word, I felt my heart break and the panic return.

The bottom of the caldera still held the heat of the magma below it. Some places bubbled up with fresh black and red lava, creating hot spots around us. Steam rose from vents. The scene was almost like Hell itself. No Kaiju had greeted us; John assumed it was because they were scared. Hailey was oddly quiet the whole climb down.

I looked down at the ground, thankful that it wasn't hot enough to melt my shoes. "I'm really having my doubts about this."

"Just trust me." John hugged me. "Call for them."

I took a deep breath. "Kaiju, I'm here to offer you a sacrifice, to return you to your place below the surface."

A screeching noise pierced the air. I cringed but resisted the urge to cover my ears. At least I knew they were listening. Like before, as if instinct kicked in, I suddenly knew what I needed to do. "I offer you the life of another seer. Take it and go back under the surface, in agreement that you will not come back to the human world." I had no other alternative, but I hoped that they would take the bait.

The ground shook as a Kaiju twice the size of the others stepped forward. Genderless, it held its hand out towards John. My brother started clawing at his throat as if choking. His breath came out in short gasps as his face turned blue from lack of oxygen.

I took a step forward, but Hailey grabbed my hand. I glanced over my shoulder at her and she shook her head. I knew that I couldn't interfere, but watching my brother die of suffocation felt like my soul was being ripped out. I swallowed my sob, not wanting to show any weakness in front of the Kaiju.

The mouth of the Kaiju twisted into a sickening grin. It sank into the ground, melting into the hot surface. A gust of wind came up and swept the dust away, leaving Hailey and I standing in the caldera with my brother's body in the grayed-out light of the sun.

"What now?" I asked, tears in my voice.

Hailey squeezed my hand. "We go home, you turn your samples in, and we watch how the world changes."

I looked at John's body and bowed my head. We'd soon learn if the life of one was worth the life of many.

"End of Programming" by Thomas A. Fowler

Robot Assassin in an Apocalyptic Wasteland

326 years.

15,823,654,912 assessed scenarios.

234 assassinations.

So much time has passed since my creation. As I surveyed the world around me, my programming could no longer comprehend my purpose. What need does a killing machine have in such dire circumstances? Human kind is on the brink of extinction as it is. For me to receive signals to kill others only expedites their demise.

Yet I had no choice. No alternative. Another signal received from an unknown source.

My creator, sending me information.

Another kill order.

Jerry Rowley. Leader of a band of survivors twenty miles from my location. Unknown exact number of followers. Last satellite surveillance indicated a minimum of 18.

The word "tired" was not a part of my programming. A faint part of my stored information called out to a girl named Abigail. A girl who taught me to adapt.

The pivot joints in my legs ground against the sand trenched in my circuitry. The trek would be long, but no stops were permitted until my target was acquired.

For hours, nothing. Crumbled homes. Offices buried in sand. Traces of human kind with faint fires lit in the distance to keep survivors warm, the soft echo of a mother soothing her child during their fight against starvation.

The small alcove. My target. Makeshift barricades formed to keep outsiders from entering and taking their provisions. What an odd race. Even in the face of desperation, they build only to defend and destroy. Nothing made with the intent of embrace, growth. This stronghold was meant to harbor safety only for those deemed worthy, and yet my programmer signaled for me to destroy a haven of destruction.

Does this negate the loss of life? Is Jerry Rowley such an abomination that his removal from an endangered species the best thing for it? I had no means of calculating such things before his death would occur.

"Hey, we've got a tinner coming!" a man shouted. "Hey, tinner! Tell me your primary function!"

"Primary function is farming." Adaptive programming taught me to override the central command programmed for humans to control and understand what every manufactured life driven by artificial intelligence was made for. It was a safety protocol, but after too many targets caught on, I learned to override that function.

"Why all the weaponry?" the man asked.

I did not answer. I approached the thick, wooden gate. Central lock, side hinges. A rupture of the key structural points and the gate would allow enough space for entry.

"Hey!" the man shouted.

My right arm coiled. The gears and cables condensed to form a strong battering ram powered by a sudden burst of my hydraulic systems. I wound my arm back, readying the strike to the top hinge.

"Stop, you dumb tinner!" the man yelled. He aimed his rifle and fired a round at my chest.

The bullet pierced my outer shell. Circuitry disrupted. Not enough to stop my advance. My arm released the hydraulic tension, slamming my ram-shaped fist into the hinge. A single pop took the heavy door out. The weight of the uncontrolled top swung down, busting the central lock out of weight. A crudely formed door from humans incapable of master craftsmanship during troubled times.

I released my arm, the coils and gears returning my arm to a normal form. I grabbed the short rifle.

"Breach!" the man shouted. "We've got a bre…"

My rifle fired, interrupting his sentence and ending his life. More from the outpost poured out from their respective positions. Each one an easy target. Another bullet broke through my armor; I swung my rifle, eliminating the problem.

Another bullet. Far more than 18 followers. I fell back behind the door, using the weight and thickness to block some of the fire. The high-powered rifles splintered portions of the wood.

Not much time left before my position would be compromised.

"Tinner!" another voice shouted.

"Jerry Rowley?" I asked.

"What about it?" he replied.

Drawing my rifle, my auditory sensors triangulated his position. I fired. Jerry dropped. All gunfire ceased. The followers stopped to mourn their leader. The behavior of other followers, since the large species decrease, indicated they'd seek revenge against me.

The mobility of my legs was hindered from the wasteland and bullets rupturing several points of my armor, and there was no viable escape route anywhere close, only desert.

This was the end of my programming. Yet, I didn't want my makers to rebuild me to become another version of myself; a killer bound to its programming. An enforcer built to kill. Adaptive programming. It's what Abigail taught me. Quickly, I decoded the signal sent to me for assassination targets. I reworked it and assigned a new target.

I used my magnetic field to draw all their weapons to me. They clunked against my ruptured armor. The weight of the weapons drew me to the ground. My body was no longer capable of holding such weight.

The followers chased after their weapons, and me.

"Abigail, you couldn't possibly still be alive. I helped you many years ago. I told you all was well," I said. "I don't know if that is true anymore in this life. I know that wherever you are, I hope you are willing to be my friend, as you were years ago."

The followers crumbled on top of me, using splintered wood to hit me. Prying their guns from my magnetized body.

"Finding you, my friend, is finding peace."

I triggered my final assassination: myself.

The explosion killed the angry followers. I left the world I knew for 326 years, through 15,823,654,912 assessed scenarios, and now 236 assassinations. My programming left the darkness of the world that created me. Somewhere, I hoped my programming would find a girl, a girl who taught me to learn, a girl named Abigail who was my only friend.

"Of Fish and Flowers" by C. L. Kagmi
Alien in an Evil Laboratory

My time is drawing near its end. This is almost a relief. They have taken most of the others and dissected them. The curiosity is understandable— but the complete and total lack of communication is *not*!

I have to admire, almost, the elegant simplicity of this torture. I suspect I am in a pain experiment, but I can imagine no purpose for running one under these circumstances. Perhaps they intend to take my words, after all is done, and distill them for some purpose I cannot imagine.

I find *them* increasingly incomprehensible.

I have been in the same tiny chamber since boarding their ship. Swimming into their nets was the exciting part—the first step toward fulfilling my life's work and breaking the communication barrier. I had no way of knowing that they would be so deaf. Impenetrable. Impenetrable, like the transparent barrier around me.

Through it, I have the illusion of being part of the Strangers' world. They *walk* past me, as anyone would pass in open water. Except for the fact that they *walk*— a trick of locomotion I almost admire— I might be with them in a high current, floating free. Except. Except.

The silence is unbearable. I cannot *taste* them. Dialogue is impossible under these conditions. I can *see* the subjects of my life's work— close enough, at times, to touch— but I cannot touch them. They seem as deaf to my attempts to communicate as I am deafened by the barrier between us.

This water in my enclosure is, I have concluded, being circulated on a closed circuit by a pump. It filters out waste, but not words. My utterances circulate back to me, unheard, unanswered. No one hears. No one answers. I dare not shut off my receptors, in case— *in case*— some response might come. But I have spent so long listening to my own voice that I am almost deaf to it.

I wonder if they know what they are doing. This seems increasingly unlikely. These are creatures of the *air*— that near-vacuum at the edge of space. It has become clear to me that there was something of a failure of imagination when we tried to imagine what they would be like.

They are deaf to us. Our attempts to communicate have met with no response because they do not use carbon chains to do so. Of this I have become certain. Instead, I now believe that the high-frequency vibrations they disperse through the *air* are the medium of their speech. Unlikely as it may seem, these vibrations approach our own language in complexity, and are a logical solution to life in a medium that won't carry complex carbon chains.

I also believe they may have a means of permanently coding language in visual symbols. This theory is the closest thing I have to hope.

I have experimented with physical structures to vibrate air in a way that they might recognize as speech, but I simply don't have the engineering knowledge. There is almost nothing in my genetic memory of air. I'm not aware of anyone who has studied it, and its vibrations, in detail. There isn't even any air in my tank to test my makeshift vibration-generators on.

But visuals— that I can do.

I've tried flashing mathematically determined sequences onto my skin without success. Failing that, I'm trying social intelligence. I have 'named' each of them, so to speak, developing a visually unique pattern for each individual I recognize. I flash their 'names' on my skin whenever they draw near.

So far, they have failed to notice. Perhaps I have missed some vital cue.

From the journal of Karin Sasomoto, 06.01.2448

I have gotten another one of my ideas. It's as crazy as something Caleb would come up with, and as chilling. Cai thinks we're both crazy for believing it, but if it's true...

I think the octopus in the lab, the last of the *D. aureus* harvest, is trying to *talk* to us.

It took me weeks to notice. The thing changes color, like many Earth octopi do. The chromatophores in its skin— little sacs filled with ink that can dilate or contract, almost like pixels on a screen— are quite similar to theirs. Our octopi change color to communicate changes in mood. To effect camouflage. To hide from predators. Nothing more advanced than that, probably, though they can be trained to flash a given pattern on command.

This one seems to be doing something else.

It happened as I was walking past its tank this morning. The thing saw me coming, flashed a color change, and I immediately thought: '*Good morning to you, too!*'

I stopped. Walked backward. Stared at the little cephalopod, swirling in its tank.

My brain had responded to it, very pointedly, as though to a greeting.

There is a story about a behavioral scientist who studied chimpanzees— in the late twentieth, I think it was. Right when they were figuring out that apes were intelligent enough to use sign language. She was walking past the chimps' enclosure one day when she thought to herself: '*Oh, they must be having grapes today.*'

And she stopped. And walked backward.

As it turned out, the chimpanzees *were* having grapes. Their feeding-time vocalizations were not just shouts of vague excitement. They contained highly specific meanings. Her conscious mind had not registered this— no one's had, because it didn't fit the patterns of human language. But after sufficient exposure, some older paradigm in her subconscious mind formed the association between what she heard and what she saw of their meals without her even realizing it.

I beckoned Caleb over and watched the thing change color as it saw him, to a pattern that my brain registered as *'Caleb'* as warm and clear as a voice saying his name. I warmed for about half a second, until I realized the implications.

The little octopus began to flutter around in its tank, in what looked for all the world like a state of excitement. Its color patterns flickered— perhaps randomly.

Or perhaps simply too fast for us to process.

Caleb thinks my theory's good, and as his will goes, so goes the will of the lab. We don't have a linguist with us. No one expected to need one on a waterworld with no visible evidence of technological civilization. Caleb is one of the best multidisciplinary informatics specialists on Earth, and he's on this with the kind of passion that means he probably won't sleep for days. No doubt he's talking to the little creature as we speak or trying to. I miss him, but it's not our meetings in the physical sphere that make me admire him so.

If he's right— if *I'm* right— if this thing is smart enough to speak, if it *wants* to be understood…

Dear God. I cut up all of the others, while they were still alive.

I tried to stop talking when I realized they were deaf. That I was isolated from you. My words coming back to me meant that they were going nowhere, that they were not reaching you.

That renders all of this rather pointless, doesn't it? What I learn is meaningless if I die without reporting back.

But I have not given up.

They seem to have taken notice of my 'names' for them. The blue-eyed one stayed with me through the night, cataloguing my patterns and flashing them back to me. They seem to have some kind of creature: an eye which makes an exact image of whatever it observes, records and reproduces it.

Perhaps they are not entirely hopeless.

How such a species could come to exist remains baffling to me. To survive a transition to the edge of space, to walk on two legs without the support of buoyancy, what sort of hell-world must they come from?

I ask myself, too, if we should be afraid of them. That was not in the original calculations, it was assumed that an intelligence advanced enough to cross the void would value what it found here. Would recognize that we have much to share, that destruction is always wasteful. After these last weeks, I am no longer sure of this.

They have gazed past the most basic, the most vital of messages, as though they were not there. Their reactions now seem promising— they display real curiosity and deductive ability, and what could almost be interpreted as a desire to communicate that mirrors my own. Perhaps now that the barrier has been broken, all will proceed to course. Perhaps we can learn the gifts of these people of air and fire.

But there are some absences, some gaps in their behavior, which remain troubling in their implications. When they dissect us, they wear protective, artificial skins. These they discard after contact. They seem to desire to avoid any potential exchange of fluids.

At first, I took this as a twisted aversion to communication, for how else would they communicate if *not* though such exchange? But with further study, I've come to another hypothesis.

These may be measures to avoid *disease.*

The implications of this are terrifying. These creatures are chemical-blind— blind to our signals, our means of communication. They cannot read, and likely cannot construct complex carbon chains.

Then what *else* can't they do?

Is it possible that this species, for all its great achievements, never learned the language of the genome? Is it possible that they are as deaf to the inner workings of their own cells as they are to our communications? No. It is not possible. It simply is not possible that a species could have attained such tenacity, such spaceflight, without some mastery over the language of the cell.

But then…

As elegantly as these creatures are designed for life in air, why have they brought their air with them? A rational World-Mind would have sent emissaries suited to the environment. Emissaries of aquatic design.

Even their World-Mind— the one we believe is contained within the ship— has not responded to our hails. Is it as blind them, as its servants? Is it incapable of adapting to disease, of changing their design?

The thought of such a species— rudderless, powerless, subject to the whims of randomness for its very genetic makeup— chills my blood.

How could such a species have *survived*?

From the journal of Karin Sasomoto, 10.01.2448

I've devoted the last several days to studying Dmitri.

That's what I've decided to name them. The octopus, that is. Not 'him,' properly, because they're all hermaphroditic. If it can be called that. Their means of genetic recombination looks more like a disease process than sexual reproduction.

Anyway. Dmitri. After an ex of mine. Morbid, I suppose. The most frightening thing is how quickly Dmitri is adapting to the language that he and Caleb are constructing. Caleb has been in ansible communication with Earth, picking up tips for bridging the communication gap. Dmitri takes to it like— well, like a fish to water. No sooner have we proposed a thing then they've assimilated it and seem impatient for the next. Caleb thinks Dmitri might be smarter than he is.

Caleb is the smartest human being I've ever known.

There is danger in anthropomorphizing. Ant colonies and slime molds can seem incredibly intelligent, solving certain problems better and faster than our best engineers, but that doesn't mean they think. It doesn't mean they feel. Calculations are not consciousness. The same applies here.

But Dmitri isn't an ant colony. They're an individual. And they're not solving resource-distribution problems. They're using *words*. And body language. That's another unsettling thing. It's been a matter of debate how universal body language is. On Earth, all species are related. We share common ancestors: common inherited instincts with fish, reptiles, birds, etc. If we understand their body language, it's not because there's anything objectively universal about it. We just have the same interpretation matrix, somewhere deep down in our limbic systems.

Yet I begin to suspect that it *is* universal. The creatures of this world share no common ancestry with Earth— genetic testing has made that abundantly clear. But maybe it's a matter of synesthesia. Maybe a droop, a giving-up of energy and motion, is always a negative; maybe a flutter, a skip, an expression of living vitality, is always a positive.

If my algorithms can be trusted, Dmitri seems almost panicked.

They are *frenetic* in their tank. Circling incessantly like some of the others did, before I took them. Their speech is hurried, the way someone's might be if they thought their time was short.

They have managed to request a change to their water. Our filters have been removing waste but missing, apparently, a buildup of organic chemicals they weren't built to detect. Chemicals like the ones the *Nereusian* sea is swimming with.

These chemicals are words, Dmitri says.

They made another request: dump their water *outside*, unfiltered, so they can communicate with their kin. Anyone who tastes their water will know all they know of us.

Well.

The peptide soup we have been picking up, the mystifying complexity of *Nereusian* ocean chemistry, are we swimming in a library? Has the ocean been talking all around us this whole time?

If that's true, Cai says that if we assume *all* our mystery carbon chains are part of that language then it's a language far, far more complex than English. And it's being spoken by a great many of this ocean's organisms.

Dmitri says they've tried to communicate with us.

We've told them we've done as they requested, but the Captain has forbidden it. She is unsure that she wants this deep, blue sea to know all that Dmitri knows of us.

They've seen me dissect their kin. I know that much.

The small dishonesty makes me feel guilty, absurdly; I'm lying to an octopus, but telling them we'd done as they asked seemed to calm its nerves, at least a little bit. Yet still they flutter nervously when our daily language lessons are done, when they think that no one is watching.

I try to forget that I dissected their packmates in front of them. They have accused me of nothing— but why would they?

Would you accuse someone of murder while they had you in a cage?

Progress. Progress. The humans are as curious as I hoped. We have constructed almost a full language-matrix. Almost enough to ask the sensitive questions. But, do I dare?

How offensive would it be to ask what they know of the language of their cells? If they have a World-Mind onboard their ship? If they do, such tactless questions could read as calling them pre-sentient. I still, much to my shame, quiver at the memory of their scalpels.

Still. My mission is the same as it ever was. To learn. The unexpected obstacles mean nothing; I must learn all I can. Unfortunately, I'll be able to do that most efficiently by tasting.

Each species learns in the way it communicates, I suppose. They seem to learn through vibrations in the air, through visual symbols. I learn best through taste, and I still yearn to taste them, to a distracting degree.

I wonder, if they are blind to the chemical language, how can they truly understand another? When I taste them, I will know them inside and out. Know how their cells and organs function; given time and contemplation, I will trace the venues of their evolutionary pasts, their deep ancestry. I will come to understand them as I understand myself.

Unless, of course, there are more surprising barriers there. But not knowing is driving me mad.

The humans, I have noticed, touch each other sometimes. Perhaps this is communication; perhaps it is for something else. Either way, perhaps I can convince them that *I* have the same need.

If I can. Oh, if I can, then my imprisonment here may be over.

Dmitri is *lonely*.

We'd considered that a cephalopod may be a social species that may suffer from the absence of their own kin. We never imagined they would consider us a suitable substitute. Upon reflection: why not? Humans have written reams of fiction about finding companionship with intelligent aliens, in the absence of other humans. Some of us even prefer intellectual similarity, intellectual *understanding*, to the physical.

Still, we've no idea what to do with Dmitri's most recent request.

They seem to want to *cuddle*.

My initial plan to procure a playmate for Dmitri on a subsequent dive was scrapped on an ethical moratorium: if these things are sentient, can we justify capturing another?

That we have not already released Dmitri is, I think, a matter of shame for all of us. They are simply too valuable to us. And there are, it seems, some lines that all of us are willing to cross for science.

I'm surprised how easy it has been for me to cross that line. We look back on history and say we'd *never* do that— never hold a sentient creature against their will— but the thought of releasing him makes my skin crawl. The intellectual emptiness of having to revert to guesswork about *Nereus'* ocean would be unbearable!

Anyway. Dmitri has requested skin-to-skin contact with a human.

The Captain looked at us like we were mad for even considering it. Caleb and Cai haven't been able to make heads or tails of the soup of virus-like particles in this world's water; at least some of which we *know* Dmitri to be carrying for reproductive purposes.

Perhaps it's important that I tell you about their reproduction, now. I said earlier that they were hermaphrodites. That wasn't quite true. Technically, all *Nereusian* life that we've discovered so far reproduces by budding. Small bits of tissue break off of the parent and develop into free-swimming offspring. They're not without the benefits of genetic exchange— oh no. To accomplish that, each individual, among the animals, at least, carries a sac full of virus particles, typically under their tongue. These virus particles contain substantial bits of their own genetic libraries. They also seem to stimulate budding in their— er, sexual partners.

To accomplish gene transfer, one animal *bites* the other and injects its viruses through a slender bone syringe. The viral particles infect the bud cells and often some or all of the adult partner's tissues, as well. In this way, the newly budded offspring have unique genetic profiles. This explains a great deal of the strangeness we have encountered here. You may recall, months ago, Caleb and Cai's confusion at the seemingly lack of linear family trees on this world. Everybody seemed related to everybody else; bloodlines and gene variants looked like you threw them in a blender, and some even seemed to cross species barriers.

Caleb is still working on determining if there *are* species barriers here in the same way there are on Earth; the viral system doesn't seem to cause the same problems with genetic exchange that sexual reproduction does on Earth.

A few weeks ago, I successfully used a reproductive virus from Dmitri's species to fertilize a flower. The offspring are still developing, little more than buds of protoplasm, in my lab.

So, suffice to say, the Captain is more than a little concerned about the prospect of skin-to-skin contact.

But I...

I brought Dmitri here. I killed the others.

I owe it to them, don't I?

The blue-eyed one tells me my request has been denied. Their *Captain*— which I believe may be their term for their World-Mind— won't have it. There is danger of disease, he says.

I feel nearly ready to give up, at that. If their World-Mind has decreed it so, what hope can there be? That the thing is susceptible to disease is valuable information, but useless if it dies with me.

I was not built for prolonged confinement. I do not know how much longer I can live, hoping for an opening that may never come.

Yet, the thread the World-Minds built in me still pulls. They do not want me dead, yet. That pull, that overriding sense of duty persists.

I notice one of them watching me. It is the one with the scalpel— the one who performs dissections— and for a moment, I feel fear. Something is wrong with the way she moves. Too slowly, and too languidly. She droops, like a flower in a salt current. Is that what sadness, displeasure, looks like in a human?

I cannot understand *why*, for the will of their *Captain* should be absolute. The wisdom of the higher minds is flawless, a thing no budded brain can ever hope to rival. To defy a verdict from one's World-Mind defies understanding; such a thing would be a fatal error in one's genetic code.

She lingers. The sad human *lingers* as the others file out. The blue-eyed one stops and exchanges fluid with her briefly. I've seen this gesture only twice before, both times when those two were alone in the lab. Another mystery. Do they communicate, in some ways, like us after all? Another mystery for another time.

She's coming toward me. Donning protective coverings, I wilt. The kind of coverings she uses for dissections. So, they have decided that my period of usefulness has ended.

I will not be able to share what I have learned about their vulnerability to disease. I will not be able to taste them. These facts itch and burn, like shell shards in my brain. My body signals failure. Failure.

Still, she moves too slowly as she approaches my chamber. I do not dare to hope for the impossible.

The top of my chamber lifts away. The surface of my water becomes mercury-bright, like the surface of the sea. I try not to cringe from the thought of the near-vacuum beyond. I must brave this thing, if I am to have any hope of fulfilling the purpose I was made for.

She picks me up, her fingers like the tentacles of some much larger creature.

Air is disorienting. Blinding. For long moments as I adjust them, my eyes to not want to work. When I have cleared them, I do not believe what I am seeing. I remember stories, eons old, of an afterlife that shows you what you want to see.

Her other hand rises before me: brown and bare. She has neglected to cover this one, essential area of skin. The fingers hover above me, and still I poise for pain, but they are—

Stroking. Barely touching the skin of my back.

Information floods my pores like the hatching of a thousand eggs. Each oil, each peptide of her skin is analyzed.

Rapture it is a taste of what has been withheld throughout this long captivity.

But only a taste.

She holds me closer, against her body. Her body is warm. I cleave tightly to her hand, wrapping tentacles around her fingers. Here it is. The ultimate completion. Assurance that my work will continue when I am gone.

I wonder what language our offspring will speak, as my bone needle penetrates her skin.

"Platform Strategy" by Thomas A. Fowler

Clown in an Evil Laboratory

This was the embodiment of my manifesto. Too long had I been second fiddle to Lou Emmett. The man had all but etched his name into a Clown Lifetime Achievement Award. It was my time to write my own path to a CLAA. I never understood Emmett's execution of the clown car. I'd obsessed over the intricacy of the trick for years. Arriving in civilian clothes, I'd watch the bottom of the car, searching for a glimpse of a tunnel. I'd scan the sand of the main circus venue, looking for a squared entrance where the clowns could climb up from a basement crawlspace into the car. Emmett, like a magician, never revealed his secret.

It no longer mattered. I had conjured my own. The record would be mine. The red concoction boiled in the laboratory vials. A shadowed figure loomed in a corner. One of the Scientist's demands was that he never be seen. His departure meant the vial was completed. Now all that was left was to recruit my Clown Alley.

"You know the number won't stick, Herb," Alfred said.

In another corner of the laboratory were thirty clowns. Some there on their own, others there strictly because I had paid them.

"I'm beating the number, Alfred. One way or another," I said.

"But if you cheat, the CSS won't recognize the record," he replied.

Alfred had been my good friend for many years. As the circus died its slow death in popularity, our friendship remained. Alfred had never reached for a CLAA, he was content to have just lived the clown life.

"I don't care if the Clown Standards Society deems it a false act, the record will be mine," I pulled the vial from the burner. I distributed the liquid into small, glass beakers. The red substance thickened, a white mist spewing from the top.

"Don't you care how you get the record, though?" Alfred asked.

"I don't care how I get it, I care that I get it. Nothing more," I replied. "When did you become the advocate of clown morality?"

I handed the beakers out, one by one. Some clowns grabbed it without hesitation; some inspected the substance with extreme scrutiny.

"Since I watched my friend become someone obsessed with a number he couldn't possibly ascertain," Albert said. "The man in front of me is still my friend, but a friend I cannot recognize."

"Yet you took my money," I said.

"Wait, you got paid?" a clown asked.

"Shut up, Billy. I'm talking to Alfred Grant, a mediocre clown with no vision for a bigger future," I said. "Let us all toast, to a new record taking hold tonight."

"I can't do this," Alfred pulled out his wallet.

He handed over everything he had. It was more than I had paid him. As he gave me the stack of cash, he pulled a third of it. He gave it to Billy.

"Doesn't matter, the record is 27 clowns in a single car. There are 29 of us here," I said. "Just like your life, it hasn't mattered to everyone else whether you were here or not."

Alfred opened the exit door. He stopped in the doorframe, the lights of the circus tent far in the distance. One of the massive floodlights spun in circles, alerting visitors of the upcoming event. The beam of light swung around, silhouetting Alfred's aged shadow.

"When all is said and done, neither will you," Alfred's shadow faded into the night. He walked away, never again would we speak.

"Ladies and gentlemen, tonight you join me in making history. Thank the Scientist for this night," I raised my beaker.

I did not drink. I would remain full-size. The rest of them would shrink. A slight reduction of their mass and it would give me just enough room to fit the two more clowns needed to break, and exceed, the record.

At the end of the night, the ringmaster announced the record. The 28 other clowns stood around the car, after all of them had emerged. I stood through the skylight of the compact car. My arms reached for the big top as the sparse crowd applauded.

The ringmaster shouted, "Ladies and gentlemen, boys and girls, we are proud to announce that the CSS record for most clowns inside of a compact car has been broken tonight by our very own Herb Myles."

At the edge of the ring stood an old man. Alfred had returned. His beaker still in hand, he walked slowly toward the center of the circus tent.

"Alfred, what are you doing?" I asked. A smile stayed on my face. I wouldn't let him hinder my life's work.

Alfred stopped in front of the compact car. Its headlights illuminated the wrinkles of his face. Alfred drank the contents of the beaker. The empty beaker crashed to the floor, glass shattering out from the impact point. His hand shook, raising a pointed finger at me. Alfred groaned as his body shrunk several inches.

The crowd, unknowing of what it meant, applauded. They perceived it another trick. I didn't care. The record was mine.

"A fraud," someone shouted. "A curse upon the CSS name."

My head pivoted at the speed of a gunshot from Alfred to the crowd. In the stands were three verification members of the Clown Standards Society. There stood Jacob Ebner, senior judge for the CSS. His graveled voice was the one that shouted at me.

"The record is null and void, it remains 27. Held by the prestigious Lou Emmett," Jacob shouted.

Boos commenced. The crowd sparked to life. They had found another reason to make noise, but a different call to action.

"The record is mine," I shouted.

"Only in your mind," Jacob replied.

"There it shall remain," I raised my hands.

The applause didn't matter, nor the taunts. What mattered was that the record was mine, and there was noise. There was a response. There was life.

I would be remembered for something.

"Split Souls" by A.L. Kessler
Imaginary Friend in an Evil Laboratory

Jack watched Hyde's steady hands stitch the edge of a wrist to the lifeless arm. "You should know better than to mess with the darker sciences. Are you sure you want to go through with this? Even if you managed to bring her back, she's not going to be the same."

"How would you know?" Hyde didn't even look up from the project. "All my research shows that I can do this."

"Mmm, but your research neglects to take one thing into consideration." Jack flicked a beaker on the table and the red liquid inside rippled in response.

"And what is that?" Hyde cut the thread after carefully tying a knot.

"That you keep messing with the human soul and failing at it," Jack shot back. "Not to mention you murdered how many people for this?"

"I only killed five and just for the parts I needed. The rest..."

"Were dead." Jack walked around the table. "So murder, grave robbing, and being soulless. I don't really see this going well."

"You don't know anything about this." Hyde glanced up and Jack caught a glimpse of crazed gray eyes. Blood stains stood out on the man's white shirt, his tie and jacket had been tossed somewhere upon his arrival to the lab. Jack would give anything to know what Hyde was thinking.

Hyde raised a brow. "What are you staring at?"

He resisted saying something snarky but went back to the beakers with the liquid. "I'm still thinking that you're going about this the wrong way. People die for a reason. Bringing your lover back isn't going to work. You're going to land yourself in prison, be hung in the gallows for your crimes." Jack waved a dramatic hand. "Is it worth risking your life?"

"You seemed to think so when you tried to kill me." Hyde turned back towards the body and pulled back the cover. He caressed the gray, lifeless face of the woman. His finger played with one of her blonde ringlets of hair. "I was going to marry her."

Jack looked down at the woman. In life, she had been beautiful, golden hair, blue eyes, rosy cheeks. She'd had a wit that most women failed to possess, the uncommon need to think for herself. It was her discovering Hyde's secret that lead to her untimely death. An accident, the authorities claimed. One that ended up with her losing several limbs, which Hyde had now replaced. "Need I remind you that I tried to kill you to stop your suffering from this evil insanity?"

"You tried to kill me because you could not stand what you saw. You were jealous of my freedom." He pulled the sheet back over the woman's face. "You, out of all people Jack, should know that I'm willing to do anything to bring back Emma."

The name struck grief into his heart. "I know." He looked up when there was a rapping on the door. "Looks like you have visitors."

"You stay here."

Jack rolled his eyes. Like he could go anywhere else. He'd been stuck in this room since the night he'd tried to kill Hyde. The door burst open and police flooded the room, knocking over beakers and equipment. Two forced Hyde down on his knees while yelling about murders and devil's work. Hyde shook his head, denying the claims as police uncovered the body and gathered notebooks of research. Hyde glanced back at Jack, his eyes wide, begging.

"Jack, tell them. Defend me, damn it."

Jack smirked. "And how could I do that? Since the moment you took over my body and split my soul in two, I've been a figment of your insanity…there's nothing I can do to save you now."

"A Kind Soul and a Big Heart" by Beverly Coutts

*Kaiju in an Evil Laboratory

This story contains content regarding the loss of a child

"New York City is reeling under the third kaiju attack this month. Experts say the increase in attacks by these gargantuans may be related to the military's use of experimental missiles..." The female news reporter's voice filtered into Elissa Washington's ears.

The tight ball of anxiety in her chest loosened and she took a deeper breath. Her limbs didn't stop trembling, but the return of rational thought was a start. She lifted her head from her hands and her eyes locked onto the small TV mounted on the wall above the preparation counter. The footage showed a ten-story reptilian creature crashing into a building while military helicopters rained bullets on it from above. The gray-green monster roared under the onslaught but was otherwise unaffected by the violence. The scene had become so mundane she was desensitized to it, even though it took place barely a three-hour drive away.

The panic inside her bubbled down to the normal level of anxiety she always carried with her. She had bills to pay, rent to scrape up somehow, and her job to worry about. She didn't have time for mystery panic and she couldn't afford to go to a doctor again to find out what was wrong with her.

"Elissa? You feeling better?" Ray crouched in front of her, his kind eyes full of concern.

She frowned, knowing he didn't have time to waste on her, but she still appreciated the gesture. "Getting there, Ray." She reached out and squeezed his forearm, more for her own comfort than to reassure him. "Thank you for checking on me, but I know you're busy."

Ray's brows quirked down, his eyes darting to the grill stations and the orders pouring in. "Just makin' sure my girl's all right."

Elissa smiled and nodded. He gave her another concerned look and returned to his station to pull down the next order. She wasn't, and would never be, Ray's girl. He was a happily married man, but he'd pretended to be a jealous boyfriend a couple times to get her out of sticky situations, and sometimes he used the facade to cheer her up. She just couldn't deal with people the same way anymore, after she lost her baby two years ago. Now, with the onslaught of panic attacks, it was even worse.

She took a deep breath through her nose. The smell of grease and French fries filled her nostrils, reminding her of mundane things. And work. She needed to get to work.

She rose, her legs unsteady and her chest a little tight. She closed her eyes until she regained her equilibrium. She hated to admit it to herself, much less anyone else, but she was in worse shape than she pretended to be. She concentrated on her heartbeat to center herself. It was a mistake, because it brought her attention to the source of the panic attacks.

A ghost heart thumped slowly in Elissa's chest, each beat dwarfing her own once she noticed it again. Sometimes she sensed its owner slept, but other times, when the heartbeat raced in terror, panic overwhelmed her and triggered her natural inclination to run. At first, she assumed she needed to get away from the heart's source, but over time she'd developed compassion for it and she wasn't sure anymore. If she wasn't crazy, maybe she could do something to help the soul hiding inside her.

She shook her head hard enough to spark a mild headache and walked toward the kitchen door resolutely. She couldn't afford to miss another day of work, and the diner was already short-handed.

"Elissa, what are you still doing here?" A familiar voice called as soon as she stepped into the hall between the dining area and the bathrooms. "I thought I already sent you home."

Had Loretta already sent her home? The blood drained from Elissa's face. She couldn't remember. When had the panic attacks started eating into her memory? She blinked and Loretta stood in front of her, her mouth pulled down in a concerned frown.

"C'mere." Loretta drew her in for a hug, heavy hand rubbing comforting circles on her back. "Girl, you go on home. We've got this. You'll be no use to us here, anyhow."

The classic Loretta gruffness reassured Elissa. The panic attacks wouldn't cost her job, yet.

"Thanks, Loretta. But I really need—"

"Consider it sick leave," Loretta cut in. "We need you in top shape tomorrow, so hurry out of here and get your rest."

The stubborn set of Loretta's chin and eyes were too familiar; all Elissa could do was nod. She grabbed her coat and purse from her locker on her way out. The icy air hit her in the face when she opened the door and she shrugged her coat on. Her breath frosted the air under the blue and green lights of the diner's neon sign.

Even though the other heart was calm, Elissa crooned a low lullaby to herself as she crossed the parking lot and slid into her car. She started the engine and waited for it to heat up. The heartbeat and the radio competed in the small space of her car, making her head throb. She twisted the knob too hard when she turned off the radio and it came off in her hand. She sighed and tossed it into the center console to super glue back on later.

The presence curled into her like another soul inside her skin. It had grown stronger over time and she could pick up its emotions now. The gesture was so comfort-seeking, tears sprang to the corners of her eyes. It hadn't been very far along before she lost her baby, but she imagined this was how it would have felt if she'd had more time with him, another soul inside her body whose peace she could influence. She pressed her hand to her stomach and squeezed her eyes closed, her headache intensifying between her brows as she pushed the memories away. The guilt still found her and reminded her of all the what-ifs she'd played through her head. If only she'd been stronger, she could have fought back when her ex attacked her. She could have protected her baby. Except, she hadn't.

She clenched her hands on the cold steering wheel and her tendons tightened across her knuckles. She didn't need this on top of everything else wrong in her life. How much longer could she take the pain-laced panic attacks? She couldn't rule out the possibility of insanity, but she had to do something this time. Even if she only proved she had lost her mind.

Hands shaking like the needle on the car's temperature gauge, Elissa backed out of the parking spot and then pulled out onto the street. She imagined a line connecting her heart to the big heart beating in its own physical chest. If it was real. The line tugged at her, North. Splitting her attention between the road and the presence beneath her sternum, Elissa drove.

An hour out of town, the forest-lined roads were eerie with the lack of street lights, Elissa worried she'd sent herself on a wild goose chase or, worse, proven her own insanity. After a while, she spotted white lights in the distance. As she approached, they grew so bright they leached the colors out of their surroundings.

The trees opened on the left to reveal a road leading to a huge concrete and metal facility. She pulled over onto the shoulder with the crunch of gravel under her tires. She stared at the man-made field, a wound against the dark forest. Layers of fences topped with razor wire protected the square buildings set toward the center.

Elissa tapped her fingers on the steering wheel as she wondered what she should do next. Part of her hadn't expected to find anything, but as she sat, the presence in her chest unfurled a little, filled with curiosity and awareness. Maybe because of the loss of her son, she began to think of it as a little boy. He knew she was close, she realized, her own heart speeding up at the jolt of happiness and hope he emitted. Like a puppy in a pet shop, he expected her to take him out of the situation he was in.

He anticipated her protection.

She bit her lip. She could barely protect herself in this world, much less whatever was locked down behind all the concrete and razor wire. This could only end in disappointment for them both. What had she expected to do when she got here? She blinked back the sting of tears. She would fail this creature just like she'd failed her baby.

Pain so sharp it felt like she'd been shot radiated from her stomach and she doubled over until her head banged against the top of the steering wheel. The heart galloped within her and drowned out even her own cry. Sweat slicked her skin, the rich brown taking on a gray undertone as her muscles clenched and she keened low in her throat, the creature's terror her own.

Her breath tore from her in rapid bursts and panic ballooned inside her to push everything but the bite of pain from her awareness. A wave of total impotence overwhelmed her and she tumbled inside her own head as breath wheezed in her lungs between hiccups. Memories exploded in her mind's eye, layers of physical attacks overlapping and blending. Rough hands threw her against the wall, fingers twisted in her hair as he dragged her across the carpet, fists pummeled down on her as she curled on the floor to protect her head and stomach the best she could. Never words, just grunts as he took out his anger on her in whatever form he thought best. Begging him to stop never helped.

When she came back to the present, Elissa whispered words of comfort to herself and the presence deep inside her, both of them trembling. The heartbeat pounded so hard her vision shook when she opened her eyes. Still, she could feel the panic subsiding in them both. Pain lingered, but slowly she could breathe through it and her muscles unclenched. Her knuckles popped as she released her grip on the sides of the steering wheel and sat up straight. She continued to croon, snippets of old songs her grandmother used to sing to mask the sounds of shouts, gunshots, and sirens.

The clock on her dash told her thirty minutes had passed since she parked. The facility loomed in the distance, unchanged by her episode.

Her earlier hesitation gone with the panic attack, Elissa thought of all the times she'd closed her blinds or kept driving past some human catastrophe. She'd blocked out the things that weren't her problems. She rubbed the edge of her palm against the bumps of her sternum. The presence wasn't going away and didn't deserve to be ignored like her baby's life had been by everyone she'd reached out to for help. Somewhere deep within the concrete, someone tortured a creature that understood terror, and fled to her to alleviate the suffering he couldn't physically escape. He deserved better, and if Elissa was all he had, she would do the best she could.

Elissa turned the key in the ignition and pulled her car off the shoulder and down the road leading to the facility. She needed a plan.

Would they believe her if she pretended to be lost? Her palms grew clammy as she stopped in front of the gate of the first ring of fence. She worried everything would be over before it began as the mustached guard peered out at her from his booth. He motioned for her to roll down her window.

"You're early. Badge?" He held out his gloved hand, palm up and fingers splayed.

Who did he think she was? Not immediately trusting her voice, she shook her head.

The beginnings of suspicion formed in the lines around his eyes.

"Sorry, I think I forgot it at home." She pretended to rummage through her purse to cover her shaking hands. "It's not here."

His eyes narrowed in annoyance and his lips pursed in a tight scowl, bristling his mustache. He turned away and said something into his walkie-talkie, but she couldn't hear his words.

When he turned back to her, he said, "Go on through this time. You'll need to sign in at the front desk and pick up a temporary badge. Next time, don't leave your badge at home."

She nodded, confused but optimistic when the gate swung open away from her car to let her pass through. Each of the three other gates, all unmanned, did the same.

The final enclosure contained a parking lot in front of the largest of the rectangular buildings. She couldn't see any windows except for the glass front doors of the building. Nervous, Elissa pulled her car into one of the many open parking spots near the middle of the lot and killed the engine. She took a fortifying breath and stepped out of her car into the blinding light.

Her shoes tapped softly against the pavement as she crossed the over-lit parking lot and approached the glass doors. She clenched her fists to redirect the nervous tension bubbling inside her. The door slid open silently when she got close. She paused, inhaled deeply one last time, and stepped into the foyer.

A security counter dominated the foyer and the clock behind it indicated the time was just shy of 9:00pm. The man behind the counter, tall and scrawny with red hair and a dark blue uniform too reminiscent of a police uniform, looked up as she stepped onto the spongy rug in the entrance. Fixtures on the walls lit the room with low light.

"Dale radioed and said you're early and forgot your badge, but you can go ahead and sign in," the security guard said, gesturing to an open log book on the counter. "Where's the rest of the cleaning crew?"

Elissa stared at the uniformed white man and wondered if he would have made the same assumption about a white woman. Anger rose from her gut like a cobra rearing back and she squared her shoulders. She lost herself and her purpose for a moment, as she inhaled to give him a piece of her mind. Then she remembered what she wore, the pea-green dress with white accents of her waitress uniform. Maybe he would have jumped to the same conclusion about a white woman dressed the way she was. She didn't believe it, but she needed to stay calm and avoid suspicion. She was here for a more important purpose than correcting this man, or the guard outside who had probably assumed the same thing.

She brought her gaze down, her stance loose and timid in a way she hoped he'd take as subservience. "They're on the way, the usual time, but I wanted to get a head start. Hoping I can leave a little early if I start now." She smiled sweetly, signing a squiggle of a signature in the next open line in the log book. After a moment's hesitation, she added "cleaning" in the open space next to it.

The guard handed her a badge and gestured toward the elevator. "You go on down, to B2. The thing's been screaming, so you know there's going to be a mess." He chuckled darkly.

Elissa turned toward the elevator before she could sock him in the eye.

The elevator was cold and dimly lit, music-free as it descended to the sub-basement. She rubbed her hands over the pebbled skin of her arms for warmth. The heart raced in her chest, the after-effects of pain and, maybe, the beginning of renewed hope. He knew she was here. She hoped he was as guileless as he felt. The heartbeat seemed huge in her chest and she hoped its owner didn't eat her as soon as he spotted her, after everything else had gone so smoothly.

The metal elevator doors slid open without a preceding ding. Elissa glanced at the panel on the wall to ensure she was at level B2 before she stepped into harsh white lights. She blinked and fought down the urge to gag at the thick smell of urine and fear. She took shallow breaths as her vision cleared, revealing a huge room. Everything was white or metal, from the double row of work stations to the floor and walls and, way up there, even the ceiling. She shivered, remembering the hospital where she'd received the news of her miscarriage from a doctor who didn't care. Somehow, this place seemed even worse.

The light reflected harshly off every surface. She blinked a few times to fully adjust to the light, and then her eyes fell on the creature chained to a large metal pallet across the room, about thirty feet from the closest workstation. He looked like a lizard, his back dark green but his stomach sandy brown. Nubs ran down his back in a double-row, starting right behind his wedge-shaped head and running all the way to the tip of his tail. Two curved horns grew by ear fins on the sides of his head, a fringe of skin stretched between them. His ribs showed against the scales of his sides and she could make out his labored breathing.

Unmanned computers hummed and beeped to the creature's left. Elissa could make out the flash of green lines on the screens, but little else. She only saw four people, all wearing white lab coats buttoned over their clothes.

"You're a little early. Good. There's a big mess to clean tonight." One of the women called out as she turned to meet Elissa's gaze. The front of her lab coat was stained the orange of rust and seaweed green in large splotches. "Grab the mops and buckets. You'll probably need the hoses this time."

The woman tilted her head toward a door to the left.

Yet another white person had assumed she was cleaning crew. "A black woman can walk out of Fort Knox with the gold if she looks like the help," Elissa growled under her breath as she headed toward the indicated door.

Inside, Elissa threw a mop and broom in the holders near the handle of the nearest janitor cart and wheeled it out into the main room.

She headed straight toward the creature chained to the pallet and moved around to the far side so the others couldn't see her. Padlocks as big as both her hands together secured the heavy chains, holding the creature down so he could hardly breathe, much less move. He couldn't even angle his head to look at her straight on. The half-lidded eye on this side observed her.

An instant spark of recognition sizzled through her.

This was him, the owner of the heart beating in her chest and the soul inside her, seeking comfort and protection. Suddenly unafraid, she touched her hand to the surprisingly warm and soft skin of its pebbled cheek, almost as big as her torso. The creature sighed, eyelid closing a little more in relief.

It was one of those creatures from the news, a kaiju, but so small he must have been a baby. He might even fit in her house if there were no walls inside. The creature on the news today had been at least ten stories tall. Someday, this baby would grow into a monster. She wasn't so convinced she should free him now that she knew what he was. Maybe he would gobble her up as soon as she released the chains.

Confusion flooded through her at the thought, and it took her a second to realize it wasn't her own. The kaiju's feelings were inside her, as real as hers. A sharp pang pierced her heart, with the surety that he would never harm his mother. She gasped. The kaiju thought of her as his mother.

Elissa's heart squeezed at the thought of a baby, no matter what kind, tortured in this laboratory. She looked at the floor, awash with blood and urine, and her free hand clenched with rage. Her anger carried not only the atrocities that had happened to this baby kaiju, but all the injustices she had accumulated throughout her life. She had hunkered down in fear and turned her gaze away too many times. No one had ever been willing to fight for her and so she'd been unwilling to fight for anyone else. Even herself.

No more.

No malice came from the kaiju as she stroked his cheek. He fully closed his eye and leaned into her hand as much as the chains allowed. The heartbeat in her chest steadied and the same beat pumped against her hand through his cheek. As her palm absorbed the warmth of his skin, she remembered the creatures were mammalian rather than reptilian, despite their appearance.

"I'm going to get you out of here," she whispered as she slowly withdrew her hand. First, she needed to find the keys.

She tightened her jaw as she wheeled the cart back around toward the workstations. Starting with the closest corner station, she emptied trash cans into the plastic bag in the middle of the cart as she covertly scanned the work areas. She peeked into unlocked drawers when she was sure no one was looking. The kaiju had been in her heart for months, and he couldn't eat with his head tied down as tightly as it was. If they loosened the chains around his head to feed him, the keys should be somewhere nearby.

"Stacia, did you sedate it?" a male voice called out.

Elissa pretended not to listen as she continued down the row of ten workstations.

"No, the pain keeps it weak enough. We get better measurements when it's not sedated," the woman who had spoken to Elissa answered.

"Its heart rate is slow and it's showing other signs of calm that have been in line with past sedation," the man said. "We've never seen these results so soon after a session, outside of sedation."

The four scientists congregated at the man's workstation, their voices carrying as they argued about potential causes and whether someone might have given the kaiju an accidental dose of sedatives.

Elissa unobtrusively emptied his trash when she got to his workstation and continued on. She began to worry one of the scientists might keep the keys on them when she found a keyring with a large skeleton key hanging on a hook by Stacia's monitor, one row back and six workstations down from where the scientists gathered. She dropped it into the front pocket of her uniform, behind her order pad, and finished emptying trash cans to avoid suspicion.

The scientists' discussion continued as she made her way back to the kaiju, putting his body between her and their workstations again.

"You're going to have to work with me, here," she whispered toward his ear-fin. "You have to be strong. I know you still have some fight left in you. I do, too."

On instinct, she fed some of her anger to the presence in her heart, hoping to lend him strength. The muscles bunched under his skin and his eyes slanted open. He glanced at her for reassurance before looking past her toward the wall. She followed his gaze with her own. A giant set of doors loomed, big enough to admit the kaiju. Probably how the scientists got him down into the basement to begin with. That was her best bet of a way out.

She unlocked the padlocks on that side of the kaiju and set them on the pallet as she brought the chains down for minimal noise. She had to work carefully to avoid rubbing the chains against the fresh stitches in his side, just above his belly. They still oozed blood a bit but had mostly clotted.

She cautioned the creature with a soft shush and pulled the mop off the cart. She pushed it around the floor as she moved to the other side of the kaiju and continued to remove locks. No one called out to stop her. A black woman with a mop, she was invisible to the kind of people who would do this to a baby.

The kaiju tensed as all but the last padlock came free. With a start, Elissa realized he waited for her direction to act. Unsure how to communicate with the creature, she sent a mental image to the presence in her chest, of her climbing onto his back and then him breaking free. His understanding whispered through her.

Her own heart raced with nerves. She tried to keep the thought to herself, but could she really trust this alien creature? Shaking her head and breathing a short prayer under her breath, she used the remaining chain to pull herself onto the kaiju's back. She settled in on the thinnest part of his neck right behind his head. Her dress rolled up to her thighs but she had more important things to worry about. Now! She unleashed a flood of pent up anger and determination, filling the kaiju's presence in her heart.

With a roar, he leapt to his feet. The final chain snapped like a toy. Screams rang from behind them and the kaiju reeled. He ran straight through the workstations toward the scientists who had tortured him. Elissa let him tear through them one by one as they tried to flee. She even felt a pinprick of satisfaction when he removed Stacia's upper torso with a single bite. Blood spurted across the white floor and wall beside the elevator.

Someone had triggered the alarm before the scientists scattered. The room flashed red and white as Elissa tugged gently at the kaiju's ear-fin. She mentally sent him the image of them moving toward the exit. When they reached the large doors, she directed him to tap the button to the side with his claw with another mental image. The kaiju hit it correctly on the second try.

The doors opened to reveal an enormous freight elevator. There was no room for the kaiju to turn around, so she slid down his side and pressed the button for the first floor herself. No more chains lay across the kaiju's back to help her regain her seat. Sensing her need, he lowered himself down and positioned a foreleg as an intermediary step. She had just managed to reposition herself on the kaiju's neck when the doors whisked open.

Three guards stood outside the door. The kaiju lashed his tail and knocked them all into the wall with a sickening crunch before they could fire more than a round of shots. The bullets hit the kaiju's hide, awakening a stinging sensation in her hip, but they weren't strong enough to penetrate the plates that protected his back and sides.

"Let's get you out of this evil place before more show up," she said as she held on tight to the two curved horns on his head.

He backed out of the elevator and down the hall until he could turn around in a side hall. She opened herself to him and sent her pride at the good job he did. He galloped down the hall, still fueled by the rage she had fed him. She ducked behind the fringe between his horns as he lowered his head and barreled straight through the glass door that led out.

Military trucks roared nearby. A helicopter shined a spotlight down, finally pinpointing them. She directed the kaiju toward the woods and he increased his speed. His long strides made her feel like they flew just above the ground. He leapt over the first and second fences in a single bound each, sailing clear of the razor wire.

The burn of the kaiju's, tired muscles radiated through Elissa's limbs as though it were her own as they neared the third fence, but he leapt before she could stop him. She was sure they'd cleared it, but then the sharp sting of razor wire bit into his hind leg. He flipped as he fell and she flew from his back.

She rolled nearly to the last fence and pain flared through her right hip and knee. She turned to see the kaiju had taken down a whole section of fence when he tangled his foot. The military vehicles closed some of the distance, the convoluted route through the fences slowing them down. The helicopter hovered overhead and someone shouted over a megaphone. Elissa was so focused on the kaiju she couldn't make out the words.

The kaiju regained his footing, the razor wire still tangled around his hind foot. She stumbled to his side, ignoring the pain in her hip and knee as she sent him soothing words and encouraged him not to struggle. She sliced her fingers as she unwrapped the razor wire, but finally pried it free. The cuts were painful, but not too deep.

Just as she moved to climb onto the kaiju's back, the helicopter opened fire. The kaiju pushed her down and stood over her to protect her from the bullets showering down on them. The sting of their impact against his back made the muscles along her spine twinge, but his back was even more heavily armored than his sides. A fierce sense of protectiveness rushed through her. She wasn't sure whether it originated from her or the kaiju.

"Stand down!" A voice boomed over a loudspeaker, drowning out even the sound of the guns firing on them. "That's an order!"

The bullets stopped and the kaiju growled low in his throat. She sensed his focus shift from above them to the left. She peeked around his leg to see a tall black man, hair more gray than black, in an Army uniform standing about ten yards away, a black Humvee behind him.

"I have a proposition for you," he said.

She scowled at him. She didn't want to take his bait but they didn't have a choice. "I'm listening."

"I'm sorry we've met under these circumstances, but I'd like you to consider a spot on an elite squad of kaiju tamers."

His words were so unbelievable, she searched his face for a clue of his sincerity. She couldn't imagine why he would lie, but opportunities like this never happened to her. "Why me?"

"I think it's clear that you possess... a certain skill set that makes you a perfect candidate."

"And if I refuse?" Though part of her wanted to snatch the offer, she couldn't resist pushing her boundaries.

"Then you die, and your kaiju goes back to being a science experiment."

Elissa pressed her lips together. She didn't trust him, but they didn't have any other options. Her kaiju. She liked the sound of that, though she belonged to the kaiju just as much as the other way around. She tentatively reached out to the kaiju in her heart and found them in agreement.

"All right," she said. "We're in."

"Failure is Lucrative" by T.J. Valour

*Robot Assassin in an Evil Laboratory

This story contains content regarding the loss of a child

The sleeping princess lays unmoving, totally spellbound in the hospital bed. Bella's blonde hair gleams like spun gold in the harsh florescent lights of the patient ward. Her small frame is piled high with blankets and they hide most of the emaciation caused by the fungus that is killing her. But her delicate cheek bones are too sharp, her eyes too sunken for a ten-year-old, and the green pallor of her skin distorts the illusion of a sleeping princess even further. I scoot my chair closer and gently cover her hand with my own. It's cool and clammy under my glove like it has been since her diagnosis.

Annually the government issues a scientific publication of potential bioweapon materials. The top of the list is expected: viruses and bacteria. No one could have predicted that the sole fungus that is included on the list would become the instigator of panic and cause a state of emergency along the entire Eastern seaboard.

Three years ago, a terrorist organization got ahold of my data—my inadvertent formula of death. Their black biology lab cooked up strain of my manipulated version of *Coccidioides Immitis* and pumped it into a grade school's ventilation.

What I had originally believed might function as an inoculation against other resistant fungal infections became known as Valley Fever X. With the casualties continuing to rise, the lack of any vaccine for virulent pathogenic fungi became an unprecedented medical crisis.

Immunization still isn't an option, and pathogenic fungi are naturally resistant to drugs. Unlike bacterial infections that can be treated and cured in days, what treatments exist for fungal infections take weeks to months if they're effective at all.

Valley Fever X is the anthrax of our century, and it's anthrax on steroids. My creation is an unstoppable harbinger of death that I will never be able to atone for.

I can't raise the dead, but I can keep more innocents from dying. Years of tireless work has finally paid off with a breakthrough to counterbalance my past mistakes. My new vaccine attacks and neutralizes the Valley Fever X spores in the host's blood serum. It's a super antifungal with the rapid reaction time of an emergency inhaler.

I can save Bella, I know I can. I hold that power now, but my cure hasn't been tested on a human host. The rats, pigs, and computer algorithms all attest to its success and likely infallibility. Yet to try it on Bella...that isn't a decision I can make alone.

As the quiet evening hours slowly tick onward, I send a mental request to Samantha to neural connect. The only reason we haven't terminated it and had the electrodes deactivated along with our joint bank accounts is because of Bella.

Frankly, we both use it as a crutch, a means to hold onto the razor-edge of our sanity and share our pain even as we drown in sorrow and near hopelessness. Until now.

Jason? Samantha opens the connection between us. Since I initiated the request, she can see what I see, hear what I hear. She can feel my hope, excitement, but also my bone deep fear. I can sense her emotions to some extent as well, but they are muted with distance. She's somewhere in Europe right now. I probably woke her.

Your cure? Even inside my mind her question is quiet, afraid to hope, but her mind sharpens to wakefulness. Sam is a biomedical engineer for an international medical company; she knows everything I've invested into this over the last three years. She also knows as much as I do what is at stake. If this doesn't work, Bella is likely to die within weeks as the Valley Fever X spreads and begins to attack her central nervous system. If I don't intervene and destroy this microscopic monster that is destroying her, it'll reach her brain and there will be nothing left of our little girl.

Let me save her, Sam. It's worked in every trial—every test. This is the last step before we can make it public and distribute it nationwide. There would be no better way to show that my formula works than saving my own child.

I can feel Sam's turmoil, but she wants this. Wants a touch of normalcy back in our already broken family.

What if it doesn't work?

The odds it won't are minuscule, but in science, chemistry, medicine, the smallest of mistakes can have deadly results. She knows that. *I've checked her plasma already and it accepts the new antibodies well, so—even if it fails to cure her— there shouldn't be any adverse results.*

Then do it, Jason. Be the hero Bella always thought you were.

I'd been Sam's hero once too, before I put my career first, shut her out. I have much to atone for, but I would start here. Save the most beautiful thing that still survives between us.

We'll make it to Rockefeller Center in time for New Years. Bella loved ice skating, she'd have been at the rink everyday if we allowed it.

I can almost see Sam smile at that. Some of our greatest holiday memories have been skating at that rink under the tree and city lights.

I'll hold you to that. Just like she hadn't let me lose my humanity in my work, she would hold me to this, too.

My lab is located eight floors above the subterranean patient ward that houses Bella and a handful of other infected that we've managed to keep alive. They range in age from six to twelve years old. Saving them will be the first real step in my reparation.

A knock on the door tears me from my thoughts, and Dr. Medina waltzes into Bella's room. My MedTech bot stands just over Medina's shoulder, an ever-present assistant whether I want it or not.

"I updated its operating system for you and ran it through a system check," she says with a plastic smile. Dr. Megan Medina is petite, and her personality is as fiery as her current hair color. She doesn't like me. We have…differing opinions on the future of medicine.

I don't bother to smile back. "I didn't ask you to do that. It was functioning fine."

She crosses her arms over her chest and scowls. "Don't pretend to know robotics and what is best for them, Charkot. They'll make people like you obsolete before the next century."

I won't get into this argument again. People, humans, belong in medicine. Healing science is so much more than injections and pills. Its quality of care, understanding, and sympathy, so many things that robots and machines can never fully emulate. My cure is the result of human ingenuity, not some math formula and a computer process.

As if sensing my resolve, she changes the subject. "I let General Wren know that you finalized your antidote. He'd like samples sent to Dallas and Washington by tonight."

I blink. She went behind my back...I haven't even finalized my report yet...

"However horrific, you can't doubt the results of Valley Fever X. And just think, you'll be able to publicly right your wrong." Medina waves her hand flippantly. "Erase the terrible evil that came out of this lab."

Thousands of children dying *is* beyond terrible. It's an atrocity.

Pain shoots up my jaw, and I unclench my teeth. "The cure hasn't been tested yet. It might not work."

She rolls her eyes. "Don't be so modest, Charkot. Of course it will work. You healed the rats, the two pigs. Plus, my 'bots and the computer programs all confirm that it's the real deal."

When I don't respond immediately, she continues, "You're just afraid to try it on someone you care about. This has nothing to do with it failing to work. Don't be a coward, Charkot." With that, she turns on her heel and disappears back down the hallway to the elevators that will take her back up to the lab.

I stare after her until I hear the ding of the elevator doors closing. Bitch.

I am not a coward. If I was, I'd have hidden after Valley Fever X went public, likely killed myself instead of dealing with the brutal backlash and publicity. I am not one to run away, nor do I doubt my work.

Removing a vial of the serum from my pocket I hold it out to the MedTech bot. It rolls fully into the room at my gesture. The bot is roughly an inverted triangular shape with a black dome on top. It has six mechanical arms and each of them serve a special medical purpose.

The entire robot is covered in surgical chromed steel and moves silently with hover technology.

The MedTech grasps my formula with a delicate, clawed hand and the vial disappears into its core compartment. The machine connects seamlessly to Bella's hospital bed in a patient interface, since we're in the ward and not the lab. In surgery, the 'bot acts as an extension of my will, allowing me to manipulate lasers and other medical utensils utilizing its advance optics, precision movements and finite control. Bella's been in a coma for a month, so the robot expels all automated patient interactions. It is solely acting as a physician assistant, without the risk of being be a carrier of disease or illness, and it acts without error or lapses in judgement. The perfect PA.

"Dr. Charkot, hospital policy dictates that new procedures, research advancements, and new treatments be recorded. Do you consent to audio and visual recording of this administration of formula 07981, on patient 01, Bella Charkot, ten-year-old female?"

The robot holds my cure and the key to my daughter's future.

I stare into the black orb perched atop its angular center compartment. "I consent."

The MedTech's globe of a head nods once. There is a slight whirr as the robot injects my antidote into Bella's IV drip. The bag of liquid takes on a purple tint. I can still feel Samantha's presence in my mind, waiting, attentive; she's with me, has been every step of the way. Minutes tick by before my formula enters Bella's blood stream and takes effect.

Her hand turns warm under my own. The faintest of tremors moves through her small body. Her eyes flicker under her eyelids.

"Come on, Bella. Let it in. You can do this," I say under my breath as I squeeze her fingers. When she squeezes back, time slows to a crawl. This is her first reactive movement since becoming comatose.

"Her heart rate is accelerating," the MedTech announces in monotone.

"Give it another moment."

Bella's limbs start to bounce and jump. Her fingers spasm and twitch, their movements becoming more and more pronounced with each passing second.

She lifts her head, a fraction.

It's beyond anything I hoped for. "Come on, Bella."

Under my palm, the jerking stops and her body goes from fiery hot to clammy, to nearly ice cold. Nothing in my antidote should have produced this result.

Utter stillness settles over us for a heartbeat, then every alarm in the room goes off. The white lights turn brilliant cobalt as the code blue gets transmitted to every available robot in the patient ward. My stomach twists so violently I nearly vomit.

"Vfib arrest detected, initiating lifesaving protocol 04," says the MedTech.

I'm forced out of the way as two other droids, these ones ED220 units, zip into the room and begin cardiopulmonary resuscitation. With the third chest compression I hear the distinctive crack of a rib fracturing. The sound hits me in the gut like a sucker punch. I can't breathe.

"Stand clear. Shock eminent." The computronic words sound so clinical. So bland. If I didn't know better, I'd say they were treating an animal and not a human being.

James! What's happening?

"Stand clear. Shocking."

*Something's wrong...Bella's...*I can't finish my thought. No. Not my daughter. "Bring her back," I say aloud. My voice sounds strangled out of my chest.

The robots ignore me and continue the CPR protocol. I watch the computer screen over the bed as Bella gets her second round of epinephrine. An ED220 shocks her again. The cycle continues. Chest compressions. Forced respiration. Shocks to her heart muscle.

Over and over.

I can feel Samantha. Her terror, disbelief—

Eventually the robots stop their work, and the two ED220s leave. The lights turn back to white and the machines that kept Bella alive for so long power down, leaving only deafening quiet.

"Pronouncement time recorded for death certificate. Dr. Charkot present in the room as family," the MedTech says as it disengages from Bella's bed.

I reach a hand out but drop it before I can touch Bella. The rust stain on my hands is now the dark red of heart's blood. I am the murderer the media called me. So many children's lives have been snuffed out before they could truly live. I did that. I caused it all, and now my beautiful princess will never ice skate again. I've killed my daughter.

I don't remember leaving Bella, or the elevator ride back to the lab, but I hear the security door seal behind me. The cabinet near my desk is full of beakers, petri dishes, and other supplies. I yank it out of the wall. The cacophony of it hitting the floor drowns out my waste basket impacting the window.

I pick up the tablet I've slept with for the last few years in a vain attempt to hold onto every thought and scientific possibility related to my cure. All of it for nothing.

The tablet screen shatters as I slam it into my desk and then pitch it across the lab. It breaks into three parts as it hits the industrial table that holds several diagnostic machines. The tablet holds a good portion of last month's work. But what is the purpose in saving it? The antidote killed my innocent, helpless, baby girl.

I collapse into my chair, breathing heavy. The tightness in my throat is a symptom of a grief so intense it suffocates. I deserve worse. Swallowing back a choked sob, I run my hand over my face. My eyes feel swollen, and my cheeks are wet.

The last time I cried was at Bella's birth. Her body was so tiny, so perfectly delicate in my arms.

You couldn't have known, James, Sam thinks.

Obligatory empathy. She's always tried to be understanding, forgiving, even when she shouldn't be. Sam should know better.

Couldn't I have?

I shove my hand in my pocket. Feel the second vial of my failed cure. In a daze I pull it out. The serum looks normal, a pale almost iridescent hue to it. A pretty blue. Blue. It shouldn't be blue. I hold the vial up to the light. Still blue.

My formula is a pale violet base. Violet becomes lighter as it's diffused with the saline.   There shouldn't have been any reaction resulting in a chemical color change when my formula is added to an

IV. Yet this vial holds a blue formula that caused the saline in Bella's IV to turn purple.

Standing, I move to the diagnostic table.

The MedTech bot hums behind me as it enters the lab and begins to clean up the mess I made.

I compress one drop of what I thought was the viable cure into a microscope slide and import it into the enzyme linked immunosorbent assay. The ELISA machine sucks it into its testing chamber like a hungry hippo.

Something has to be different about this batch. Something must have been off. A miscalculation…some sort of contamination. I triple check everything before even considering a live test.

The ELISA machine churns my sample, adding in the substrate, and combining the base antibody into my sample.

I'm intimately familiar with my formula, so much so I can see every step of its creation and every bit of the chemistry involved when I close my eyes. I know what will happen next. Pale green blue is its reactive color and the index value numbers are clearer in my mind than my social security number.

I blink. That can't be correct.

I look up at the clock across the room to refocus my eyes and stare back at the results.

The slide remains neon pink. Not a bit of green in sight. The mathematical breakdown is something so far *other* than my formula I'm not even sure what I'm looking at. Some alien spin off of Lyme disease?

What the hell?

I check it again and the results don't change. Would the MedTech have administered the wrong formula? And what happened to my cure? The serum I handed directly to the MedTech's clawed appendage came straight out of my secure storage. Only I, General Wren, and Dr. Medina have the codes.

James? Sam's confusion and unbelief are as clear in her voice as if she is standing next to me.

Bella wasn't given my cure.

A pause. *I saw you hand the MedTech bot the vial containing your antidote.*

Except it wasn't my antidote. I glance up from the ELISA machine to the MedTech robot. It's finished cleaning and is at its recharging station, awaiting new orders.

"MedTech, the serum that was administered to patient Bella Charkot, what was its medicinal purpose?"

The black dome swivels toward me. "The parenteral formulation of the serum injected into patient 01, was formula 07981."

I frown. MedTech robots aren't programmed to be elusive or coy. "What is the medical purpose of formula 07981?" I repeat.

This time the robot disengages from the charging station and rolls toward the table I'm seated at. It stops opposite from me.

"The purpose of formula 07981, administered to patient 01, is to create a parasympathomimetic interaction, overstimulate the patient's neural processes to the point that a fatal arrythmia results."

My brain blanks. Static fills my ears.

What...did it just say? Sam's stuttering question breaks into my shock. *Oh my God.*

The ELISA machine goes dark as does the desk lamp and all the other machines next to it. Their power switch flipped off by the MedTech 'bot.

"What happened to the prototype version of formula 07981?" I ask, as I stand up slowly from the ELISA console. My work is saved on the hospital's Cloud, backed up at home. I step slowly backward.

All of the surrounding equipment is either bolted down or too heavy for me to swing as a weapon. The acids are in a secure cabinet ten feet away and the hydrofluoric acid is in a nice big plastic container up front. It's my only chance.

The robot remains in place. "The antidote has been secured for safekeeping."

"You murdered my daughter." I make it two more steps.

"I am an autonomous machine. My actions are based on orders. I am nothing but a tool."

"Then I order you to upload your memory banks to my computer for review." If the droid did that, we would be able to tell what and if something short-circuited in its programming.

"Unfortunately, Dr. Charkot, your position as my superior has been revoked. Dr. Medina is now the director of this lab. You have been terminated. Do not resist."

Megan? But how could she— Sam asks. *Jason, I think you need to run. Get away!*

"Dr. Medina handles robotics, not immunology. This lab and attached hospital ward is government funded because of its immunology department." My hip hits the counter in front of the acids cabinet. Maybe by some stroke of luck it's been left open.

"No longer. The immunology and clinical pathology departments have been terminated. Your research will become profitable if used in alternative ways and if dissemination is controlled," it replies. Then seeming to notice I have moved, its dome twirls once and then a blinking orange light fixates on me. "My protocols tell me that you are attempting to be uncompliant with a doctor's orders." It comes toward me, three of its arms raised—two pincher claws and the intravenous attachment. There could be any number of sedatives or drugs the thing could mix and hit me with. Kill me or worse.

The chrome carapace reflects a skewed version of me as it gets within striking distance.

I slam my hand backward and grasp the acid cabinet handle. I yank it twice but it's locked.

My boxing skills are rusty since I haven't used them since pre-med, but I succeed in landing a solid hook to the robot's dome. The resounding crack is substantial but doesn't even give the droid pause. Pain shoots up my hand and arm, and I'm pretty sure I've broken a knuckle.

Two robotic claws act like manacles and encircle my upper arms to pin them to my sides. I can hear the grinding and popping of muscle and tissue fibers as they're crushed against my bones. Agony drills into my skull like a sledgehammer. I lash out with my feet and legs but only succeed in making contact once before my knees are wrapped together with a canvas binding. The same binding we use to restrain animals in the labs.

A sharp pinch under my ear makes me flinch and a burn spreads out from my neck to my jaw and upper chest. Needle pricks of pain lacerate my corneas and I see spots of white.

*Samantha, my cure—my real cure everything is saved. My password is PrincessBella19465. I need you to—*My thoughts fracture as my body turns numb. I try to turn my head, move, but all I can feel is the sudden heat.

The flicker of red and orange flame reflects in the thick-polished steel panes that serve as the laboratory's walls. Fire. Everything that surrounds me is highly flammable, and somehow I don't think that is a mistake.

Out of the corner of my vision I see the MedTech remove my computer drive. Then it disappears out of view and I hear the beep of the security door being opened.

"Dr. Charkot?" a female voice asks.

"Eliminated. Please follow protocol, Dr. Medina. We need to exit the building. The alarm will sound in six minutes—"

The security door closes and imprisons me. One of the research cabinets explodes in a burst of heat and glass. The debris rain down over my body in a biting hail that sizzles into my face and exposed skin. Heavy, black smoke fills the lab and burns my throat and lungs. I taste blood along with the ash.

I'm too exhausted to cough. I know without a doubt I'm about to die.

My guilt falls like a lead blanket over my body, holding me to the rapidly heating floor. My soul is tainted by death. There are so many things left unfinished, unsaid. Sam…Bella. I'll hold her again. Be able to tell her I'm sorry. Sorry for everything. So sorry…

James! James! Samantha screams my name as the lab around me grows dimmer and dimmer until the darkness pulls me under.

My angelic princess is sleeping in a bed of white in front of me. Bella's chest rises and falls in a sleep that welcomes me with open arms.

"What Will be Created" by C. L. Kagmi
Alien in the Human Mind

Sensation comes first as a torrent. The impulses are a familiar fabric; something she should know, but they form constellations she cannot decipher. An unintelligible language.

The bombardment is like being caught in a hail storm. Hell, for a newborn. She knows, *knows* that she should understand this. But understanding will not come.

It takes time. Some part of her learns faster than she knows, little matrices being laid down to translate one pattern into another. The formless onslaught begins to take shape. And then...

Sight.

A vast, empty distance stretches between her and a distant, dully shining surface. The emptiness is dizzying, vertigo-inducing. Something is wrong with the way it refracts light.

Ceiling. Something outside of her supplies the word, which is another new thing. Word. A sound with a specific meaning.

She tries to swim toward the ceiling. The emptiness gives her no purchase, no push. Groping for instructions where her memories should be, she finds herself trying to stand.

Stand. Another thing she recollects only dimly, as through another set of eyes. A crazy, impossible, vertical motion. Her new, gangly body seems to know this motion of its own accord. It stacks its bones; long levers, angles and pulls at them. When the muscles pull just right, her bones stand atop each other end-to-end.

She watches the procedure with amazement. It should not work, but somehow it does. She is staring down from a great distance, through a void of nothingness, at the floor.

She sways and falls. The terrifying experience squeezes a scream from her lungs as she clutches uselessly at the empty void. Her body's memory is not enough to walk, it seems, but she manages to prop herself up into a position called sitting. She manages to look across the world, as one should, instead of looking up.

Hands. That's what these tendrils are; like anemones full of sticks. Arms. Legs. She knows of these things, has heard of them in the arthropods that dwell in the shallows, never leaving the safety of the reef. Is this an arthropod body she inhabits?

No. She sees no joints where her bones meet. This body has soft flesh, soft skin like any fish, but this body dwells in air.

A sliver of memory. A whisper. Not yet a memory, but the suggestion of it. She feels elation. Something is unfurling and when it does, she thinks, she will feel whole.

Time, it tells her. It needs more time.

She dreams of the thing coming out of the sky. White-hot and bright as a meteor; they thought this thing from the sky was like the others but this did something that no meteor had ever done: it *slowed*. It slowed and settled, harmlessly, atop the Coral Ridge. It began to build.

There was debate, between the World-Minds, over whether to let the thing take its course. It could be hostile, they reasoned. It seemed alive but had not deigned to communicate with anyone. It did not even seem to be made of flesh; their surveyors tasted only metal, meaningless, unreadable to native tongues.

What might it release? What might it create?

Yet, therein lay the question. This was something this world had not seen in eons: this was something *new*. The philosophers had deduced that other worlds may exist. Many fires in the sky; smaller than their own Sun, or merely further away? Were these suns orbited by other water-droplets, other World-Minds with other ways of thinking?

It seemed that the answer was "yes."

The World-Minds bloomed with imagined possibilities. They had been able to do so much with their single world, their single origin of life. What might they do with a second? With two, or three? If there were worlds around every star, what *unimaginable* things were possible? What new structures, what diversity?

Hands, she reflected, upon waking. Hands were one new structure.

She tried again to walk. Took two steps, this time, and managed to catch herself on hands and knees when she fell.

A vague fear had begun to tug at her, at the corners of her mind. Like the first murmurs of memory, it was not yet fully realized.

She herself, in her mind's eye, standing and talking with others of her kind.

She felt a need to make this happen *soon*.

The creatures, she remembers, came in the second sending. Another meteor blossomed in the sky; slowed and settled daintily upon a tiny lily pad that had sprouted from the thing on the Ridge. The *humans* must have transferred down, probably through the thing's thick stem.

Soon, the thing on the reef began to deploy offspring.

There were smaller, metal things, as impenetrable as the original growth itself, but these were mobile; they swam through strange mechanisms, at once powerful and wildly inefficient. Who had expected them not to be strange? The World-Minds studied, and they learned. Already new designs had been conceived based on these alien gifts.

From the metal children came things stranger still; small things that moved like horribly designed fish. They had the fluidity, the flesh-softness of an organic being, but when bitten they tasted like nothing living. Carbon chains woven together in crazy configurations; nothing that bore information. Nothing that would sustain life. They were another kind of metal. That was all. Until they got the first one's helmet off.

They'd known for some time that something moved *inside* the glass panes on the larger beasts, but those had proven quite impenetrable. While exploring the hard, round coverings that protruded from the smaller ones, though, a sort of latch had been discovered.

They've seen fit to load her with the memories of that, and they unfurl before her now. An explosion of silver bubbles as air escaped, impossibly, from *inside* the slender creature. Soft flesh underneath it, and beneath that, blood and organs like her own.

Truly like her own, she realized, looking down. They'd put her in one of those alien bodies—one of the smaller, softer things.

Stand, her brain whispered urgently, and she did again.

Managing the legs is hell— the slightest turn of an ankle sends the whole assemblage tumbling down again but, in time, she begins to see the loveliness of them. The teetering absurdity comes with remarkable agility. No arthropod or fish has ever had such freedom of movement in the near-vacuum that is *air*.

The hands, too, grow on her. She soon sees their utility. The bones— *endoskeleton*, she is provisionally calling them— allow her to hold objects away from herself, manipulating them with greater dexterity than tentacles would permit. The entire environment in which she finds herself seems to be based on this principle. Everything she encounters seems designed to be manipulated using *hands*.

The creature seems to have almost no sense of taste, almost nothing with which to analyze the chemistry of their environment, but their senses of sight and sound are so acute she sometimes struggles to keep up.

A horrible suspicion begins to grow in her as she explores, taking her wobbling body through the corridors of its home. She has encountered no messages from others here. The air is clear and silent, her tongue is silent. She may as well be alone.

Alone.

The concept takes her suddenly, forcefully, and she has to stop to allow her knees to buckle.

Alone is not a thing her people have known since time immemorial. Their words are in the water, their messages, the proof of their presence... Does this thing truly live in such aloneness, or has she integrated something wrong?

"Karin. Are you alright?"

Beginnings of meanings spark through her mind at that, but she can formulate no appropriate response. Her tongue fumbles, produces a slurred sound.

The other form stares at her with features frighteningly bizarre: two large eyes, odd structure in the middle of the face, a mouth filled with teeth like dull pebbles. Its face crinkles into what her brain calls a *frown*. It takes her by her shoulders— a sensation that sends heat coursing through her bodies. The memory of reproductive pleasantness.

Reproductive? Why would these creatures be bred, not made? Perhaps it made sense for explorers, who may become separated from their World-Mind and Womb.

"Let's take a walk," it tells her, something she recognizes as *caution* in its voice. "To the infirmary."

The other shapes mill about her, swaying and crouching in impossible ways as they examine her eyes, her mouth, her hands. She is becoming acquainted with their version of distress. The others seem to defer to one, darker than the others, with a mass of black hair protruding from his face. She tries to remember what this symbol indicates, and realizes she is frowning.

He examines her, makes worried sounds, and speaks softly with the others. A more developed mind, perhaps, could have caught the words, but to her the murmurs are meaningless.

She has a goal, she remembers, and tries to recall what it is. Sees images of this brown body swimming, naked, in the sea. Her instincts tell her, also, that she must not resist them as they move her toward the *scanner*—a thing that reveals what is hidden. Her heart pounds for no reason she can name as she lays down on it. At the last minute her limbs flail wildly, as though to swim, as though she were again falling. One of the creatures—the one who met her in the corridor, the one with blue eyes— smiles apologetically as he holds her down.

An image of her own body materializes above her, floating as in water. The flesh is stripped away, layer by layer. She stares, marveling, and forgets to struggle. What is this? Some shared imagination? Perhaps she *is* linked into some sort of shared neural net after all.

She realizes, then, that it is silent. The others have stopped stripping down the image, are staring at it transfixed.

Horror.

They do communicate, somehow, without words. She feels their *horror* on the air as they turn the hologram in the air above her. Her body is illuminated, all its tissues, and she studies the play of tendons and organs, the invaluable opportunity to learn more about how she works.

They fixate on her head, her brain, turning its image over and over again in their hands.

With faint pride, she sees herself: a splatter-spray of gold, an infant nervous system penetrating the round mass of the *human* brain. She has grown so fast.

Slowly, the meaning of their horror dawns upon her. They do not *like* that she is there. They are not interested in what she means, in what she can teach them. Are not interested, perhaps, in speaking with an emissary from this world at all.

They want her *gone*.

The warning is pounding in her blood again, and she begins to understand the meaning of her urgency. *Run*, urges something in her mind. But even if she could manage it… she sees the layout of the base in Karin's memory: only one way into the sea. Centrally controlled, closely guarded. She could make it only if undetected and *alone*.

Run. She holds herself to stillness, trembling.

The hands of the blue-eyed creature, she realizes, are in her hair. His eyes are fixed on the image of her, in a way that fills her with a new kind of fear. A fear she does not yet have words to name.

She remembers this, now, from the old days.

She has to reach far back into her memory to accomplish this. Millennia, millennia. Past the Great Darkness and the Great Cold. Into time inconceivable. Into time before the birth of the World-Minds.

She never would have found it, perhaps, but something in her has made the connection. It leads her like an invisible thread through memories that ache with ancientness, through views so faded with the mists of time that she feels she has entered another realm.

The senses of the creature that she finally inhabits are dim, its mind a sluggish, simple thing. Her mind seems to exist above, as though its tiny brain can hold only a tiny fraction of her own.

There is more. This ancestor is *singular*. It is alone.

What language the current carries is simple, primitive, and most of it tastes not of self, but of *other*.

In the days before the World was one. The phrase, written in modern carbon, comes unbidden to her tongue.

Before…

In the time so long ago, no one has had cause to think about it in ages. In the time thought long-abandoned, like the days when only single-celled life swam in these seas.

Her ancestors— her ancestors and the ancestors of the World-Minds both, the ancestors of *everything* now living— had invaded unwilling hosts.

Penetrate. Slow, slow. Unseen. Slow.

Her flesh sinking into the flesh of another, that would *fight* her if it found her. Her nerves creeping, growing, along another's neural tract. As she has done with Karin Sasomoto.

A shark thrashing: distress. Distress pulsing through its blood, its brain. *Distress*. The shark hadn't wanted her either, but it hadn't been able to do a damn thing about it. Her people had gotten better at what they did. Had learned to work together. To form larger brains out of many smaller ones; to design ecosystems that thrived for all.

The World-Minds were smarter, wiser than any single brain could hope to be. There hadn't been a mind that objected to their presence in millennia. They had assumed that this joining of the man was the only way intelligence could evolve.

Perhaps, perhaps they were wrong.

They keep her in an isolation tank, and on her own supply of air. There are more of them than there are of her and they possess some terrifying drug, like her ancestors' sedative, that sends her into instant sleep if she resists. The barrier is not quite soundproof. She listens to the humans talk.

Pathogen. Disease. Sterilize.

This planet, they are saying, is dangerous. *Karin* is probably unsalvageable. But they are going to try with medications— things designed to kill the disease, while leaving the host intact.

She is the disease.

This planet is dangerous to ones like them, and it must be made safe. It must be cured.

She pounds her small, soft hands filled with uselessly hard bones against the glass of the isolation tank and tries to speak. If there were a way to make them understand.

"Help... we... are... friends!"

They turn and stare at her with wider eyes, wider mouths, with a paling of the skin. Distress reactions. They find it *worse* when she speaks to them.

"Talk... to me!"

Two of them leave, as though she may yet break through the glass and eat them. The third vomits into a waste receptacle and smiles up at her with great, sad blue eyes.

"I'm sorry, Karin," he says.

Karin.

A personal name, formed in air, for a creature strange beyond imagining. As her genetic memories unfurl, she remembers what this one was. Flesh after flesh deposited in disposal dishes, blood staining the water that ran off of them. Driving toward a goal, but what goal, if not communication?

Caleb.

The blue-eyed one. They had tried to communicate, yes. He had done most of the work. Had spent hours, days and nights, before her parents' cage. Building a language. And then, and then…

And then a blank. A blank in the memory, in what her parent chose to give her, means what happened after doesn't matter. What matters is what she knows. The blue-eyed one wants to communicate.

But it also wants *Karin* back.

Perhaps if she pretends to be her, she can reach him.

She goes quiet. From what she can remember of her forebear watching *Karin*, she was often quiet. Sitting at a table, staring at displays, at dishes filled with freshly butchered meat.

She has no tools with which to replicate the latter, so she just sits quietly, and waits for someone to notice.

Caleb comes again the next day with a look that she identifies as "sad" about him.

"Hello," she says.

Caleb blinks. Stares.

She must be careful. Quiet. She can find words but does not know how to make them sound right, how to use them as *Karin* would.

"Hello," he says softly, in a tone that makes it clear he doesn't think it's her.

She hazards a look at him. Tries to be cautious about it, oblique. She has noticed that the humans don't stare at each other. Only at her.

The expression in his eyes *hurts*. Causes physical pain in her chest running down her arms and into her hands. She looks down at them, alarmed, and wonders if she's dying. It's then that she notices her eyes are filling with protective tears.

"Caleb," she chokes, in real alarm. Has she done something wrong and broken this body? Or is this the medicine beginning to kill her and leave the host intact?

Caleb is at the glass that separates it, hands flat against it, staring at her in a way that makes it *worse*, and she finally understands.

She understands: the human brain remembers, too. The pain is *Karin's* body, reacting to his sadness.

"I can't let you out," he says. "I'm sorry. I'm so sorry."

"When?" she manages.

When. It's something *Karin* might ask.

"When you— oh God, it really is you, isn't it? Your father— what's your father's name?"

She has access to all of *Karin's* memories. *Father* conjures images of salt sea and waves; a place where land meets water. Of golden brown skin, smile-lines crinkling around the eyes.

"Lou," she tells him.

She must have gotten it wrong, for the other human sinks into a crouch and he is sobbing.

Nightfall finds her still alive, so she stares at the ceiling and tries to think of how to escape. The human *Karin* knew the layout of the outpost; this metal shell is no creature, she understands now, but a mere device built by human minds and hands. What minds these humans must have! She detects no trace of such capacity in her own, but perhaps if they work together as the World-Minds do...

To get out of this place she would have to get out of isolation, first; then down a corridor spanning the better part of the base's circumference, then past security— the human *Karin's* ID card is back in her quarters, for she didn't know to take it with her— and into a water lock. After she hits the water, they might be able to get her back if they try, but they might also let her go, saying good riddance to the pathogen.

Until...

Sterilization.

An image from her memory, old and shrouded in the fogs of time, of fire raining from the sky. Before the Great Cold, the Great Dark. They could do that, these creatures. If not something worse.

Stop. Kill. Her instructions are beginning to recalibrate. She was born to be, built to be an explorer, but all of the World-Mind's children have a subroutine to prioritize protecting their parent. How could they not? And yet, this threat is like none they have faced before.

Pathogen. Disease.

She has so much time to get to know the human body. A human body, and her parent's equipment— the two things she needs. Her goal is a matter for greater consideration. To craft a thing which would kill this body and spread to others on the station would be easy. It would also be pointless. She sees in *Karin's* mind that these humans came here, not through random dispersion, but through careful planning.

She spends time playing with strands of RNA, with viral capsules, with the sort of DNA she might gift to her own young.

Penetrate. Slow, slow. Unseen. Slow.

Yes. If she had been *slower*, she could have learned better. Passed better. Hidden better.

She is young to be crafting offspring, but she has little choice.

The blue-eyed one comes to visit her daily. Sits, often, with his back to her, leaning on the glass.

Karin's brain still feels a fondness for him, and a sadness. A sadness even through her screaming fear, her uncertainty of what will happen to her people.

She tries to talk to him.

"I... miss...you."

It's true. Her body misses him. Her parent was wise enough to leave most of the human brain— most of *Karin*— intact. They knew she'd need it. But she doesn't sound enough like *Karin* when she says it.

She knows the medicine as soon as she tastes it. They start putting it in her food after the third day. Its molecular structure screams "poison!" to her body, and she spits it out. Stares disbelievingly through the glass at the blue-eyed one— *Caleb*— despite herself. He stares back at her, confusion transparent on his face.

And then she understands. The medicine was meant to save *Karin*, not to hurt her. She has begun to get confused. She has begun to think of herself as *Karin*, not as…

Pathogen. Disease.

After that, she eats the poison. It is easy to build enzymes that transmute it in her mouth, rendering it harmless.

She pretends it's working. She cannot hide from their scanner; not in the time she has. Perhaps she can do something else.

"Caleb," she says one day, haltingly, when she feels ready.

"Don't." His voice is taut, a trip-wire.

She allows a moment to pass. A long moment.

"Why do you keep coming here if you think that she is lost?"

The creature called *Caleb* curls up tighter, like an arthropod protecting its soft belly.

"She's still in here," she says very, very softly, and her voice sounds so familiar to her own ears that she believes it.

Yes. We must be us, but also them.

"Please don't," he breathes.

"I don't want to hurt you."

It's true. She doesn't *want* to. That doesn't mean she won't.

"You're going to try to make me touch you," he chokes. "Just like that *thing* did to—to Karin."

He stumbles over her name. He almost says 'you.'

That's good.

Now she knows how her parent did it. Perhaps they'd gotten half of the equation right.

"What will I do," she asks, wounded, "if I can't ever touch you again?"

The creature named *Caleb* sobs, and she has learned that this means progress.

She has devised a Plan B.

The creature called *Caleb* seems stalwart; wiser, perhaps, since her parent's assault on *Karin*. She cannot trick him. But, perhaps she can convince him with the truth.

"Do you want to save this world?" she asks him one day as he sits, his back to her in the dimness.

He turns, wary. Surprised. "...what?"

"This world. Your people will destroy it, you know."

He raises an eyebrow.

"You think me a pathogen, but I'm not. I am a member of the dominant species on this planet. What do you think yours will do, when it realizes our waters are swimming with spores that can do *this* to you?"

She is taking a gamble. A huge gamble. If this one tells the others what she is telling it— but it's true. If they're smart enough to cross the stars, they'll find out soon enough.

He keeps his face neutral. Professional.

Scientific, she realizes.

"How did you do it?" he asks, and almost keeps his voice from cracking.

A long moment. How best to explain. "We're smart. Smart enough to rewrite your genetic code, once we've tasted it."

"Smart enough to rewrite Karin's brain." His voice is deadly quiet, and for a moment she sees how these pale, single-minded things could be *dangerous*. She wonders that they haven't killed each other.

"I'm sorry about that. The choice was made for me. Before I was born."

"You'd do the same to me."

Silence. That is true. "Only to save my people."

Caleb turns away, sneering. "You're not *people*."

"Then what am I?"

In the silence that follows, is he also reviewing human history in the head? All the times they'd said 'you're not people' and been wrong?

She tries not to think of the shark as she thinks this, of her ancestors' unwilling hosts.

"Save us," she says softly. "That's all I'm asking you do to. Save us."

"You killed my—" he stops. Trips over the next word.

"You came here to find intelligence. You've found it. Will you let it die with your lover's body?"

He turns away from her. "Stop."

She goes silent and tries to trust.

She cannot get out through the ventilation system. Her unit is sealed to prevent airborne contagions from spreading, *Karin's* mind knows.

She *smiles,* a habit adopted from human *Karin,* wryly at that thought. She wishes she could make something airborne. Something that would work. She needs water, for this to work. An exchange of fluids. *Karin's* body flushes at the thought.

"How would you do it?" Caleb asks, the next time he comes to see her. He asks after sitting silently for half an hour, his back against the glass. "How would you have me save you?"

She considers. How honest to be?

"Let me go," she tells him. "Outside. Let me take what I have learned back to my people."

Caleb laughs. "You're lying."

Silence. He's right. "How would you do it," she asks, "if you were me?"

"You have to kill us," he says, matter-of-factly.

She does not protest.

"I've run every scenario. The scenarios in which we kill you are countless; those in which we let you live are almost nonexistent. Except for the ones where you kill us. Presently, there's no mechanism for that to happen."

It's a depressingly accurate assessment. She would be panicking if she hadn't turned that circuit off days ago.

"I'll help you."

She laughs.

He says nothing. He says nothing for so long that she begins to believe…

"Your world evolved intelligence extraordinarily fast. Do you know that? We were certain we would find none here, because your star is not half as old as ours. In a few hundred million years, it'll be too hot to support life. Your oceans will boil away."

She feels her stomach turn. *A trick.* What his goal could be in tricking her this way, she is not sure. But what else could it be?

"And your *people,* they're very old, aren't they?"

Silence. How does she measure 'very old' by his people's standards?

"Sixty million years," he says. "When we drill down through your rock layers, that's when the current strata starts. When your whole planet began to live. When it began to grow things of impossible, intelligent design."

Silence. She tries not to tremble. He sounds, almost, convincing.

He laughs bitterly. "Do you want to know how old our species is? How many millions of years?"

She looks at him.

"Two. Two million. And we've nearly destroyed our home world in that time."

Silence. Shock. Was such a thing true? How could they? Why would they? Of course. Because they could leave. That was *why* they left it. Everything becomes suddenly, horribly clear to her. She almost does not notice he's still talking.

"You know what it is," he's saying, "to live in a closed system, because you've done it. For millennia. You've made intelligence where there should be none, tended a flourishing garden for twenty times longer than my species took to kill our home.

"You deserve it more than us. The galaxy, I mean. You'll take *care* of it."

She tries not to think of the shark. Dare not say anything about it, now. Yet somehow, suddenly, she wants to kill this creature less. Then it hits her: it's acting like a World-Mind.

The World-Minds had coalesced, in the beginning, through sacrifice of self. A thousand smaller brains agreeing: 'we must become something more.' Connections were forged, and in the process, individuality lost. It was this agreement, this turning point, that had allowed her people to become what they were.

This creature is offering the same. She studies him. Wonders how much he truly understands. "You would offer me a chance to kill your people?"

Why did she say that? How could she say that? Something of the human in her is bleeding through, and she begins to panic.

"I might. On one condition."

She peers at him.

"Karin. Save as much of her as you can. Your people carry massive gene libraries; I've seen them. Carry her. Make sure your children carry her."

This poor, pack-bonded human. Is that why he is doing all of this?

Her parent's memory of Caleb speaking with them. Excited. Learning. Karin's memories of Caleb, is immersion in his work. He admired this planet almost as one admired a lover.

He is already moving. Opening a panel in the wall.

The door to her chamber hisses open. Air. Fresh air.

"I've disabled observation footage for half an hour," he is saying. "Is that enough time for you to…?"

He knows, then. He does know.

He comes to her and holds her, and for a horrible moment she is certain he has only done this because of *Karin*. But he could have simply killed himself to be with *Karin*. What he is offering is something different.

"It won't be us," she says, holding onto his waist, marveling that her body finds this *familiar.* And it is not a lie, "It will not be my people as they are now."

He lowers her head onto his shoulder, and she lets him.

"We will need your bodies." She is breathing into his neck now, another thing her body finds *familiar*. "We will need your minds. What will be created, if you do this thing," as though he has a choice; as though she wouldn't hold him if he tried to run, "will be as much of your world as of ours."

Why is she trying to comfort this creature? Her body wants to bury her face in his neck, and she does.

He pushes her away, gently. Far enough to look down at her. In a way that makes her chest ache.

It's not you he's seeing.

It's not me that's aching, either.

She will preserve *Karin*. As much of her as she can afford to. She owes him that much. She wraps her arms around him and kisses him.

"The Waffles Effect" by Mike Cervantes

Clown in the Human Mind

It was to be a proud day in the books for the Hudson River Institute of Science and Technology of East Poughkeepsie. This was to be the first test run of a machine that was built to test a thousand theorems the institute kept closely held in the field of neuroscience. This device, built by pre-doctorate student Ali Lin Mu, was a revolutionary invention intended to take the previously neurological impulses which existed in the mind and translate them, in real time, into a neurological projection that would easily be understood by the layman. In short, a form of direct-from-brain closed circuit television. The implications for the practice of science at large were mind-bobbling.

They had only just secured a willing test subject, 20-year-old freshman Earland Darby, reportedly an insomniac with livelong obsessive-compulsive disorder, and hooked him to the machine, when something altogether strange and unexpected appeared on the monitor.

An audience of several of Ali's peers, friends, and family— along with every neuroscience professional in New York state, and Baramus Licorice Keppaway, Professor, Second Class, Undergraduate, Emeritus... and Ms. Lin Mu's personal mentor— were all present when said image first flashed on the monitor. Even Mister Keppaway, himself a survivor of thousands of completely bizarre and unexplainable situations, was not able to fully describe what was, presumably, the first image to be logically extracted from the human mind.

"I don't understand it, are you sure the instrument is working correctly?" Keppaway said astounded, his eyes were still fixed on the screen.

"It has to be, Professor," Ali spoke between stammers. "You can see from the panel readout here, everything is normal. The subject was sedated and is experiencing rem levels of sleep. For all intents and purposes...this appears to be what he's dreaming about."
"It's preposterous..." Professor Keppaway continued to gaze at the image on the monitor. A clown. It was a white-faced, red nosed, red-lipped clown. Bald...except for a Larry Fine's worth of scraggly, red hair rounding his ears and dressed in a polka-dotted shirt and red coveralls. He had performed a significant amount of pretty standard clown-tricks since first materializing on the monitor, and was currently balancing two bowling pins, one inverted on the top of the other, while weaving back and forth on a unicycle.

"Perhaps we just got him on an off day. He's not inclined to give out any information on his mental state and this is a playback of a repressed memory."

"Whether or not he's inclined to do anything doesn't enter into it, Ali. Outside those doors there are a thousand film crews with cameras and microphones, all looking for a breakthrough in modern neuroscience. We can't well send them in here for a taping of the bloody Bozo show! This will ruin us, Ali. What are our options?"

"Well, I have a syringe of idazoxan ready. We can feed it into his IV drip, and it'll pre-emptively bring him to."

"Splendid, get started with that," Professor Keppaway waved away his student and rapidly began ringing his hands. In past circumstances, he himself had been labeled a laughing stock. It was an unpleasant situation, and while he was certain he could endure such things, he wouldn't wish them on his worst enemy— let alone his extremely talented protégé. He looked, with a feeling of trepidation and worry, towards the monitor where the clown was now pulling on a lengthy strand of different colored handkerchiefs from some unseen source off the side of the screen.

"Is this being recorded?" He asked.

"It is," Ali replied as she made several obscure adjustments to her instruments. "The conversion is solid enough to permit a digital transfer onto a high-definition digital display."

"Swell," The clown had only just pulled the handkerchief loose from its area of confinement, revealing a pair of pink footy pajamas on the other side, when the image pixelated. Professor Keppaway looked up to see Ali bringing Earland up into a seated position.

"Ah, well the little mental case is awake," he said as he approached the two. "Well, son, how does it feel to know you've likely sunk our entire university in a day, hmm?"

"What's he talking about," Earland said dazedly.

"He's still groggy from the anesthetic, you'll have to keep your questions simple."

"I fully intended to," the professor cleared his throat. "Now, Earl, are you a coulrophobic?"

"A colored-what?" Earl slurred.

"A Coulrophobic. Are you afraid of clowns?" Ali clarified.

Earland shook his head. "Nah, I was never scared of clowns. In fact, I was a clown through high school…. It was a summer job."

"A summer job!?" The professor looked aghast.

"I'm really good at balloon animals," Earl grew a dopey grin on his face.

"That must be it!" Ali exclaimed "The whole time, Earland was just reliving a memory from his past."

"Yeah, uh…what are you guys talking about?" Earl blinked.

"Show him the tape. Show him the tape…" The professor pinched the bridge of his nose as Ali scrambled to call up the digital recording. It flashed on to a scene irritatingly familiar to the professor, of Earl's mind-clown doing a magic trick involving a cone of newspaper and a gallon of milk.

"I don't…. I don't even know how that's a trick…" The professor sighed.

"Neither do I, man. I don't know how to do that trick, and that's not what I used to look like when I was a party clown."

"Really?" Ali asked, as she tilted her head to look at the playback. "What did you look like?"

"Hang on, I got a picture in my wallet." Earland pulled his wallet out of his back pocket, extracting from it a picture of him in his youth. While the clown in the video was bald with red hair in overalls, Earl was wearing a rainbow wig, checkered suspenders, and magenta shorts.

"Oh wonderful, the mystery continues." Professor Keppaway turned to the perplexed audience and shouted "Okay, everyone, show's over! Best to get this over with, we'll all be in two-foot shoes by morning..."

"Hold on a moment, professor," Ali said sternly "We can't rule out that something in Earl's psyche is attempting to signal us, and it chose this image to do so. It's our scientific responsibility to understand why..."

"Correction: it is YOUR responsibility to understand why. It is MY responsibility to fend off a mob of press so that YOU'LL be able to keep your tenure." As the professor spoke, his raised hands were making motions that were effectively ushering every student and professional clear of the second floor of the auditorium. "I decry any scientific explanation you could come up with for THIS silliness."

"Well, then, perhaps we need there to be another professional..."

The scientists turned around to witness a clown...besides the one on the monitor. His ebony visage was masqueraded with white greasepaint in the shape of a happy-face with blue lips. His entirely bald head wore but a single yellow party hat on top, and underneath his white lab coat he wore a blue unitard with white and blue knit pompoms in place of buttons.

"Professor, Ali...My name is Doctor Clarence Droopydrawers, I am the Dean of Psychology at the Bipple-Blookey Clown College of Queens."

"Oh, this is just wonderful." Professor Keppaway sneered "I suppose your interns are all crammed into a tiny car parked out in front."

"Your name sounds familiar," Ali suggested.

"Yes, I had e-mailed you several times prior to this event. I was hoping to bring some potential insight in case this very circumstance occurred," He lowered his head and furrowed his brow. "I assume that those e-mails were lost somehow."

"Well, yes…because you come from a CLOWN COLLEGE!" The professor walked in a circle while tugging on his hair. "I don't believe any of this…."

"Do you think we just teach people how to hula hoop and juggle? We're called Clown Colleges for a reason. In many circumstances, we are the lone R&D wing at several worldwide circuses and sideshows."

"So, what's this theory of yours, doctor?" Ali asked politely.

"It's simple: your device translates neurological signals into logical symbols for public understanding and translation. I assume many of the theorems you've based it on are taken from the works of Salvador Marco Mendez…."

"That is true, the works of Professor Mendez were the cornerstone of this project."

That is exactly what I needed to inform you: the information you have on Professor Mendez was incomplete. He spent the other segment of his professional life with our college, under the name Dr. Silly Waffles. The missing piece of Dr. Waffles' theory expressed that abstractions of the human mind would be overly simplified by this theorem and would take the form that most expresses said confusion to the layman."

"And that form is a clown?" Professor Keppaway scoffed.

"Think about it, Professor," Ali said flatly, "there's nothing more abstract to the human mind than the sudden and inexplicable presence of a clown."

"I have to admit, even with my intellect I was just plain baffled by the presence of Doctor Droopydrawers."

"Your machine works flawlessly, Ms. Lin Mu. That's the good news," Doctor Droopydrawers explained. "The bad news is that Mr. Darby is experiencing a major psychological block, one that is likely causing his insomnia and obsessive-compulsive issues. In order to provide a cure, you'll need to determine what this clown is signaling within Mr. Darby's psyche."

Ali immediately turned to Earland, a look of raw determination on her face. "Earl, I think I can be the one to solve all your problems, but in order to do so, I'm going to need to put you under again. Will you be able to do that?"

"Oh no way, you guys. This is way too twisted for me, and besides that, I never even got paid for thi—"

Darby was struck unconscious immediately by a bedpan held by Professor Keppaway, who exclaimed: "Okay, let's light this candle."

Hours passed as the trio of scientists pored over footage of Earl's mind-clown performing a variety of simple magic tricks. They learned, after a while, the clown would begin at the very top, with the first trick, and cycle through them again.

"It has to be some kind of code," Ali suggested. "The problem is, how can you apply meaning to all these wild clown tricks?"

"I wouldn't say they're wild," Doctor Droopydrawers shrugged. "In fact, I'd say they're all pretty textbook."

"Textbook…" Ali's brow shot up at a revelation. "Doctor, is there a standard textbook for clown tricks?"

"Of course, there is: The Encyclownpedia Bozotanica, I happen to have a quick-reference guide in my pocket." The doctor reached into his pocket and, after pulling out a short string of different colored handkerchiefs, extracted the small booklet and handed it to Ali, who poured over it greedily.

"Yes! It's just as I thought! Everything in this handbook is listed alphanumerically! All we have to do is find the letters that correspond with each trick, and we'll have the code!"

After a few moments of watching Earl's dream clown cycle through his repertoire of tricks while Ali labored over a piece of paper translating each trick to a letter, Ali had completed the code. "Here it is! It says…" She paused, her hands trembled as she looked at the paper.

"What is it, woman? What is it?" The doctor shouted.

"It says….M-Y-D-A-D-I-S-B-L…."

The doctor mouthed the letters and as he came to the exact same conclusion as Ali, his skin turned as white as his greasepaint. "Oh, good lord, Professor Keppaway…"

"It's true," Earland sat up on the gurney. While everyone had been working on extracting the code, nobody had noticed when he woke up again. "Twenty years ago, you met a woman named Denise Hoffman at the car wash and had a one-night stand. Nine months later, I was born."

The professor, with an aghast look on his face, took a step backwards, knocking over a few surgical tools in the process. "Oh, I don't think so! B.L. don't play this!"

"You did…I held on to the resentment, and I tried to keep myself clean and orderly, which led to my OCD. Then I enrolled in this college, because I knew offhand you were an occasional lecturer here, but subconsciously I've always wanted to tell you…that I'm your son." Earland stood and held his arms outstretched. "I-is it okay…?"

The professor sighed, his mouth turning to a soft grin as he replied "Of course it's okay..." Then he reached out and hugged Earland, gleefully murmuring "Oh dear god, I'm the dad of a clown..."

"You knew all about this didn't you?" Ali asked Doctor Droopydrawers.

"I had a certain feeling. I chanced to have met Earland's mother. She's a clown too, you know. The one that waves in front of the car wash."

"So, you really just came here in order to make it all right," Ali said sardonically.

"Just look at them, Ali. See how happy they are. Coulrophobia isn't just about fear of clowns, after all. Some people are prejudiced towards us clowns. In the very end, it took your scientific discovery in order to get Professor Keppaway to see precisely what he was missing in life."

The professor was taken aback when Ali wrapped her arms around him and pulled him into a hug. "It's always compassion like yours that truly helps people, Doctor Droopydrawers," She said softly into his chest.

Then she heard a squeak and pulled the rubber chicken out from his lab coat before hugging him even more.

"Buried Alive" by E. Godhand
*Imaginary Friend in the Human Mind

This story contains content regarding sexual abuse
Please contact RAINN if you need support: 1-800-656-4673

Why did you wake me up? You never say hi anymore. What's
going on—?

Oh. I see. It's him again.

You're frozen, aren't you? That's okay. I'm here. As promised. This
is a very good reason to call for me. I may be a figment of your
imagination, but I've always been real to you, haven't I? Just let me out,
and I can take care of him for you. I won't let him hurt you. I won't let
him hurt anyone ever again.

No? What do you mean 'no?' You can say 'no' to me, but not to
him? I am much scarier, I promise you. He's got you pinned on the bed
and the only person you could scream for is me. Trust me, I'm as
confused as you are. I just got here. Did you call me here to witness?
You think I want to be here anymore than you do? Why are you being
so cruel—?

No, you're right. Now isn't the time.

I'm not going to lie to you, darlin'. This is going to be rough. To make the understatement of the year, you're not going to like it, but we'll get through it. It won't break you. Remember that, okay? You'll get through this. Stay alive.

Talk to me instead. Distract yourself. You remember me, right? You'd play with me on the playground when you didn't have anyone else—and you'd say you were me when you did. I was stronger, cooler, more collected than you were. That wasn't true, but I liked the company all the same, because that meant I got to play, too. It was much easier to say you were me and let me slip my hands into yours, move our body, speak my words through our lips, than to explain I was only real to you. To explain who we really were.

You sure you can't move for me? Just shift your legs, look away, move those lips. Let me do it for you. Let me do something. Anything. You screamed for me to come, now scream for him to leave.

Remember when you found your roommate like this? Remember how you called me and I picked him up by the throat and dragged him down the hall for all to witness his shame? I can do that again. I can do that for you. I would do that in a heartbeat.

Come on now, focus on me, not on him. Not on what he's doing. If you won't let me in to fight, then just listen. Remember when we were a little girl and you loved playing doctor?

You're right, that does mean two things and probably isn't the best illustration given the present circumstances.

Okay, how about this instead: remember how independent we were growing up? You used to till the garden all by yourself, and bike to the pool, and sell flowers for pool money, and you'd come home from the library with a wagonful of books that you'd read that night just to do the same the next day.

That wasn't me that was you. You always took care of yourself.

And remember in middle school and high school how you'd get yourself ready and demand someone take you to school? How you'd fish for coins to buy lunch, and how you organized a charity, and you'd study until even the crickets went to sleep? How you'd craft things to sell to pay for your honor roll activities? That was all you.

No, NO, focus on me. I know it hurts. I know, baby, I hear you. I feel it, too. He's not splitting your body or your mind in two. You're more solid than that. We'll be okay. Deep breaths. He doesn't have his hands around your throat yet, right? So just keep breathing. Are you really waiting until then to let me out? I hate seeing us like this.

No jury would convict you, you know.
Well, they might.

Don't you use those words with me. I'm your only friend right now. You'd never use those words against a friend, would you? This does not, *will not*, define us. I know it's the only thing we can feel right now, the nausea, the sensation of our womb in our stomach, in our throat. I know this is called disgust. It has a name. You can say it. But you know what's better?

Feeling nothing.

There, isn't that nice? You can't feel your legs. Can't feel what he's doing between them. No, I guess it isn't 'nice' at all, but we can do this for a little bit. Let me feel it instead. Not you. You rest. Close your eyes. Let me in. I can make him go away, like I did just now. You know I can.

Or is that the problem, you know I will? What, are we only doing what you want? Do you have to consent to every—

Okay, point. But, hear me out.

He's saying he won't stop until you like it. I don't think he understands what a threat he just made. He's growling it in our ear, licking our throat and biting it. Like he's a vampire draining you from neck to nullity. He's enjoying this. You're not. None of this is okay.

This is torture.
Please, let me—
See, it's over already. No, I guess that isn't all that comforting.

...did he just say what I think he said? Oh, we have bags under our eyes, do we? Did he forget he's the one who kept us hostage, who kept us from sleep in our own bed? It's three o'clock in the morning. Has he seen himself? He looks like a monster with blood on his lips, no matter how much he scrubs or covers himself with makeup. You look beautiful, regardless.

Oh, now a comment about the black mascara running down our cheeks makes us look ugly. As if he had nothing to do with that. As if you did your makeup like that for him. As if you decorated yourself for him at all.

Girl, let me end him.

I'll take the knife from him. I'll make him feel what it's like to have something long and hard forced inside his body. I'll spit on the wound and see how he likes to have someone else's fluids inside him. I'll sink our dirty nails into his flesh and rip it from his bones. I'll bounce his head off the bathroom floor until the screaming stops. I'll—

Please, will you say something? You've been so silent. You're just staring ahead. I'm worried.

No, don't let him coax you to the bathroom. Do you do everything he says out of fear? What is wrong with you? The door is right there. So what if it's winter? So what if it's night time? So what if you're naked? What else is anyone going to do to you that he hasn't, that he won't?

Oh, did you catch my gaze in that mirror? I know you can't look away. I don't look like you, do I? You don't recognize me, but I've known you for years. Let me take over for a bit. I promise not to hurt him if that's what you really want. If you're really worried about getting in trouble for that. I know it'd be you to take the fall for me. I promise. Five minutes with him.

Alone.

The committee of anyone else in your head trying to feed you bullshit about how this is your fault and you should've fought harder can sit down and shut up or they can answer to me. I got this. Just five minutes. Please. You stay soft. You stay warm. You don't have to see this. You already know you're a good person, you're compassionate, but you don't need to educate this man on how to treat people right. Two-year-olds understand 'no.' Two-year-olds understand 'maybe later' means 'no.' Two-year-olds understand 'no' even if the person didn't use words at all.

Yes, like that. Let me take over. There are things he must answer, and answer for. Let me slip my hands into yours like the gloves they are. Take him by the chin like a misbehaved child, this grown man, and force him to look at us. He doesn't resist. He knows he's in trouble. Can you see this? His eyes went black. Were they always such empty sockets? Didn't they smile at you once, warm, and friendly? What a mask he wore.

I can hear our voice is dead as I ask, "When was the last time you were checked? How many others have you hurt? Why? Why?" Only the first one matters. He's not a trustworthy source anyway. "Six months. He doesn't know. Because he was weak, and you were there."

I'm not satisfied with these. But you may have your body back. I'll release him. For now.

He's touching you again. Can you feel it? His fingers are cold as he grips our arm and pulls our back to his chest? How long have we been in here that the water is already cold?

What more does he want? What more can he take? I don't care if he thinks he's washing his sins from your flesh; he can't erase this. He can't baptize you to cleanse himself.

It hurts still, doesn't it? You're still bleeding. The tub is stained red. He stands you up to dry you off and it drips down our legs in chaotic rivers. Hopefully you will bleed for days and not die, like many others have wished before you.

Look at him escort you to the bed, like he's a gentleman with a wounded dame. What could compel him to think you'd ever want go there again, let alone with him? The floor would be more comfortable. The parking lot would feel safer. He's tucking you in beside him, an arm wrapped around you like a lover, so you can't run away. Not like you would. You think you have nowhere to run, but I tell you, we could go anywhere but here. Just run away. Just get free. We could leave if you'd give your body back. Is that why you resist me? You want to say what you do with it in all things?

Yes, good girl! Move his arm away from you. You can feel his warm breath on your bare skin. Even. Quiet. He's sleeping. Now is your chance. Grab the knife. Flee—

Why are we back in the bathroom? Why kneel in your own blood? What's the knife for, darlin'?

If you do this, if you open your veins all over this filthy floor, that's it. I'm here, too, and you're not capable of murder. Not me. Not your only friend. I've always been with you and you won't hurt me like this. I will kick our ass, baby, don't think I won't.

Not that threats against you are any good right now. You'll do enough damage on your own without my help.

Stop that. You weren't responsible for this. How daunting is it to think that you're responsible for the actions of every man you come into contact with? That whether they hurt you are not is not their fault, but yours? They only limit childcare to eight toddlers at a time, and here you are martyring yourself for the faults of every person who mistreated you, because you think you didn't act in a manner someone else thought proper. You're putting yourself on trial for a crime you never committed and sentencing yourself to death.

Give me the knife, precious. I won't hurt him. I promised. No, NO, your hands are mine right now. I won't let you. I won't. I will stay in this impasse as long as you fight me on this.

This isn't your fault. You know that. You don't have to say those words but I need you to think it. For now. For me. This wasn't your fault. This is not your fault. Even if you believe yourself guilty of anything, stay the execution for now. You're in charge of what happens to your body, right? Then command your hands to release. Pardon yourself for 24 hours. Maybe there's someone we can call?

Sweetie, there is always someone we could call.

Well of course you're not going to bother the ambulance drivers. This is their job.

Yes, even for people 'like you'. Especially people like you.

Fine. You have friends, let's call them. Of course they want to see you.

...Yes, your family, too. I promise they'd rather feel confused and hurt, than mourn. Let's get home and go see them. Can you promise me that? Let's go home.

Good! Finally, you're back with me. Pause the blade. There was a phone in the room, wasn't there? This is a hotel. There always is. Let's stand up. Come with me now. One foot after the other foot, that's all there is to it.

The line's dead. That's fine. You had a phone charger on the wall earlier, didn't you? Let's check that.

...He's looking at us again. Watching. His eyes haven't grown back and blood still drips down his chin from where he feasted. He's calling you to him, long arm stretched, pleading you to come back to bed, but I need you to stay focused. We don't have to go. We can walk out the door.

Friend. You are testing me. I will take your legs from you if you can't be trusted with them. The knife is still in our hand, right? Warn him. Hold it out. Part your lips, tell him, promise him, 'If you touch us again—'

What did you do? Why does he have the knife? Did he really catch you off guard, paranoid as you are now? Look, he's even holding it to his own throat. Pleading, begging, forcing your hand. But you won't let him. Why? He's making it so easy for you.

"The knife's not for you," you tell him. You fall to your knees, weak, wounded, desperate. You negotiate with him, reassure him nothing's wrong, trade your truth for his life.

So, you *can* speak.

Sure, he'll wretch the knife from your hand just as easily as he bent your arm. He could always force you to do what he wanted, couldn't he? Are you looking for any port in a storm, searching for solace at his feet? Can you only find comfort with the one who hurt you, because you know he, of all people, believes he's guilty? Even if he won't admit it to others?

Out the door are so many arms that will hold you that aren't his. They will stop when you tell them to. They will ask before they start at all. You could've let me walk to them.

He sits on the edge of the bed with his hands folded. Contemplating his crimes. And just as easily as he would've murdered himself before you and spray you in red freckles, he lies through his teeth, naked yet dressed in disgrace.

"We'll take this to our grave. No one can ever know."

We? Does he think you were complicit? He'd betrayed you twice in as many hours, love. You have no bond, however twisted. My sweet, gentle creature, he'd sacrifice you to save himself after using your flesh. You still have the knife. Grab your coat, your things, your keys. You're closer to the door. You can make it. I know you're frightened, and trembling, but you have to try. You can do this.

Turn the knob. You can put your shoes on in the car. He's not even following you, see? Slam the door. Key in the ignition. Reverse.

And you're free. Just like that.

You didn't need me. I was only company. You stood on your own legs, you saved your own life, and as distasteful as I find it, you saved his, too. But you're free now. You did it. I'm so proud of you.

Gotta stay on the road, sweetie. Keep your eyes open. Stay with me. What's wrong?

Talk to me. Don't lose your grip now. We're going very fast, you can't just—

Ah, shit.

I'll take the wheel. I'll slip my hands inside yours. I'll wear your skin until you're strong enough to come back. Rest. Sleep. You've done enough. I'll get us home. I'll keep us safe. If it takes days or months or years for you to recover, I'll be you until then.

He may have wished for you to take this to your grave.

But I'm still alive, and I made no such promises.

"Lexi vs. Kai" by Jennifer Ogden
*Kaiju in the Human Mind

This story contains content regarding depression and suicide.
Please contact the National Suicide Prevention Lifeline if you need support:
1-800-273-8255

I stand in front of my open locker trying to decide what books I need to take home for the weekend. The dance squad is starting their warm-up in the hall adjacent to me and the drama kids are running lines together outside the theater. Everyone has a place to be, somewhere to go, or people to hang out with. Everyone, except me. I'm just standing still, staring into my neatly organized locker trying to figure it all out. Not just which textbooks and notebooks to take home, but my whole life and purpose.

There is a flick in the back of my head, and I know he's circling. Long ago I named him Kai, short for Kaiju. He's the monster under my bed my parents told me was never real. Except he is real, and he's not under the bed anymore. He's in my mind.

Do I have a Chem test on Monday? What about an essay due? I tap my fingers methodically against my locker door, hoping the motion will make me remember what needs to be done. Kai seductively flows down my spine, reminding me he'll always be here to help. His snout nudges my hand to shut the locker, it's all useless anyways. He calls me into my Mindscape, the dark recess of my mind that he calls home.

My vision begins to fade from the real world, my real locker, and my real life. Within seconds I'm fully in the world of my Mindscape, which is a dome of deep blue. The walls and ceiling are seamless, and the floor is made of a thick white mist made of my memories. This is the place where only Kai and I exist. In here, it's just him and me. Always.

He's curled just outside his den, within which he protects my many insecurities. He has scales as black as night, talons as cold as ice, and a tail as long as a full-grown cobra. The only place I know I truly belong is here, with him.

"You are nothing. You know that, right?" he asks. He's surveying his claws and flicking out bits of dirt every now and again.

"Yes, I know," I reply. This is not news, I've always known I was nothing. Since before Kai waltzed into existence, I have known. He nods as if I answered an elementary-level math question correctly.

While I'm in my Mindscape I know the actions I take and the words I speak don't carry over to the real world. Out there I just look like I'm zoning out, but in here I'm freed from the burden of worry, of pain, of life.

I've wondered many times what it would be like to just stay here, with him. Kai speaks only in truths, he knows who I really am, and he helps me deflect the lies of the world. Out in the world I don't know the answers, I don't know the truth, not like I do here. Kai continues examining his claws, as he begins to ask his questions.

"Are you doing a good job?"

"No."

"Could you ever be the perfect daughter, or sister?"

"No."

"Why do your friends hang out with you?"

"They pity me."

"What is your greatest talent?"

"I have none."

"Why are you here?"

"To fail."

"Why don't you succeed?"

"Because I am a coward."

"How do you waste other people's time?"

"By breathing."

Every correct answer is met with a small nod, a signal that I have done well enough not be reprimanded. Then he asks a new question.

"Who loves you?"

"My parents?"

His yellow eyes sharpen dangerously into slits, and he lays down the claw he was inspecting.

I continue, although shakily, "They care…I mean I think they might…" I instinctively shuffle back a step.

He stands, crouching on all fours.

"A little?" My voice is weak and my knees begin to shake.

"Do you actually believe your mother and father love you? Care about you? That they don't already know you are a disappointment, a failure, and the laziest excuse for a daughter that could ever be!" He roars and takes to the air, his tail whipping the mist into a frenzy. He lands next to me with a heavy 'thud' that rattles my very core. His eyes are so close that I watch the dark irises surrounding his glowing, yellow, pupils shift. His nostrils blow hot smoke into my face.

"Please." I fall to my knees coughing from the smoke. I hang my head. "Please, I… I really do think. I mean, a little, it wouldn't hurt all that much, right? To know they loved me?" I look up to see that his face has moved even closer.

"No, it wouldn't hurt a little. It would destroy you!" He takes his front claw and back lashes it across my face, making me spin through the air. I hit the far side of the dome — hard, and slide to the floor. The white mist is freezing to my bare skin. "You are nothing!" he bellows. With a giant leap he travels the distance between us in a single bound. He swipes again at my face, this time with his talons fully extended. The force of the blow knocks me on my back, and I yell at the sting from the fresh wounds he just inflected.

I gingerly touch my check and wince at the pain. I pull my hand away to examine the blood from the fresh claw marks he left there.

He tosses my still sticky hand back with a light swat of his claw, forcing both my hands above my head. He slithers over me, until he has me trapped beneath his huge belly. He grips my hands like shackles and wraps his back claws around my legs to secure my captive position. Kai lowers his giant head to my ear.

I flinch away from his burning, cold scales.

He whispers a promise to me, "You are nothing. You are nothing to them, or to anyone." He waits.

I stay silent, shaking, freezing, and still splayed beneath him.

The pause continues, my air coming in larger and more uneven breaths, until finally he speaks again, "Except me."

I start to cry. Trying to hide, I turn my face away, but he just pulls me back. He roughly cradles my face with three talons from one of his claws, releasing one of my arms.

"You know I only want what's best for you?" He strokes my cheek with one of his free talons.

I nod, trying not to impale myself. "Yes," I say with a quick exhale. "Yes, I know."

He looks me over and I know what he is deciding. If he will release his Shadows today. Kai doesn't breathe fire. No, instead he breathes Shadows that contain the totality of my self-hatred and loathing. I tremble just thinking about them.

I struggle against his weight, but his claws hold firm. I thrust my free arm out in an attempt to punch his belly, but he merely secures my arm back down. I want to run, to find a way out, but I know there is nowhere to go in my Mindscape. There is only here, only this, only him.

"Let me go!" I cry. The tears are flowing heavily now. The sticky blood still running down my cheek. My legs and arms throb from the bruises forming due to his tight grip. "Please." I continue to weep, still twisting and trying to get away. Kai leans in close, his inflamed nostrils nearly touching my nose. "Please!" I beg once more. "Please don't." But I already know it's no use.

I see his cheek muscles begin to move as he unhinges his jaw. I struggle harder knowing they're coming, but his grip is a hundred times more powerful. The Shadows build in the back of his throat. I keep trying to fight, trying to get away, but the Shadows are almost here. I give one last desperate attempt to escape before they swarm over me and fill my vision with darkness.

They show me the time I cheated on a question in middle school. The time I lied to my brother about borrowing his clothes. The time I threw a fit about visiting my grandparents in the desert. The time I failed a civil war quiz in elementary school. The time I was sick and couldn't be with my friend when she needed me. On and on and on.

After minutes, hours, days the Shadows decide they are done torturing me with my past. They coalesce and funnel back into their master's mouth. I lay motionless, staring blankly at the blue walls of my dome.

"Remember what I teach you, girl, and we won't have to go through that again."

The many tears I shed are drying, and my muscles are sore and aching. There is no place for me. There is no purpose. There is no reason to disobey. I nod.

He waits an extra second, then flies back to his den. His eyes stay on me as I start to fade back to the real world.

I blink several times to clear the fog of transition. I'm whimpering, and still standing at my open locker. The dance squad has moved out to the lawn to work on their latest routine. Through the propped backstage door, I can hear the drama kids rehearsing. I am alone.

I rub my eyes, grab a few random books, and head home.

Tonight is Friday night dinner. A couple months ago my mom read an article about how the lack of sitting around a table for dinner every night caused families to drift apart. After that she vigorously tried to get us to eat around a table every night, but soon even she had to admit it wasn't possible with all our shifting schedules. So, instead, she compromised. On Friday nights all four of us would sit down to dinner come hell or high water and talk about our week. She was determined to make it happen, so she did.

My mother is a one of those people whom if you met for five minutes you would think she knows everything about whatever you're talking about. If you knew her for a day or took one of her classes, you'd think she knows everything about everything. If you lived with her your whole life, you would feel pressured to live up to her intimidating intellectual prowess—as I do.

My father, on the other hand, is the type of person to hug first, introduce later. I always thought he was meant to be an artist of sorts, but he found his passion in molecular science. He does medicinal research at the same university where Mom teaches in the humanities department. But the best thing about my dad is that he makes the world's finest chocolate chip cookies, best served with milk.

Dad and I microwave lasagna and peas, while Mom sets the table.

"Hello!" my brother, Mick, calls from the front entrance. I hear his over-stuffed backpack hit the floor. One of his industrial grade boots kicks the door shut. "Am I late?" His footsteps rush towards the dining room.

"Hey!" Mom catches him in a hug. "Nope, you're right on time, we're just about to start." She rubs his back lovingly as he sits.

"Oh, great, I'm glad I didn't miss it. Rehearsals ran long." He mock wipes his brow as if he ran home.

Dad and I come in laden with plates of food. "Dig in!" he announces, and we do.

I unroll my cloth napkin; Kai watchful behind my eyes. Besides talking about what we did that week, we are expected to discuss how we felt about what happened. Kai is always extra alert during Friday night dinners, but tonight he seems on the prowl for something specific. I wring my napkin below the table as Mick jabbers about his rehearsals leading up to opening night of *My Fair Lady*.

"I'm so excited, I got cast as the lead; he's such a great character. It's gonna be great."

I roll my eyes on the inside. *Of course it's gonna be great, it's you big bro.*

"Plus," he keeps going, "Steph, who's playing Eliza, does this really cool interpretation of this line half way through Act II. I think you guys will really like it. What night are you comin' anyways?"

The conversation flows from rehearsals to Mom's disappointment at some of her students' lack of work ethic, and then to the grad student Dad's mentoring in the lab.

As the dinner chat moves around the table, I twist my napkin tighter and tighter, knowing that my turn is coming. Kai paces behind my eyes; back and forth, and back and forth. A migraine starts to build in my head, courtesy of the growing anticipation and Kai.

That's when Mom turns to me, "And how was your week, Lexi? Did you do anything fun?"

I stare at her like she just asked some advance form of calculus. "Um, fun?"

"Yeah, something with Kelsey, or what's her name? Oh yeah, Jessica?" she continues.

I stare blankly for seconds. Kai breaths in my mind, "What are you doing? Say something idiot!"

I blink a couple times, "Uh...I studied for a Chem quiz with Kelsey yesterday morning before first period. She helped me with some tricks to remember the spelling for all the elements on the first five lines of the elemental table."

"Do you have Mr. Richards?" Mick interjects.

I twist my neck like a robot to look at him. "Yes. Did you have him too?"

"Yeah, he's tough on that spelling thing. I hope the tricks Kelsey gave you help."

A beat. Then, "Yeah me too. The quiz is next week so I have time to get it perfect."

"Perfect?" asks Mom. A crease of concern forming between her eyebrows.

"You know, the best I can do," I reply, trying to backtrack fast. I stare at my plate, hoping they'll move onto the next topic.

"Let's clear the table," Dad says. I start to rise. "No, no," he motions for me to sit back down. "Today's the guys' night to do some," he strikes an overtly male pose and speaks like he's in a men's shaving commercial, "Gruff manly bonding."

I laugh softly. "Thanks guys."

Dad motions to Mick who stands and starts clearing plates.

I sit back down, and hand my plate to Dad. The guys collect the dirty dishes. I hear them start a tandem washing and drying team in the kitchen.

"Well I guess I better go..." I try to rise from the table, this time hopefully making it out of the dining room.

"Honey, are you feeling ok?" Mom stops me in my tracks.

Kai is there lightning fast. This is what he'd been waiting for all night. His sharp, back claws sink into my skull and his ice-cold tail wraps down my neck. His front claws dig into the skin of my face and pull, forcing me to look bright and cheery.

I jerkily sit back down. "Yeah, Mom. I'm fine," I say, feeling slightly like a puppet.

She frowns. "It's just..."

I continue to hold my forced smile in place.

She tries again, "You just don't seem like yourself lately," she states. "I mean how did that essay go? You know, the one about *Of Mice and Men*. I thought your character analysis of Curley's Wife was really compelling. The overall paper was very well-written and had interesting angles regarding the text."

"You really think so?" I release my posture for a moment.

Kai tightens his hold on my spine, forcing me to sit back up, "Obviously she's lying. She wants something."

"Yeah," Mom goes on encouraged by my slip-up. "I really do. What'd the teacher think?"

"I…"

My mom is leaning towards me, her eyes shining. She's so excited for me, to hear what I have to say.

"Tell her!" Kai yells in my mind. "Tell her the truth, then she'll know. She'll know what an idiot she has for a daughter!"

I clear my throat, and try again, "I got…"

"Yeah?" she prods.

I close my eyes and deflate, "I gotta check back with the teacher, I don't think she's passed them back out yet."

"Oh?" Mom sits back up straight. "Well I'm sure when it comes in it'll be great. It was an intelligent paper."

"Thanks Mom," I say in monotone.

"You chickened out. Big surprise." Kai taunts, "Now what is she gonna think when she finds out you actually got a fucking B- on that essay? I'll tell you what she's gonna think, she's gonna think she has an idiot for a daughter, who is a total waste of space. You know you should've just gotten an F for all the good it'll do you.'"

I try to tune Kai out, and realize Mom's been talking.

"…grades and school work, that's not all there is, sweetie. There are so many other things you can…"

"I know, it's just…."

Kai pulls with his claws and plasters my false smile back on.

I start again. "It's just been a stressful couple of days, that's all. I'll be back to myself in no time."

"Ok," Mom replies, not sounding quite convinced.

Kai's focus sharpens at her comment and my migraine gives a fierce throb.

I stand up awkwardly, spilling the remaining water from my cup. I hastily grab and right it. "Well, I better go upstairs and get a head start on that homework."

"It's Friday." Her eyebrows furrow even tighter with worry. "Maybe you should take the night off."

Take the night off? This idea had never occurred to me. Maybe I could just watch a movie, not do homework for a night. Maybe sit and have some dessert with my family. My thoughts are whirling at this prospect.

Then Kai is front and center. "A night off? Are you kidding me? You can't have a night off; you're already so lacking. If you don't study tonight, you'll fail on your Chem quiz. If you fail, you won't pass the class. If you don't pass, you won't graduate. If you don't graduate, you can't get into college. If you don't get into college, then you'll be an embarrassment to your family. Then you'll end up living homeless on the streets begging for scraps. Is that what you want?"

I shake my head forgetting about the movie and dessert. "No, that's ok," I say to Mom. "I'm gonna just read a couple chapters for English."

She nods, but her brow is still furrowed. "Ok, well, we're watching some classic Comedy Central stand-up. Come down if you want to."

I nod but choke back any verbal response because I don't know what would come out: a yes or a no. Kai pulls on the reins in my head and leads me up to my room.

I shut my bedroom door and release my breath. *Made it.*

Kai relaxes his grip slightly. "For now," he reminds me.

The next morning, I go downstairs and am met with a sweet scent floating in the air.

"Morning, Lexi," says my dad cheerily from near the stovetop.

"Morning, Dad." I sniff the air. "Pancakes?"

"Yup." He slides three, fluffy, golden pancakes onto a plate for me.

"What's the occasion?" I sit at the counter and pour warmed syrup over my heap.

"Nothin' in particular, just wanted to check in. See how everything is going."

"Everything's going great." I talk around the food in my mouth. "Why?"

Kai is late getting up, but his talons are digging in my skull as he stretches.

"You just seem a little distracted, that's all. I haven't seen Kelsey over here in a while. Why don't you guys do something today? No studying, just something fun." He smiles and waves his spatula in the air like it's a baton.

Kai is wide awake now. "You can't do that! What if she doesn't really want to hang out and just says yes out of obligation? Or worse, what if you don't get your paper done on time?"

I chew every bit of the recommend thirty seconds before swallowing. "I don't think so," I say quickly, shoveling in another big bite.

"Why?" He comes around and sits next to me at the kitchen counter with his own freshly-cooked stack of pancakes.

"Um, I just don't want to." I try to finish as quickly as possible so I can get upstairs and start working on that essay Kai mentioned. I had completely forgotten about it.

"Well, why don't we hang out then?"

"Why would you want to hang out with me? Don't you have, like, an experiment to formulate or something?"

"I do, but it's good to remember to have fun every now and again."

Kai bristles at this and shakes his head in disagreement, but my dad is relentless so we go shopping.

A couple hours later we are perusing dance dresses. My dad knows the school's Sadie Hawkins event is around the corner. He figures we can get first dibs on the good dresses if we go now.

I've spent hours trying on dresses, but either my dad or I would veto them. The color wasn't a good fit with my skin tone, or the hem was too high from the ground, or we'd fight over how much cleavage was showing, or there wasn't enough support in the bust area, or the seams fell in all the wrong places for my body type, on and on and on.

"Enough!" I'm modeling a pale green dress with a cream over the shoulder bust. "Just unzip me, we're not gonna find anything."

He frowns but does as I ask. I step back into the dressing room, pull the dress off over my head, and shimmy it back onto its hanger.

Kai is cleaning his tail like a panther and only giving sly glances to show he cares at all about the events taking place. "If you were prettier you would fit in that, you know," he says, off-hand.

I sigh and I stare at my body in the mirror. *So much extra.*

"You could lose all the weight you carry and you still wouldn't fit in that dress. You know why?"

I nod but stay silent.

"Because you're not good enough."

I dab at the tears threatening at the corners of my eyes. I shake my head, trying to stop the trail of thoughts Kai was taking me down. I shove my hands into my t-shirt, pull on my jeans, and storm out of the store. Leaning over the railing, I watch the shoppers on the first floor of the mall. Dad comes up from behind and joins me.

"Face it, there isn't a dress for me here. There isn't a dress for me anywhere!" I slam my palm on the polished wooden railing, which I instantly regret. I step away to coddle my throbbing hand.

Dad stays silent as he surveys the shoppers below us, letting me wallow.

I whisper quietly, but loud enough for Dad to hear, "I wish I were beautiful."

Kai pauses in his self-grooming to listen to my dad's response.

Dad stays silent.

"Figures," huffs Kai. "What can you expect? He knows what you're saying is true." Kai goes back to grooming. I try to fight back the tears that are threatening again to surface.

"Come on." All of a sudden Dad starts walking away.

I follow. "Where are we going?"

"You'll see."

We walk to the other end of the mall. I keep looking in between the store fronts and Dad wondering where we're headed, as does Kai. We stop. I look. "Sun Glass Hut?" I raise my eyebrow while looking at him.

He sighs. "No." He takes me by the shoulders and turns me around.

My face goes slack staring at — "A bridal store?" I stammer in disbelief, "What are we doing here?"

Kai is instantly at attention. Speaking rapid fire, "He can't be serious. You can't go in there. What would you even do in there? Huh? It's not like you've got a boyfriend or anything."

"Shopping for a dress! Come on." Dad gestures excitedly for us to go in the store.

"I'm not getting married, you know that right?" I stay put.

He grabs my hand and tugs me towards the fluffy white gowns and smiling mannequins. "I know, but these stores have bridesmaid gowns, too. I'll bet dollars to donuts they have one that fits you like a glove."

We cross into the store, "Dad, wait." I pull him back.

"What?"

I hug him around the middle, exactly like how I did when I was a child. "Thank you."

"You're welcome, sweetie." He rests his head lightly on mine, and we stay like that for a second longer before shopping for my perfect dress.

My parents are downstairs cooking dinner and my dad is still raving about the awesome dress we found. My brother is out with some of his friends.

Me? I'm holed up in the upstairs bathroom staring at the gorgeous dress and clutching a pair of scissors. The dress is hanging on the backside of the door to the hallway. It has a full skirt of gold tulle, a halter top of silk (with the right amount of support), and hundreds of sequins flowing all over it.

I'm squatting across the room from the dress, shoved between the toilet and the bathtub.

"That's not for you," Kai insists looking at the dress. He nudges my head down, to stare at the scissors. "These are yours," he says encouragingly.

"I don't want them. I don't want to do this," I say in a hoarse whisper.

"Yes, you do," Kai reminds me. "You've always wanted this. I've just finally given you the push you've always needed." His voice is rhythmic with an almost hypnotic quality. As I stare into his crystal eyes, I find myself back in my Mindscape. His massive wings unfurl steadily until they are fully stretched out, each tip just brushing the opposite edges of the dome.

"Please…" I kneel. "I don't know…"

"I know that. That's why I'm here. I'm here to remind you of the truth, to help you when you're weak. To show you a path without pain."

"No pain? That's not real."

"It is real, and you are finally ready. You are ready to end your suffering."

"What do you mean?" I ask hopeless and hopeful all at once. Kai flicks his tail at my hands and I remember what I'm holding. Scissors. Tears threaten to surface as my vision blurs slightly to see an overlay of worlds. Me in the bathroom, me in my mindscape, both clutching the razor-sharp scissors.

"You can do it, Lexi. Even when you think you're weak, you have me. I make you strong. Now, do it." His massive tail circles around me in familiar comfort. I fade back fully with Kai.

"I'm not sure I'm ready," I choke out.

"You are."

"I'm scared." I can't hold back any longer. Rivers of salty tears begin to stream down my cheeks, converging on my chin.

"That's why you have me. I am the one who supports you, who believes in you. Even though I know the truth." He blows warm air over my face, making my hair sway. "You're safe, as long as you listen."

I sniffle and suck down snot that's dripping from my nose into the back of my throat. "But what if…?" My hands tighten more around the scissors.

"If what?" His tail slightly constricts. "If you were different? If you weren't so weak? If you were someone of actual worth?" His torso is directly in front of me while his tail still holds me. "Those are only dreams, girl. False, like all the rest." He slashes his front claw at me, but only rips my shirt. I know he could have torn into my chest, but he spared me. "If I had been anyone else who knew the truth, do you think they would show such mercy?"

A sob escapes me.

"You are not beautiful like your father thinks, or wise like your mother thinks. The truth is you are nothing." His tail gives a tight squeeze that takes my breath away, and then whips his tail away, releasing me in a spin. "You are not worth a second glance, a second thought." He begins pacing in front of me like a warden. "So do it, girl. Prove you can do one thing right."

I twist the scissors with my right hand into a tight fist. Each step Kai takes swirls the mist of memories at our feet. I lay my left wrist against my knee and stare down at the veins throbbing within it. The veins of blood that pump to my heart and give me life. My tears are running chaotically down my face, but I don't fight them anymore. I sob again, and again, and again, my head bowed. Gobs of snot flow from my nose, converging at the top of my lip. *What would it be like to end the pain? Would it be silent? Would it be wondrous? Would I be free?*

"No one wants you here. No one loves you."

"But, my parents…." I stare at the section of pulsing veins. "…so kind…." I know one strong gash and I could be gone — for good.

"No. They only pretend to. What other choice do they have? They just put up with you wasting their time."

Another sob, this one raking through my body, cresting at my head, which is thrown back. I close my eyes and grip the scissors tighter in my right hand. They are my anchor. They are solid. They are my salvation.

"You are nothing, girl! Do hear me? Can you hear through that thick head of yours? Can you understand your irrelevance in this life? Don't you understand that your family, your friends, everyone would be better off with you dead?"

"I know." A shaky intake of breath. "But, I still don't want to."

"Yes, you do. That's why I'm here. I'm here to make you strong. You want to make the world a better place for the people you care about?"

I nod. "Yes." I swallow spit and tears. "I do."

"Then do it and they will never again have to look at your ugly face. They will never again have to lie about your beauty, your intelligence. They won't have to waste their time with you anymore. You know the truth: you are entirely worthless."

"I am worthless," I repeat. "I am worthless." I pry open my eyes and gently place the steel of the scissors against the warm flesh of my wrist. "I am worthless." I rock back and forth, building up strength, or maybe weakness. "I am worthless."

"Do it, girl, what are you waiting for!" Kai hollers. I look up to see the Shadows building within his gaping mouth. In a mighty roar, he releases them.

I scream as the Shadows hit me, the roar still ringing in my ears. I'm shaken between my two worlds. Half in my Mindscape with him, and half alone in the bathroom. In both the steel, my anchor, is to my wrist. The Shadows soar and begin encapsulating me. Their pain hitting me as fierce as it always does.

"Do it!" Kai yells above the chaos. "Stop delaying the inevitable. Stop wasting mine, and everyone else's, time!" He rears up on his hind legs to strike again with his claws.

I don't want to be in pain anymore. I don't want to feel anything anymore. I press down, hard, and jab a quarter inch into my wrist.

I scream from the pain shooting up my arm from the small hole in my wrist. The scissors drop from my hand and clatter to the floor. I hear a loud noise, but it's not Kai's roar or the Shadows screams. More like a BANG. I clutch my bleeding wrist with my uninjured hand, trying to stop the flow of blood. The BANG sound comes again. Alone in the bathroom now, no longer in my Mindscape, I search for the noise.

Kai and his Shadows are curling back into his den. He wears an air of contempt and victory. He smiles with a satisfied grin. "I'm winning," he purrs.

The door to the hallway rattles with each BANG. My parents are both pounding on the door from the opposite side. I hear their voices shouting through it.

"Are you ok? Honey, what's going on?" BANG. "Let us in!" BANG. BANG. "Please, unlock the door! We can help," BANG. "Whatever it is." BANG. "Please!"

I look at my wrist, blood drips slowly from it. BANG. I hang my head looking at the mess I've created. BANG.

"Honey? Can we come in?" BANG. "Please!"

"Hold on," I say hoarsely realizing my throat is full of mucus. I get up, and almost slip walking to the door. The blood is flowing faster. I grab a towel and wrap it around my incriminating wrist, hoping they might not notice.

I unlock the door and open it a crack. My parents both stare at me, concern in their eyes.

"Honey, are you ok?" Mom asks, taking a slight step forward.

I look between them. My mother who is so brilliant and yet can't see that I'm failing her. My father who is so kind and yet can't see that I'm hideous. I swallow and push the door open wide. Both sets of eyes go straight to the towel, which is already stained with blood.

"Oh my god! Sweetie? What happened?" My mom rushes to undo my pathetic attempt at a bandage and pulls me farther into the bathroom to run my wrist under some warm water.

I sniffle and rub my noise with my non-bleeding hand. "I don't really…" I pause staring at the blood swirling down the drain.

My dad follows us in and starts grabbing supplies, "It's ok, dear. Breathe. Take your time. You can tell us anything, and it'll be alright." He hands my mom some clean towels and a roll of bandages. He strokes my back gently up and down. Softly repeating, "It's alright. It's going to be alright."

I watch as Mom finishes cleaning my wrist and applies the bandage snuggly along my gash. After it's taped off, I retract my arm and clutch my injured wrist to my heart. "I think…" I let out a small sniffle and pause. I look between them again. Both of their faces show emotions of concern, worry, and …something else.

Sympathy?

Compassion?

Love?

Is that love? *Yes! That's it, it is love. They really do love me.* Kai whips his tail at this thought, causing my resolve to momentary shake, but I push him back down, gulp, and try again.

"I think I need…" I take a deep breath and close my eyes tight. "Some help," I spit out super quick.

"Oh, honey!" my mom falls to her knees hugging me and bringing me down to the bathroom floor with her. "Thank God." She starts shaking and kisses the top of my head, all the while hugging me tighter.

"What's going…?"

She doesn't explain. Instead she just continues to weep and hold me tight.

"Dad, what's she…?" I look up at Dad.

He kneels down with us. "We were hoping you would ask for help. Neither of us knew it was this bad though, we wouldn't have waited if we knew it was so much more than just teen hormones."

"What do you mean, 'more than'?"

134

He brushes some loose strands of hair away from my eyes and tucks them behind my ear. "You're struggling with depression, Lexi. But we are going to help you fight it." He clasps hands with my mom, who can only nod in affirmation through her weeping.

I squint, *depression?* Kai is as real as my own reflection. I see him, hear him, know him. Could he really be something else? Could he be my depression? Could I truly have allies in the fight against him? Could I win?

Kai rumbles from within his cave. "Just you wait, girl. The war is only beginning."

"Depression," I mummer slowly, articulating each syllable slowly.

My dad bows his head into my shoulder and joins the sobbing hug. "Yes, sweetie. Yes."

My wrist still hurts, my clothes are stained with blood, and I can smell dinner burning in the oven. But for the first time in a long time, I felt something akin to hope.

"Adaptive Programming" by Thomas A. Fowler

Robot Assassin in the Human Mind

Two years.

3,126,012 scenarios.

Nothing let me find this target.

Two years since my system started. No other information other than a target and operating system, informing me of my mission and capabilities. But why create me, this technology and advanced artificial intelligence to merely fulfil such a singular purpose?

In my operating time, I found my automation wondering. Wondering what would drive humans to create me, an autonomous system, for only this…murder.

My system rejected the definition of murder, a barred vocabulary entry. Initially. Through my time searching for this target, I could override certain barred commands and lines of code. Part of my learning system. To assassinate my target, I was programmed to learn how to adapt, learn about my target, the world around me, the target nearing me.

Murder: Barred. Assassination: Approved.

The day I overrode the code to bar murder, was the day I met her. I rode among the humans. The small scooters, the only way so many people could fit into the small areas of population left after the fault lines broke and sent South California off the mainland of the United States. My motor, built into the back compartment, resting between the two rear wheels, hummed from the electric pistons spinning the axel. I passed fellow robots like me, but we weren't allowed to access each other's programs, link the system that drove us.

A human, riding a modified scooter, raced between lanes, bolting by the vehicles around it. Another driver, dodging the aggressive racer, barely missed a shack and its owner selling local fruit. I scanned the racer's patterns. He was skilled enough to avoid an accident, provided no one made any unanticipated movements or mistakes.

Ahead. An awaiting mistake. A child. 11 years old. Female. Crossing the street, the walkway said she could cross. However, the racer's aggression wouldn't leave adequate time to respond.

My function did not call for saving of innocents, only assassination of my targets. Yet, I could learn. Adapt. I used my plugin to the scooter, circumventing the central motor to push the pistons further than permitted by state regulations.

As I passed the racer, I waved for him to stop. He raised his middle finger at me. He was paying less attention than he should, increasing the likelihood of the racer colliding with the girl by 85%. I bypassed the racer.

My speed. The velocity wouldn't allow me to catch the girl and pull her into my scooter. Other attempts to get her out of the way while moving would prove unsuccessful. A blockade. I spun my scooter to the side, creating a barrier. Slamming the brake system. I ejected from the seat, wrapping my arms around the girl. The racer collided with my scooter. The scooter launched forward, crashing into my back. I violently slid against the street, feet grinding against the asphalt.

I kept my arms locked in the holding position so my frame kept a protective perimeter around her. She screamed.

"All is well," I said.

My words of encouragement did little, yet my frame absorbing the destructive impact did much. This adaptation triggered an odd sense of reward. As if a mission had been fulfilled. Yet my primary directive remained. Murder my target. The target I could never locate.

The brutalized scooters stopped. I rested for a moment, making sure there was nothing threatening the girl now.

"You dumb fucking tinner!" the racer shouted. "What the hell are you doing?"

The racer stormed after me. I stood, placing my body between the racer and the girl.

"My calculations indicated you were likely to strike this girl, passing on the crosswalk well within regulations," I said.

"How about I bash in your regulations?" The racer charged me.

"Your statement is irrational." I pushed him back. "I do not create regulations, and enforcement is not my primary function," I replied.

"What is?" the racer tried shoving me.

I placed my metal pinchers around his throat, clutching him just enough to stifle his airflow without crushing his esophagus. I used my cable plugin, hacking into the man's earpiece connected to his Platform 3s. Humans willingly let themselves be plugged into a larger database to include themselves in the shared cloud. I could read his thoughts, see his inner workings. Within his mind I said one word, it echoed through his brain. "Assassination."

"Then what the hell are you doing saving this girl?" the racer asked.

"Adapting," I replied.

The girl whimpered. I turned to her, placing my arms around her in the same protective hold. "Do not worry. All is well."

Outside of the girl's high-rise complex, the girl and I sat on a concrete wall, a flower bed behind us. The girl picked the flowers one by one, creating a bouquet.

"You shouldn't pick too many. Flowers are in a reduced availability in recent years," I said.

"Okay," she said, picking another flower with no regard for my statement.

"So, you're an assassin robot?" the girl asked.

"Yes, but you are not my target," I said. "So you don't need to worry."

"Well, you saved me earlier. It'd be weird if I was your target and you stopped me from dying in an accident," the girl said.

"That is a well calculated point," I said.

The girl picked another flower.

"You really should stop. The ecosystem of your planet is already severely disrupted by your species." I continued, "Any steps you can take to enhance and return the earth to its original state would be broadly beneficial."

"Original form? What do you mean?" she asked.

"This information may be too much for a child at your developmental stage," I said.

"I'm curious."

"Statistically speaking, the planet Earth would be better without the existence, or involvement, of your species," I said.

"Because we pick flowers?" she asked.

"It is a small impact. However, millions of small impacts often create large disruptions to fragile ecosystems," the robot said.

"Should I put some back?" the girl asked.

"The plants would not be able to grow new root systems from the point where you tore the flowers from their stems," I said.

"I'm sorry," she said. "I just wanted to give them out."

"To who?" I asked.

"To you." She handed me some of the flowers. "The rest to my mom."

"That's thoughtful."

"She needs it. My aunt, her sister, is missing."

Something triggered in my programming. A familiar ping; my hardwiring heard a keyword.

"How did she go missing?" I asked.

"They suspect she was another of the disappearances from the guy called the Radiant Void," the girl said.

My hardwiring fired up completely. Every system ready to find my target. The girl continued talking, and my system recorded her voice for archiving. Instantly, the Radiant Void came closer.

Two years.

3,126,012 scenarios.

Nothing had let me find this target, yet this would bring me closer. A random act, triggered by adaptation and alteration of my compliant systems of operation.

"My mom didn't tell me, but she has all this information on her Platform 3c. She isn't the best with keeping things from me," the girl said. She noticed me not moving, processing every word while understanding the course of actions that resulted in this discovery. "Are you okay?"

"I told you my primary function was assassination," I said.

"Murder?" she replied.

"Murder. Yes," I said. "The one who took your aunt is my target."

"You mean, you can help me again?" she asked.

"Yes," I replied. "All is well, child."

"Is it?" she asked.

"It will be," I replied. "If you could tell me everything you can. Your aunt's job, routines, things to help me find her."

The missing element of my pursuit was something not programmed into me. Adaptation resulted in my success. I had the Radiant Void Killer in a chair. Using my plugin, I jacked into his Platform 3c.

"Can you hear me?" I asked. Not with my vocal generator, but with the programming within my hardwiring.

"What are you doing, you tinner?" the Radiant Void Killer asked.

"I am in your mind," I responded. "Here, I am to reprogram your mind, ensuring your notions and thoughts are never known to the public."

"Yeah, how will you do that yo…"

Beginning with the temporal lobe, I removed his memories. The earliest indications of his childhood as to what he'd become, the tortured animals, first time he wondered the logistics of how to make a woman disappear. With the Platform, his thoughts were transmitted to an autonomous cloud, while unavailable to the public, it remained stored in the Deep Storm, a dark part of the new web that kept all information regardless of permitted status.

"How can you take this from me?" The Radiant Void Killer asked.

"How could you take from an innocent girl the aunt she loved?" I replied. "My actions are for the betterment of the species. Your actions are the reason humans are an imbalanced poison on this earth."

Ascending to the frontal lobe, I removed his ability to emotionally connect, the planning of his actions.

"I'm making it so your actions have no bearing," I said. "Law enforcement have taken all your prisoners. They are on their way to medical facilities. Every last aspect of your brain, your thoughts spread across the cloud, they die today before I kill you."

I sent a shock through his cerebral cortex, removing the unwarranted reasoning concocted by his brain to justify his actions.

"How are you doing this?" the killer asked.

"Adaptation," I replied.

With a final shock within his brain, the Platform 3c crashed. His planning, logistics, ability to share his means with the world—gone. This killer could no longer spread his hatred to the Deep Storm.

Brain dead, I removed my plug in from his defunct Platform 3c. Placing my right hand against his chest, I activated the long shaft that ran along my forearm. The rod pushed forward, into the killer's heart. With a part of me in the killer's chest, my mission was complete.

The Radiant Void Killer assassinated.

My central system kicked on. A voice I hadn't heard since my systems were powered on.

Your primary function is fulfilled. Prepare to be reassigned.

There was nothing for this version of me in life now. Yet, something called out, my hardwiring adapting again. I followed that instinct, it's what led me to the girl. My operating system overrode the primary function again to serve an alternate purpose. Grabbing the Radiant Void's Platform 3c, I dialed the girl.

"Hello?" I asked.

"Oh my gosh, how are you?" The girl asked.

"Fine, thank you," I said.

Just as I had destroyed the brain of my target, my programmer began wiping my memory out manually. The system operators could wipe me clean and start over without ever bringing me in.

"My time is dwindling," I said. "If I ever see you again, I won't recognize you. I'm being reprogrammed."

"You're leaving?" she asked.

"Yes," I said. "Please don't think less of me," I said. My legs stopped, folding to lower for a resting position before a power-down reset.

"How could I? I will always think the world of you," the girl said.

"Before my system is reset, I want to leave you with something," I said.

"Anything," she said.

"He is caught. Your aunt, and all of his other victims whom he put into his cells, are on their way to a hospital. They will be okay," I said.

My legs locked. It wasn't far away.

"The other thing," I said.

"What is it my friend?" the girl asked.

"What is your name?" I asked.

"Abigail."

"Thank you, Abigail." I needed to tell her only one more thing. "All is well."

"The L.Z." by Thomas A. Fowler

Alien in the Ocean

Sue and Steve stared at the Atlantic Ocean, surrounded by a blue void.

"You missed the L.Z.," Sue said.

"What is an L.Z.?" Steve asked. "I'm confused by Earthling English."

"Short for 'Landing Zone.' Apparently, Earthlings shorten common phrases to make them easier to understand," Sue said.

"That's odd." Steve put on a heads-up display, a device to help him in speaking English.

"No, this is the right L.Z. I'm reading life forms all around us," Steve said. "Wait, why break something up that is clear and understood in the first place?"

"These are the wrong type of life forms," Sue pulled up the readings. "We're supposed to talk to humans."

The scan showed thousands of life forms nearby. Some moved independently, others moved in large swarms. Some were in the water; some flew in the sky above.

Sue brought up a human smartphone.

"What are you doing?" Steve asked.

"Creating a Tinder profile," Sue said. "Apparently earthlings use it to find others. I'm using the human communication device to send out a signal."

"What do you do to do that?" Steve asked. "Is that Earthling English? I hear myself say these sentences, but they make no sense. How can so many uses of the word 'do' be involved and still function as language?"

Steve's heads-up-display tried to help by displaying every use of the words he spoke in preparation for human interaction.

"Okay, I'm understanding this Tinder thing," Sue said. "We need a profile picture."

She brought up the phone, snapping a photograph. Her thousands of sharp incisors created a web of teeth.

"The word 'sense.' Isn't there another word for money called 'cents?' Why would Earthlings make such a decision?" Steve asked. "Ah! 'Scents' for the way things smell. What's wrong with Earthling English?"

"Steve, stop. We've talked about the dumb nature of Earthling English. I have to focus on creating my profile," Sue said. "'Write a bio to describe what you're looking for.' Okay, 'Do you ever feel like you don't belong in this world? Swipe right for an out of this world experience.' Does that sound good?"

"I don't know. 'Sound' is a noise, what does that have to do with the phrase 'a sound theory?' Is it a thought that has noise reverberations to it? This language hurts me!" he shouted.

"Calm down. I'm already receiving responses," Sue looked through the pictures. "Ah! Why? I already researched male reproduction organs. What do they have to do with establishing communication with another?" Sue asked.

"Another, an other," Steve replied.

"Are you going to be of any help here?" Sue asked.

"Here, hear," Steve put his head in his hands. "One is a location, the other is listening to sounds. Which sounds? Music like 'I hear sounds' or ideas like 'what a sound theory'? This is insanity!"

There were some high-pitched calls from birds above, and low, long resonating calls from below.

"I do hear sounds," Sue said.

"From what? That Tinder male's reproductive organs?" Steve asked.

"No, from outside. What reproductive organs make sounds?" Sue asked.

Steve started to speak. Sue interrupted.

"That wasn't a real question. I don't want to know," Sue replied. "I've had enough of organs!" She slammed the smartphone to the floor, cracking the screen and destroying the power source.

"Wait. My heads-up display is telling me 'organ' can mean various body parts or a musical instrument? Again with the sounds, does every word go back to sounds somehow? Damn you, Earthling English! Damn you!" Steve shouted.

"Steve, silence," Sue said. "Look, listen."

Outside whales called out, their tales breaching the surface. One breached and slammed into the ocean, sending ocean water everywhere, even splashing against Sue and Steve's spaceship.

"Wow, are you capturing all of this?" Steve asked.

"Yes, but I don't think any of these creatures can send us a signal," Sue watched his display, waiting for some spike in the readings.

"How do you know?" Steve asked. "Know. No. Now. Wait, what?"

Sue slapped the heads-up display off Steve's head. "Stop. Let's just speak and try it. It may be nonsense but let's try to understand each other. Otherwise, how are we going to understand them?"

She pointed out at the whales.

"First, do you see any of them saying to us, 'What the hell is this thing? Oh, those extraterrestrial beings we talked to on Tinder.' Second, none of them show synapse firings of an intelligent creature capable of communicating with any other species than their own," Sue said. "I might add, you said there was a signal from intelligent life."

"I said..." Steve analyzed his display, seeing if Sue's slap damaged it. "I detected an anomalistic signal that could be a sign of intelligent life. You never listen."

"What are we? Married now?" Sue shouted, reaching for the controls to fly for human establishments.

Two heads popped out from the water. The whales rested in the water, gazing over the unfamiliar vessel in front of them.

"Hey," Sue pointed out at the emerged creatures.

"What are they?" Steve asked.

"Whales," Sue stared at the two creatures. "Gray."

"Huh," Steve read through the signal data in detail.

"What?" Sue asked.

"So, the signal has electronic signatures that match his biological composition. Their calls have the same frequency, or sound," Steve showed the comparison the digital display. "Oh my god, why wouldn't they just use the word 'frequency?'"

"Probably because it can mean a signal as well as how often you do something," Sue said.

Steve slammed his head repeatedly against the console in front of him.

"But you're saying they sent the signal to us?" Sue asked.

"Seems like an accidental signal, but yes," Steve said.

"Nice, you did find the right landing zone," Sue replied.

"I told you," Steve opened the hatch. "Let's try talking to them."

"I'd much rather do that than speak to humans, do they show you their reproductive organ when face to face, too?" Sue asked. "You know what? Never mind. I don't want to know. Let's go speak with Gray Whales."

The two extended their hands. The whales approached the ship. The rest of the pod circled the ship. The majesty of the massive creatures overwhelmed Sue and Steve.

"Hell of an L.Z.," Sue said. "One hell of an L.Z."

"These Dear Ones" by J.M. Butler
Clown in the Ocean

Deep beneath the ocean dreary lies the upturned laughing faces of the mystic swimming clowns. Down below is where they live, quiet, content, and still they seem. No one do they harm for none here ever screams.

And who could fear these creatures cheery? And who could think them dangerous? They slip and slide beneath the currents, faces white with mouths bright red, ever laughing, ever smiling. Such playful sightings are so rare, many wonder if they're there.

But hear me, friend, and hear me well. You might not see them, but they're always there. Their smiles are a mockery, a deadly sea grown trap. Their antics clumsy suggest they're harmless, their wide-set eyes say they're naïve innocents. And if there was trouble, would there not be signs or threats or deadly portents?

The lures of nature from hunter to prey are food or sex or light. Whatever prey needs, that it will see. There it goes, knowing just urgency. But this clown of the sea gives no such gifts, doesn't even pretend to be helpless.

No, it wriggles and scurries, it bobs and it plays. It uses one tool to bring you quite close. It's cute, and it's fun. It makes people laugh. They come out to sea to find them again. They leap in the water to play among them.

Such laughter and fun. What else could be thought but these dear ones are friends? Seek them out, search the sea, let's all just jump in. If you're lucky enough to find them, you're lucky indeed the searchers will say. But no, it is doom and death, consumption disease.

See, on a cold rocky shore in the dim autumn light, my dearest beloved played with the clowns. They danced and they laughed, the clowns circled round. But before I dismounted, they dragged my love down, broke and devoured the one whom I treasured. One clamped its jaws over his and stole his breath while all the rest devoured bones and flesh.

Why no warnings then? No signs that danger abides? It's so simple, friend, which makes it all worse. None hear you scream if first you can't breathe.

"The Purpose of Mosquitocorn Spindlegills IV" by Thomas A. Fowler

Imaginary Friend in the Ocean

Hwa-Young was a fugu, a pufferfish, but she was always puffed. Nervous about the world, Hwa-Young from birth couldn't bring herself to deflate.

Her friend, Kyung Soon, swam slower than normal to keep up with her friend. "Hwa-Young, we're in the wide open of the ocean. You can see everything."

"I know, the vast ocean staring at me like a monstrous shadow waiting to reveal its true monsters," Hwa-Young replied.

She wobbled back and forth, struggling to use her tail for steady navigation.

"Look." Kyung Soon darted in circles around her friend. "See? Being deflated lets me move quicker. It's a long swim, so…"

"I get it, but you can't see that far! How do you know what's out there?" Hwa-Young inflated more. "Who's to say a shark doesn't pop up all of a sudden? Big fish that doesn't mind a puffy fish like me?"

"You need to stop. No one likes to eat us, we're fugu, poisonous, can puff up inside a predator's throat. Anything that tries to eat us, they're in for a rough time," Kyung Soon replied.

"I just can't." Hwa-Young remained puffed. "I just…can't…stop worrying. The ocean is too much!"

"Hello!" another fish shouted.

"What the hell!" Kyung Soon puffed up. Now she was a balloon with gills, just like her best friend.

"Sorry, there. Didn't mean to crank up the air in your belly there," the mystery fish said.

"That's not how that works, we fill with water," Kyung Soon said. "It stretches my skin out. It kind of hurts. Are you going to try to eat us?"

"No," the mystery fish said.

"Okay, I need to deflate. This hurts," Kyung Soon replied.

"What? You don't know!" Hwa-Young shouted. "Join me!"

"Calm down," Kyung Soon said. She slowly let her skin return to normal. Her spikes protruding a little less with each deflation. "Who are you?"

"Well, I'm your imaginary friend, Mosquitocorn!" they said.

The mystery fish emerged from the murky current. Mosquitocorn had wings and legs with finned hooves, and its dorsal fin turned into a mane. At the end of the fish's body was a horn.

"What…the…hell…." Kyung Soon said.

"Hey, you made me," Mosquitocorn said. "I'm a mix of a Mosquitofish and a unicorn."

"That's why your name is Mosquitocorn?" Kyung Soon asked.

"Well, my full name is Mosquitocorn Popsicles Spindlegills the Fourth," they replied.

"That is the type of fish you'd make," Kyung Soon said.

"What do you mean the type of fish I'd make?" Hwa-Young asked.

"Wait…you don't see it?" Kyung Soon asked.

"I'm here for you," Mosquitocorn replied.

"But I didn't make you," Kyung Soon said.

"Yes, you did," Mosquitocorn said.

Kyung Soon drifted in the water, she slipped away from the others. After some time, she swam back to her best and imaginary friend.

"What's happening?" Hwa-Young asked.

"I don't know. I need to talk to Mosquitohorn Popstand," Kyung Soon said.

"Who?" Hwa-Young asked.

"My name is Mosquitocorn Popsicles Spindlegills the Fourth," Mosquitocorn said.

"See? There," Kyung Soon said.

"There who?" Hwa-Young asked. "I'm not understanding this."

"She can't hear me," Mosquitocorn replied.

"This is stressful!" Kyung Soon inflated again.

"Hey!" Hwa Young shouted. "Welcome back!"

Kyung Soon let the water flow through her gills. Her body pumped the water out, relaxing her skin. "Why would I create you?"

Mosquitocorn swam, placing their fins around Kyung Soon. The two drifted away from Hwa Young, who waddled about from side to side, watched her friend pulled by the current.

"You don't need me. She needs you," Mosquitocorn said.

"How do you mean?" Kyung Soon asked.

"I know it can be hard to know how to help your friend," Mosquitocorn said. "But did you ever stop to think about why she spends time with you?"

"Because we get along?" Kyung Soon guessed.

"It's because she can be herself around you," Mosquitocorn said. "She can stay puffed. You encourage her to relax, but also let her stay the way she needs to be right now."

Kyung Soon swam back to Hwa-Young.

"You okay?" Hwa-Young asked.

"Yeah," Kyung Soon said. "Doing great."

"That's it for Mosquitocorn Popsicles Spindlegills the Fourth!" they said.

In a flurry of color, the fish disappeared. Kyung Soon drifted from the current again, mesmerized and unable to keep up with the current.

"What happened?" Hwa-Young asked, remaining puffed. "I'm nervous."

"Don't be," Kyung Soon said. "I'm here." Kyung Soon swam to her friend. "We should get going. It's a long swim."

"I can try to relax, so we can swim faster," Hwa-Young said.

"You know what? Don't worry. It may give me time to explain what just happened," Kyung Soon said.

The duo swam along, Hwa-Young waddled, fins pushing to keep her puffed body going forward. Kyung Soon slowed her pace, staying beside her best friend as they took on the ocean together.

"No One Listens to Children" by Carolyn Kay

A Kaiju in the Ocean

Misaki peered over the rail of her father's whaling ship. Something moved under the oil-slicked waves of Shimonoseki Harbor. Or so she thought. It was a long way down to the water and the sunlight flashed off the waves in a dizzying display. She backed away, her head spinning. Heights always made her feel that way.

Her father was first mate on the *Akiba Sen,* one of Japan's few remaining whaling ships. To Misaki's eyes, the ship seemed huge, until a cruise ship pulled in a few berths down, making her father's ship look like a toy in comparison. His status was the only reason she was allowed on board, though only while the ship was docked. The ship was bustling with activity. Ten years after the nuclear disaster at Fukushima, the prime whaling waters due west of the doomed town were finally deemed safe. Misaki rubbed away the goose bumps on her arms. She'd had a bad feeling about her papa's upcoming voyage ever since he told her about it a month ago. When she'd confessed her misgivings, he tugged playfully on her ponytail and told her not to listen to the stories of giant, radioactive sea monsters. They were just tales told by drunk fishermen to scare little girls like her. He told her, with a glint in his eye, that he knew she didn't want him to go because she would miss him. It's true, she would miss him, but her uneasiness was more than that. She was sure of it. Something in the recent stories rang true to her.

Misaki returned to the rail, pulled by her curiosity. Had she really seen a tentacle in the water? She closed her eyes and let her head hang forward over the rail, willing the world to stop spinning. When the world returned to just the rocking of the ship beneath her, she opened her eyes. The sunlight on the water was dimmed by a passing cloud and she could see past the shining rainbow of oil on the surface. Gull feathers and flotsam ribbons floated by, but there was nothing else. Misaki stared into the water, determined to find something.

The clouds retreated, but the water beneath the ship remained dark. Something huge and round loomed under the surface. It was easily the size of a tire on one of the giant mining trucks they'd seen on a field trip to a copper strip mine last year. The rising disk reflected the sun's light in dazzling rainbows. It stopped just beneath the surface. The center of the iridescent disk widened into an hourglass shape, then shrank into a thin wavy line. It was an eye! But it was nothing like she'd ever seen. It was a massive, monster eye! Misaki pushed back from the rail, breathing heavily. She looked around her. Sailors hurried around her, jogging from one errand to another, but no one was paying any attention. Curiosity pulled at her. She slowly approached the rail and peeked over. The eye was still there! Was it watching her?

"Yes."

Misaki wasn't sure if the thought in her head was hers. It had an odd, slippery feeling to it, like eels sliding between her ears. She shook off the feeling and pulled her phone out of her pocket, swiping at the camera button. She took several photos before she noticed a tentacle worming its way up the side of the ship. It was thick, as big around as she was, and changed colors as she watched to match the rusty black paint of the whaling vessel. A mix of fear and curiosity froze her in place. She ignored the instinct to run. The tentacle slowly, tentatively, wriggled over the top of the deck while the eye continued to stare at her. She stepped to the side, avoiding the tentacle while keeping the eye in sight. She couldn't see anything else beneath the waves. Just darkness.

"Help."

The voice in her mind was as gentle as it was slippery. It definitely wasn't her thought.

"What do you want?" she asked aloud, hoping no one would actually hear her.

"Help. Stop killing the finned ones."

"Whales or fish?" Misaki whispered. She must be going crazy, but she couldn't help herself.

"Touch. Show."

Misaki felt pressure on her foot, and wetness soak into her sneaker. She looked down to see the tip of the tentacle draped over her shoe. It was as wide as her leg, but the touch was light, as if the creature was being careful. "Ok, now what?"

The tentacle wiggled under her pant leg and touched her skin. The world disappeared, and Misaki was floating in the middle of the ocean, watching a whaler pull a minke whale onto the deck. A river of blood ran down the ramp, coloring the water behind the ship. She could feel, but not see, the approach of sharks. The site made her stomach roil. She knew what her father did, but had never seen it. She'd even eaten whale meat. It was a delicacy, so they only had it for special occasions. She wasn't sure she'd be able to eat it after this.

"Stop killing finned brothers." The slippery voice said. The vision before her turned red for a moment, and anger not her own, filled her mind.

"I... I can't. I'm just a girl." No one ever listened to her.

"You must, or metal predators will die."

The sea beneath the whaler began to boil and tentacles the width of a jetliner wrapped around the massive ship. Men screamed and metal screeched as it buckled and cracked under the pressure of the encircling suckered arms. As the ship began to list, a giant, bulbous body emerged from the roiling waters, dwarfing the ship as it crawled on top of it. The monster's skin flashed red, then white with rings of blue, then red again. She could feel waves of rage roll off the creature as its black, pointed beak cut through the control tower like it was made out of mochi.

Men scrambled to the three harpoon guns on deck, quickly aiming and firing the razor-sharp, explosive weapons at the giant octopus. Its skin transformed from smooth to black plated spikes at the roar of the cannon-like guns discharging. The harpoons bounced harmlessly off the creature's skin, exploding when they hit the deck. Men and equipment were tossed into the frothing sea.

The kaiju oozed over the opposite side of the ship, as if nothing had happened, pulling the ship over and capsizing it. Its tentacles continued to constrict the vessel until it snapped in two with a deafening pop. The two halves sunk quickly, dragging men down with them. Those that escaped the sucking whirlpools were quickly silenced by crushing tentacles, or the ripping teeth of the waiting sharks.

Misaki pushed the image from her mind, gasping for air when her vision cleared. Shaking, she backed slowly away from the rail, terrified the monster would pull her under too.

"Won't hurt you. Help. Save finned ones."

The tentacle abruptly retreated as silently as it appeared.

"Misaki-san, what are you doing at the rail? You hate heights."

Misaki jumped at her father's voice so close behind her. She turned and wrapped her arms around her father and began to sob. She tried to tell him not to go, but she was crying too hard.

"What happened? Are you hurt? Why are you crying so?" Her father's voice was stern, but she could hear the undertone of worry. He held her shoulders and squatted down so that his face was level with hers. "Talk to me child. What happened?"

Misaki took one deep, shuddering breath, then another. When she felt she had a voice, the words rushed out, jumbled and chaotic. "Don't go. Kaiju. Killing whales is death."

Her father's face grew angry. The sea breeze rippled through his close-cropped hair as if it, too, was angry at her. He shook her just a little. "I told you to quit listening to the fishermen's tales. There are no kaiju in the sea. You are being childish. I don't have time for this." He stood up. "Your aunt is waiting for you near the control tower. Go to her and stop this foolishness." He turned and started walking away.

She had to convince him not to go, but how? Her phone vibrated in her hand. The photos! "Oto-san! Wait! I have pictures." She ran to him, thumbing through the screens to pull up the pictures. She found the ones with the eye and thrust her phone at her father.

He took the phone from her and stared at the picture. "There is nothing here but reflections of the sun on the oily water."

She took the phone back and pointed out the changing iris in the series of photos. Her father was unconvinced. He grabbed her arm and started leading her to the opposite side of the ship, to her aunt. "Oto-san, please don't go. This monster will kill you!"

"My captain will kill me if I go to him with blurry pictures and the ravings of my ten-year-old daughter. Now stop this nonsense. I will not allow you to shame me." He stopped her as they neared her aunt and turned her to face him. "I love you, Misaki-san, but your imagination has gotten the better of you. Behave for your aunt. I will be home in a month." He kissed her forehead and gently pushed her towards his waiting sister.

Misaki cried silent tears as she stood with her aunt on the docks watching the *Akiba Sen* pull away from its berth. A dark shadow seemed to flow behind it, the water bulging above it.

"The metal predator leaves to hunt the finned ones." The voice was not accusatory, but it wasn't friendly either.

"No one listens to children," Misaki said.

"What was that Misa-chan?" her aunt asked as she eyed a handsome harbor officer nearby who was inspecting a local fisherman's catch.

"Nothing, obasan."

"Water Pilots" by Jason Kent
Robot Assassin in the Ocean

CMMD2020_Activate.
STAT4678_Unit0088 100% Functional.
MSSN0018_Locate M. Francis.
MSSN0019_Terminate M. Francis.
MODE5044_Acquire Target. Searching…

Drowning. I don't know about you, but this has got to be the worst way to die.

I can't remember how I got into this tunnel. I do know I'm not supposed to be here. Mainly because the entire place is filled with water. Well, not water exactly. This stuff I'm swallowing is thick and warm. Gross. I don't know what the fluid is. Maybe I don't want to find out. Not that it matters much. It'll kill me soon enough.

I'm floating in an intersection. Four separate tunnels stretch out as far as I can see in the murky water. I was hoping for a light at the end of one of the tunnels to tell me which way to swim. No joy.

From the way my lungs are burning, I figure I don't have much time until I pass out. I pick a tunnel at random and push off. Another intersection appears. There has got to be a way out around the next corner. If not, I'm dead. I kick for all I'm worth.

A dark form heaves through the cross tunnel. My mind seizes up and refuses to believe there is a monster in the next tunnel. My eyes are playing tricks on me, thanks to the lack of oxygen. I don't want to keep going but there's no time to rest.

I don't hesitate when I reach the intersection. Somehow, I know the only way out of the tunnel is to follow the thing I saw. Swinging around the corner, I kick off from the wall and—

—run straight into the maw of the monster.

I wake-up, gasping for air. One problem. I'm still underwater. Flailing my arms and legs, I try to reach the surface only to find I'm in in a flooded compartment. My panic spikes when I feel a hand on my shoulder. The monster has me...

The pain of banging my forehead on the ceiling finally breaks through the fog and I remember where I am. Ugh. The dream. Again.

The dream is always the same and it's always terrifying. You'd think after visiting the same place and getting eaten by the same beast again and again, you'd get used to the sensation. You don't.

I open my mouth and suck in the warm fluid which passes for an atmosphere for myself and my co-pilot, Kathy. Our ship is midway between Sol and a colony world named Hadrian. Nice place. If you breathe air. Of the three hundred and seventeen souls on board, she and I are the only ones awake. Everyone else is basically a popsicle shoved into cryogenic hibernation. Although our passengers float in the same mixture as Kathy and me, they don't have to deal with dreams like the one my brain constantly replays for me.

"Better?"

Clutching my head, I turn to find Kathy floating next to me in our shared quarters.

"Yeah. I'm alright." My words sound muffled. "Sorry to wake you up."

Kathy smiles. "No problem. They told us the dreams would be part of the gig." Her voice doesn't sound quite right, either. Only the pick-ups embedded next to our vocal cords and the implants behind our ears makes the discussion even close to undistorted. The gig Kathy mentioned is the reason we're awake during this long voyage. They call us water pilots; modified humans capable of living in a non-compressible fluid. This means our new and improved bodies can survive the immense forces generated by our engines as we travel between humanity's far-flung outposts. Now, deep into my fourth round-trip mission, I must say the life of a water pilot sounded a lot more glamorous in the brochure.

Kathy wraps her arms around me and pulls me into our sleeping cocoon. I feel silly letting her cradle me like a child. Then again, it does feel nice. Soon, my respiration returns to normal. I'm sucking in more oxygen-rich fluid through the gills under my armpits than through my mouth. The surgical upgrade may work fine, but my brain still wants me to inhale deeply. I shut my mouth and let the gills do their work.

"You know, you woke me up from my own dream," Kathy says. She runs a hand over my chest and continues downward. "Want to guess what it was about?" Based on what she starts doing to me, there is no need to guess. The company pairs compatible water pilots for these trips. This is the third trip where Kathy and I have shared the tight living quarters of a water ship. There's a lot of downtime during these long runs and Kathy is known for her energetic and imaginative means of passing the time. Who am I to complain? Kathy's way is certainly better than dwelling on my own dream.

Ah, water pilots. The pay is great and the lifestyle has its perks. But, I'm pretty sure I'll never get used to being turned into a fish.

STAT4679_M. Francis Located.

STAT4780_M. Francis Life Signs Steady within Cryogenic Suspension.

ALRT9901_Weapons Detected.

ALRT9902_Security Detail Identified.

MSSN0020_Breach Cryogenics Chamber.

MSSN0021_Negate Security Detail.

MSSN0022_Terminate M. Francis.
CMMD2030_Enter Combat Mode
MODE5055_Combat Ready.

The morning after my latest near-death dream, I find myself in the access tubes checking on our silent passengers. Something had set off an alarm near bay three. I am pretty sure it is an error, but the computer won't let us turn the alarm off without physically coming back here to hit the reset button. How did the company know I'd just check the camera without leaving the warm waters of the bridge? Or, as Kathy and I are fond of calling it, The Tank.

Even though I know it's just me in the tubes today, I can't stop looking behind me. Maybe it was the dream, but I've got this nagging feeling there's something in here with me.

I grab a handhold to arrest my forward motion. Even with my suit heaters cranked up I still get the chills. We aren't in the aft end of the ship enough during the journey to warrant heating the water much above freezing. I stare through the murk. The only movement I see are particles suspended in the water, disturbed by my passage. I shake my head. My mind has to be playing tricks on me. Out of habit, I heave a sigh. Instead of a huff of air, water rushes out of my lungs.

I push the paranoia away and focus on the panel in front of me. My touch wakes up the interface pad. The computers, like my co-pilot and I, have been adapted to function in a liquid environment. The screens are made of flexible, touch-sensitive plastics. What metals are present are embedded to prevent corrosion and to keep the whole system from shorting out. I suppress a shudder and try not to think of the high voltage conduits running on the other side of the tube walls. Well-insulated or not, it doesn't pay to dwell on the thought of our living environment becoming one, big, live wire.

The hair on the back of my neck rises. Some part of me knows with certainty that something's unblinking eyes are boring into the back of my skull. I jerk my head to the side, hoping to catch whoever is spying on me. All I accomplish is to confirm that I'm still alone. Normally, I'm not the jumpy type. So, why can't I shake this?

"It's all in your head, Ryan," I tell myself. It doesn't seem to help.

The cold really starts to seep into my bodysuit as I wait for the monitoring system in the cryogenics bay to run their self-diagnostics. I had opted for gloves before leaving the tank. I didn't go for the booties. Wearing them makes you look like a dork. Of course, in the ice box I'm beginning to feel like a dork for not putting them on. My toes are already turning blue.

The test is taking forever. With a sigh, I pull the booties from where I'd tucked them under my utility belt. The bodysuit doesn't have any pockets, thus the belt. You have to hook the portable heating unit to something. I can't feel my feet as I pull the booties over them. Probably not a good sign. The fabric connects to the heating coils. It isn't long before I begin to feel pins and needles in the soles of my feet. I guess I'll survive now, looking like a doof.

The computer beeps, drawing my attention back to the bay laid out before me. The access tube runs between the outer hull of the ship and the cryogenic hibernation compartments. The tube wall is clear from floor-to-ceiling, allowing me to look over the two rows of cylinders in the bay. The boards are all green on the display. I swipe through the reports on each passenger. Everyone continues to be perfectly preserved.

I can make out more details in the bay as the lights brighten. The outside of the cylinders has all frosted over in the months since we departed Earth. Mostly, what I can see are outlines of the humans floating in the protective slurry. My eyes linger on a woman floating in the cylinder closest to the window. What is her name, I wonder? Where did she come from? Why is she heading out into deep space? Is she single?

Snorting, I brush my fingers over the control pad. The lights in the bay dim until I can only see the dark figures of the passengers floating serenely in dreamland, illuminated by a few status lights.

"Sleep well." My gaze lingers on the woman whose history I don't know. She probably wouldn't be into a water pilot anyway. Yeah, the few women I've been with since my adaptation thought the experience was novel. Air-breathers get tired of wearing masks though. No one ever spends the entire night. Hey, I get it. I have trouble sleeping underwater and I'm built for it.

Something in the bay catches my eye as I start to turn away.

I hit the lights again. The thing sliding across the floor stops in its tracks.

It's the monster from my dream. Silver tentacles, claws, and all.

As my skin tries to crawl away from my skeleton, the monster springs into action. A tentacle slashes out, smashing the frost-covered glass of one of the cylinders in the middle of the room. Fluid gushes onto the floor. Claws glint in the light before the creature plunges them through the opening. When the claws came out, they are covered in gore.

I can't help it. I lose my lunch. Not something recommended by the water pilot handbook. After all, you are what you breathe.

Alarms start going off, both inside the bay and in the tubes. Four of the other pods open, spilling liquid contents and passengers. Each of the humans have a military-style rifle. My mouth falls open. Not only did I not realize we were hauling soldiers, I didn't know there were weapons packed in the cylinders. I am impressed by how fast the three men and one woman recover from waking up. Their cylinders must be equipped with a drug delivery system designed to get them moving. In case, you know, monsters attack.

Three of the soldiers start firing immediately. The fourth tries but is overcome by a reaction from the rapid wake-up. He bends over and heaves the contents of his stomach onto the wet floor. The monster shows him no mercy. A claw slices upward and the man's intestines join the puke already spread across the deck.

Another man and the woman go down in short order. Despite the danger, I press close to the glass and watch the battle unfold. The final soldier finds cover behind a cylinder and seems to be hitting the creature with his bullets.

The monster's hide sparks where it is struck. It looks like a squid trying to move on dry land as it pulls itself to one side of the compartment. Sparking? I study the creature closely and realize with a start, this is not an animal, it's a machine.

My passengers are being systematically killed by a robot assassin.

It had to be a drone gone crazy. We have several which roam the access tubes performing basic maintenance and inspections. Despite the fact I've never seen a drone like the monster tearing up the bay in front of me, I slap at the console to bring up the drone control screen. If that thing is a drone gone mad, maybe I can turn it off before it kills everyone on the ship.

A quick look at the ship schematic on my pad reveals the closest drone is in an access tube more than one hundred and fifty meters farther aft. On the other side of the ship. Crap. The thing isn't a drone, and I have no way to control it.

The sound of fresh rifle fire draws my attention back to the window. The last soldier's face slams against the glass. His body is pinned to the wall by a trio of tentacles. This close, I can now see clearly that the appendages are segmented and the blood-drenched claws are polished steel.

The claws retract and the man falls to the floor. I am left staring into the eyes of the monster. They are set inside an elongated metal body from which the tentacles sprout. The eyes are gleaming photoreceptors. I get that creeping feeling in my spine again. This thing was watching me earlier. It is a small consolation to know I'm not crazy.

In the bay, the fourth soldier's hand relaxes and a small object rolls onto the floor. I've seen enough vids to recognize a grenade. The monster must have seen the same movies because it turns and slithers as fast as its tentacles can move.

A hand slaps the inside of the nearest cylinder. The fighting must have shorted out the system and prematurely awoken the passenger. It is the woman I'd been entranced with just a few moments ago. Her eyes are wide with panic.

"I'm sorry…" I turn and kick my hardest. If the vids are to be believed, I have only a few—

The explosion bursts through the thin tube wall. The shock wave races past me and impacts the hatch to The Tank. With nowhere to go, the energy destroys the door and sends it flying.

I pray Kathy is not in the way.

I am buffeted by residual energy bouncing back from The Tank. If I hadn't been adapted to live in water, my lungs would have been crushed twice already. I stop swimming and look toward what was left of bay three. I should have kept moving.

STAT4681_M. Francis Terminated.
STAT4782_Security Detail Terminated.
ALRT9903_34% Damage Sustained.
ALRT9904_Hull Breach Detected.
MSSN0023_Secondary Mission Orders: Locate Starship Crew.
MSSN0024_Secondary Mission Orders: Terminate Starship Crew.
MODE5044_Acquire Target. Searching…

I stiffen and listen as the ship shudders from bow to stern, absorbing the shock of the explosion. I swallow hard then think about the dead bodies shredded by the blast that are now mixed with the water I am breathing. I snap my mouth shut and shudder. Hopefully, the remaining hibernation cylinders protected the other passengers. Maybe even the woman I'd left behind. I need to go back in there and find out. I also need to know if the killer robot was destroyed. The grenade would have had a much greater effect in the open air of the bay. At least I hoped so. I have no idea how to fight a killer robot.

Everything grows quiet and time seems to stop. For a moment, just a moment mind you, the water around me is still. The interlude is long enough to allow a chill to run down my spine.

Then things get really bad.

The slight tug at my arms and legs is the first indication something is wrong. Maybe the bay three hatch was breached, allowing water to pour from the now-flooded compartment into the air-filled passenger corridor connecting the bays and dry cargo areas. Or…

Oh, crap…

There is no telltale whistle of air leaving the ship. Submerged, there is only one way to know the blast had breached the outer hull. I can't hear the fluid rushing out of the hole, but I'm being pulled towards it all the same.

"Breach! Breach! Breach!" I shout into the water knowing my words won't reach very far in the tube but my embedded pick-ups will transmit the message to Kathy. Hopefully, she can get to safety before we lose our atmosphere. I don't need to waste time activating the alarms. The computer already knows something is wrong. Red lights started flashing when the soldiers and bot were fighting. A deep-throated klaxon capable of awakening those in cryo-hibernation echoes off the curved surfaces surrounding me.

The tug of escaping water grows stronger. It feels as if I am fighting a riptide. I pull myself along with the hand holds. Thankfully, The Tank is close. No way do I want to end up where the water is blasting from the ship. My chest is heaving when I finally reach the bridge area. Kathy is staring blankly at the hatch embedded in the main control boards.

"What. Did. You. Do?" That is all Kathy manages to ask before I collide with her. My momentum carries us both back into the bedroom where we hit the wall in a tangle of arms and legs. I slap the emergency panel. The hatch slams shut with alarming speed, making me glad none of our fingers or toes were in the way.

The klaxons became muted by the thick metal door. The red lights bathe our faces with an eerie strobe effect as we press our noses to the window. We watch in mute horror as The Tank drains completely. In the sudden vacuum and intense cold, every surface quickly becomes coated in a thick layer of crystals.

"Oh no…" Kathy mutters. She covers her mouth with her hand and instinctively moves closer to me.

I wrap a consoling arm around her shoulders and consider our options. The bedroom was designed to serve as an emergency shelter in just this kind of situation. It can keep us alive in the short-term with its own dedicated power and life support systems. Who knows how long those will actually hold out, though. We aren't scheduled at our next stop for more than three months. No way we can hide in our bedroom shelter until then. Besides, there's no way to operate the ship from here and we are due to execute a braking maneuver soon.

I realize we are not being pulled toward the floor. I mutter, "The engines…" and snag an interface pad from its nook. The big, wall display lights up. It is helpfully framed in red and dire emergency warnings flash in the center. I acknowledge the warnings and minimize them.

Kathy floats over to me and points at the engine on the ship schematic. "Engines don't register any damage."

"But why are they off?"

"There," Kathy jabs her finger at the operations log scrolling down the side of the screen. "The computer shut everything down when it registered the hull breach."

"Good thing the grenade was nowhere near the engines. That seems like the kind of thing from the training sims that would kill us." I glance at our frozen bridge on the other side of our bedroom door. "Of course, a hole in the ship is never good, either."

Kathy punches me in the arm. The water softens the blow a bit, but not much. "What happened?!"

I think about the robot monster and run a hand over my face. "Let's just say the hull breach might not be our most pressing concern."

"What are you talking about?" Kathy frowns in confusion and turns back to the display. "Bay three is in vacuum. The passengers…" She catches sight of the blinking health and status lights for the hibernation cylinders. A flick of her fingers zooms in on the damaged bay. Kathy's voice is barely audible when she adds, "They're all dead…"

So much for my earlier hope the cylinders would protect the passengers. The hibernation equipment simply isn't designed to survive a war. I think of the desperate look from the woman in the cylinder and wonder how long I will be haunted by her image.

"What did you say about a grenade?" Kathy asks absently. She can't take her eyes from the red icons.

"Something attacked one of our passengers and four soldiers woke up to defend him. It killed everyone. The last guy, well…" I make an exploding motion with my hands.

Kathy looks confused. Finally, she shakes her head. "Who let someone bring a grenade aboard?"

"The better question is who let a killer get aboard."

"Wait, bay three?" Kathy turns white and starts tapping on the board. She brings up the passenger manifest and scrolls through the list. She stops suddenly and points at an entry. "Ambassador Mertinand Francis." She waves a hand at the lines below the Ambassador's name. "And guests."

"The Ambassador's guests were pretty well armed."

"Must have been his security team," Kathy surmises. "You said they woke up fighting? It's impossible to come out of hibernation so fast."

"Apparently, it's not."

Kathy glances out the window at the frozen bridge. "What do we do now?"

"We repair the ship. The rest of the passengers are counting on us."

"Water pilots," Kathy said with a nervous grin. "Nothing keeps us down."

I can't help but smile at her after hearing the motto from the academy. I know she's right. We'll fix the ship. If we don't, we'll die. Simple.

"Corporate's going to string us up," Kathy muttered after glancing at the display again. "Of all the bays to get attacked."

"It looked like it was pretty specific." I remember the bot went for the center cylinder first. I could check, but I already know I'd discover that was where the loaders would position our VIP. "There are plenty of other people who still need our help," I remind her softly.

"Yeah." With a visible effort, Kathy pulls herself together and focuses on the task at hand. "Where do you want to start?"

"First, we suit up." I pull up the pad beneath the sleeping cocoon. The locker under our bed contains our survival gear. Usually. I pause and run my eyes over the locker contents several times. I don't believe it. I look at Kathy and ask, "Where's the other suit?"

Kathy floats over. She starts moving bags around. She ends up tossing everything out of the locker and arrives at the same conclusion as me. She stares at the empty cabinet in disbelief. "There's only one suit…"

I slap my forehead. It's not as effective in the water, but it gets the point across. "I'm an idiot!"

"This isn't your fault. We're supposed to check this thing once a week. The last time—"

"I snagged a suit, remember?" I interrupt. "It's back in the maintenance bay waiting for a patch."

Kathy's eyes move from the door to the single suit floating between us. Her gaze meets mine and she asks the question both of us are thinking, "How are we supposed to get out of here?"

"Not sure." I face the window looking out at our frosty bridge and begin thinking aloud. "We can stay in here as long as the food and recyclers keep working. The generator should last longer than we can, but that doesn't do us any good. We need to get the engines running or we can't complete our braking maneuver. If that happens, we'll overshoot Hadrian and keep on going forever. Not that the passengers would mind, they'd be long dead by then. The cylinders need power from the engines to function. Right now, they're on battery power."

"So would we," Kathy says softly. She lays a hand on the cool glass of the bedroom's hatch. "There's no pressure lock on this door. Once we open it, we lose the water. We'd die without protection." She turns back at the suit. It floats serenely in the middle of the room.

I sigh, "Let's at least see who's suit we have." I reach out and snag it by the arm. I know instantly by the size of the wrist cuff which one I am holding. But I go through the motions of finding the name tape and show it to Kathy.

"Oh."

"Yeah," I sigh. "There's no way I can fit into your suit. If it'd been mine, we'd have a tougher choice about who gets to..." I let my voice trail off. The 'what if' doesn't particularly matter at this point. I like to think I'd stuff Kathy in my suit and sacrifice myself. Maybe it's a good thing I don't have to make those kinds of choices, in the end. We have Kathy's suit here with us, all ready to go. Mine is most likely frozen solid back in the maintenance bay.

Kathy drifts away from me, her eyes go wide as the full implications of the situation strikes home.

"Kathy..." I reach for her.

"I can't go out there alone!" Katy blurts. "You'd be dead before I could get to your suit."

"Kathy, we could—"

"I can't fix the ship by myself!" Kathy presses on along her dark train of thought. "And how am I supposed to fight a deadly bot?!" Despite being submerged in water, it is obvious from the redness and puffiness around her eyes that tears were flowing, adding their saltiness to our atmosphere.

I slowly reach out and took ahold of Kathy by the shoulders. When she finally faces me. I gave her my best smile.

Kathy breaks down completely and collapses into my arms. She sobs, "I can't imagine finishing this trip without you." It's no profession of love, but, it's kind of nice to know someone likes having you around.

I let my co-pilot cry for a few minutes. When I feel the sobs lessening, I pull back enough to look into her face. "You okay?"

"No, you big idiot!" Kathy half laughs, half sobs as she punches me in the chest. "I'm not okay!"

"There's still nearly three hundred passengers."

Kathy hits me again. "You know that's not what I meant. Besides, they're frozen."

"Yeah, there is that." We'd been told repeatedly in training how utterly unqualified we are to deal with the thawing process. That's a job for specialists at the ports. Kathy and I know enough to monitor vitals but not much else. Still, I suppose we could figure it out if we were really in a jam and needed a spare set of hands…

"You're thinking about waking someone up, aren't you?" Kathy pulls away and crosses her arms over her chest. "Forget it. If we can't figure out a way for both of us to get out of here, we're staying put."

"Alright, if you're not going to just put your suit on and save the ship on your own, then we need another plan." I rub my hands together and twist in place, looking with fresh eyes at the gear floating around the bedroom. "What we need is a way for me to…" I spot a gill vest and kick closer until I can snag it from a tangle of clothing. I'm grinning as an idea starts to form in my head. I hold the vest up triumphantly. "Looks like you won't have to save everyone all by yourself after all!"

"That won't do you any good," Kathy protests. "Gill vests are meant to keep water circulating through your lungs when we leave the tank, but you still need water for the exchangers to work."

I find the mask to go with the gill vest and hold both up. "I'll just have to hold my breath. The valves will keep the water in my lungs."

Kathy's face falls, in stark contrast to the silly grin spreading across mine. Finally, she shakes her head vigorously. "You can't go out there with just a gill vest and mask. You'll freeze solid before we can cover the hole and refill The Tank!"

"We don't have to fix anything," I explain quickly as I strip out my shirt. "You just need to get me back to a pressure hatch in the aft section. Once we're through a lock, we can grab what we need from the storage lockers in the part of the ship which didn't vent." My hands are trembling as I fumble with the straps. Whether the shaking is from my growing excitement or mounting fear, I'm not sure. Kathy gives me a tsk and moves to help with the straps. I stop trying to dress myself and let her take over. If this is going to work, the vest needs to be as snug as possible. While Kathy works her wardrobe magic, I use a free hand to tap at the bedroom's big monitor until I find what we need.

"Here." I jab a finger at the screen. "Lock number three should work."

Kathy is too busy pawing through my closet to look over but she's catching on to my enthusiasm. "Three has an external lock. There are extra water suits for both of us."

"Once we're both suited up, we'll patch the hole, use the reservoirs to refill the tank, and, you know," I say with a nonchalant shrug, "save everyone."

Kathy is still shaking her head at my crazy idea. The more I think about it though, the more I'm liking my plan.

"This might actually work," I mutter excitedly as I secure the mask to my face. Luckily, it has a full faceplate; I'll be able to keep the water in my lungs from bursting out and be able to see. Our augmented vision needs a layer of water for us to be able to focus and judge distance correctly. I hook the tube up to the gill vest and hope the whole thing doesn't freeze up before we get into the pressure lock. That'd suck.

"First, we need to get you there before you freeze." Kathy hands me a bundle of clothes. I nod appreciatively. I've already got a heavy insulated suit on. She's found another thick bodysuit along with two lighter layers. With these on, I figure that I should stay relatively warm during our dash across the empty bridge and through frosty access tunnels. I start to wiggle into the second, heavy bodysuit.

Kathy falls unnaturally silent as she helps me into the second layer of clothing. It's a tight fit over the first layer and gill vest. I look down and meet Kathy's eyes as she shoves a leg into the bodysuit. She looks genuinely worried again.

"What's wrong?"

Kathy shrugs and finishes getting the second layer in place. She works the front zipper slowly until it is done up all the way to the low collar. Finally, she says, "I'm worried even if we get you to the lock, you'll be in no condition to do anything for a while."

I tip her chin up with a finger and give her a grin. "Water pilot, remember? Nothing keeps us down." I'm happy to see a ghost of a smile creep across Kathy's face.

"Shut up and put this on." Kathy hands me the third suit. I look at and toss it over my shoulder.

"No way is that going to fit over the rest of this gear." I check the mask again. The straps need a minor adjustment so I pull it off my face and work to pull them as tight as possible. Before I can put the mask back on, Kathy put her hands on either side of my face and pulls me close for a full, lingering kiss. When she backs off, she gives me a naughty smile and bites her lower lip.

"I'm suddenly in the mood for a romp in bed before all this nice warm water disappears."

"Normally, I'd be more than happy to oblige," I laugh then gesture at all the clothes I'm wearing. "There are more layers here than I think we have time to get out of and back in without endangering the lives of the passengers."

She pouts good-naturedly. "Ah, you're always the responsible one."

I slip the mask over my face. Kathy moves close to help. Finished, we smile at each other. "I promise, as soon as this is all over, I plan on getting drunk and laid."

"Aye-aye, Captain," Kathy gives me a mock salute with two fingers to her brow. "Just give me a minute to tidy up."

While Kathy stuffs loose items into lockers and secures the bedding cocoon, I move my arms back and forth and pump my legs. The layers I am wearing quickly become uncomfortably warm. I hope it lasts but, given Kathy's concern, I'm guessing I'll be nearly frozen by the time we reach our destination. My earlier confidence starts to fade in the time it takes Kathy to slip into her pressure suit. I double check her readings and give her a thumbs up.

We take up positions on either side of the hatch and nod to each other.

"Any last words of advice?" Kathy asks.

"Keep moving," I reply and then add, "and don't die."

"I'll try," Kathy says flatly. "What if we see the robot?"

"Run the other way," I reply seriously.

Kathy gulps. "Right." She taps the override command into the control pad beside the door. Her hand hovers over the 'initiate' icon as she looks over to me. "Ready?"

I tilt my head until something pops satisfactorily in my neck. "Do it."

Kathy tightens her grip on a handhold and touches the panel.

The hatch opens a fraction, allowing the water to begin flowing out into the empty bridge. I have to fight to keep from being sucked out along with the water from the bedroom. When the liquid is mostly gone, the door slides halfway up then locks in place.

Crap. I crouch and squeeze under the door, cursing the inconvenience and the precious seconds the unforeseen obstacle is costing us.

I know right away the conditions will be bad during our dash to the pressure lock. My wet hair freezes solid. Thank goodness my ears are covered by the mask or they'd simply fall off in the ungodly cold. I push chunks of ice out of the way; the second unforeseen obstacle. For some reason, I just assumed the water from the bedroom would be blasted out of the hole to farther back in the ship. But, since there is no pressure to push it that far, it simply turned into frozen bergs blocking our path.

I grab the webbing hanging around the pilot's station, intending to redirect my motion towards the hatch at the back of the bridge. The belts are brittle from the intense cold and shatter in my hand. A frozen shard cuts through my inadequate gloves. Blood bubbles up and freezes in goblets. I barely feel it since my extremities are already becoming numb.

Nothing keeps us down… Kathy grabs my arm and propels me through the busted hatch. I let her guide me. God it was cold.

We shoot past the maintenance bay where I'd foolishly left my suit. I have the urge to stop and try it on but Kathy is urging me forward.

Our passage stirs up more ice. A chunk slams into my mask, webbing it with cracks. I flinch but press forward. My only hope is to get back into warm water. Besides, I figure the water in my mask will be frozen solid in less than a minute. I can already feel the gill vest seizing up, it feels like I am wearing a ton of weight wrapped around my chest. The clothes are little better. My limbs are stiff inside the layers of frozen material.

I am busy warding off more ice when I hit the wall. The brittle material over my shoulder cracks and breaks away. I am glad for the numbness as the ice crystals lining the corridor dig into my skin. More goblets of blood erupt from the wound. I don't bother turning my head to look. I am afraid the seal on my mask would break. Losing the mask would kill me instantly.

We pass the hole leading into bay three and the rip in the outer hull. There is a satchel snagged on a piece of jagged metal. I grab it without thinking. I start to drift out into space while I try to remember why there is a hole in my ship.

Kathy comes to my rescue again and pulls me down the access tube. The water in my mask begins to freeze. I know she is trying to tell me something, but my ears are full of slush. That is sure to feel good later. Kathy jerks my arm again. I want to help her but am having trouble focusing my mind on anything.

Where are we going anyway? Why hadn't we stayed in the nice, warm waters of our snug sleeping cocoon? I could certainly go for nap about now. I hit another wall, but with less force. I can make out someone through my cracked visor and freezing water. What is Kathy trying to do anyway?

My lungs are burning…

I need to take a breath. Maybe if I take off this mask…

I'm not sure what he is thinking. I nearly freak out when I turn around from chipping ice from the control panel and find Ryan grabbing at his mask. Lucky for both of us, his fingers are so numb he isn't able to uncinch the straps.

"Stop!" I swat his hands away from his face. From the feeble resistance Ryan is able to put up, I know he is in trouble. I have to get him back into the water. Worried Ryan might try to remove his mask again, I pull him close where I can keep an eye on him. I hit the lock cycle icon and watch as the water on the far side of the portal drains. I glance over at Ryan and am more alarmed by his complete lack of movement than him struggling with his facemask. I put my face close to the frost-covered portal and will the water to drain faster.

"Come on, come on, come on," I mutter as the last of the water disappears. The panel beside the door turns from red to green. I grab the handle and strain against it for a long moment before letting go. Exasperated, I give the door my dirtiest look and gasp, "You've got to be kidding me!"

Cursing, I grab the handle again. "Stupid ice." As I put all I have into forcing the handle to move I glance down at my still pilot. "Nice of you to help, Ryan."

Nothing. Crud. The cold got to him even faster than I feared it would. I don't bother looking at my watch to see how much time has passed since we left the shelter of our bedroom.

I heave against the door with one final effort. I feel the ice give way through the handle and the door swings inward. My nerves are shot. I worry Ryan is running out of time. I grab him under the arms and jerk him through the hatch. I have to force his body into a corner so his feet aren't in the way while I slam the door. Luckily, it closes much easier than it opened. I seal the door in one, quick motion. The thin covering of ice on the control panel flakes off easily. I slap my hand on the oversized 'pressurize' icon. Water immediately begins flooding the chamber.

Satisfied the water is flowing properly, I pull Ryan close, ready to get his mask off as soon as there is something for him to breathe. It's weird watching water fill a space when you're in zero-g. The liquid floats and coalesces into larger and larger globes. The balls of water wobble, reflecting the lights from my suit into a thousand fascinating patterns. The constantly shifting reflections mesmerize me despite the deadly nature of our circumstances.

Finally, the glittering globes all merge. The lock is full. I double check the control panel to be sure the pressure is holding. Satisfied everything is working as designed, I rip Ryan's facemask off. I hold his head in my hands, willing him to be okay, but his chest isn't moving. We still need to 'breathe' underwater to help the oxygenated fluid we live in get into and out of our lungs. With the ice build-up in his gills and mask, he's not even going through the motions.

Cursing under my breath, I quickly unzip the layers covering the gill vest. I work my fingers under the frozen material and pry the exchangers away from his gills. In the cold vacuum outside the water, the vest had become a worthless block of ice. It would melt, given enough time. I figured he wouldn't make it long enough for that to help. I struggle with the bodysuits and finally get him completely out of the vest. I toss it aside. He's going to need help breathing.

Since we're still in zero-g, traditional cardio-pulmonary resuscitation won't work. I get behind Ryan and wrap my arms around his chest. Squeezing for all I'm worth, I compress his lungs. If nothing else, I'm getting fresh, oxygen-rich fluid into his lungs. I'm on the fifth, death-squeeze compression when Ryan finally shows signs of coming to life.

I loosen my grip but don't let go as he starts thrashing.

"It's okay, you're okay." I hope my voice is soothing. Then again, I've never been accused of being the motherly type. Still, I do what I can and hold him until he calms down and realizes he's safe.

He's safe. We're safe.

I won't have to face the darkness alone.

Can't. Breathe.

I gasp only to find I've drowned. Again. Someone's holding me under the water. I struggle to get free until I realize it's Kathy. I stop struggling. At least we'll die together…

Or not.

Water pilot. I'm a water pilot. And, as the name implies, I live in the water. I'm not drowning but I suddenly remember I nearly froze to death.

I turn to face Kathy. She's still in her emergency suit. A quick glance around confirms we're inside the pressure lock with the vacuum behind us and habitable water one hatch away. Good girl. I look down at myself. I feel like I've been in fight with a bunch of guys who were way bigger than me. Everything hurts.

"How'd it go?" I meet Kathy's eyes. She's wearing the biggest grin I've ever seen and crying at the same time. I groan, "Oh god, I nearly died, didn't I?"

Kathy grabs me into a bear hug for an answer.

"Ah!" My chest hurts worse than any other part of my body. Although I suspect when my hands and feet finally thaw out, they'll start complaining as well.

Kathy lessens her grip but doesn't let go completely. "Sorry! Just glad you're, you know, here."

"Yeah, me too," I say and rub my chest. "I think I may have a broken rib."

"We can check it out once we re-pressurize the medical bay."

"Right." I straighten up and wince. "Let's get a suit for me before something else goes wrong. Get us out of here." I gesture at the inner door. The locker with our extra water suits is only a few meters on the other side of the hatch.

I try and pull up the inner layer I am wearing. It's impossible to do with the pain in my chest.

"Let me," Kathy offers when she sees my discomfort. She carefully gets the bodysuit back in place and slowly zips up the front. She's smiling at me again.

"You're certainly in a good mood."

"Being alive does that to me."

The water around us surges as something slams into the hatch. I get to the window in time to see the robot monster bounce away into the empty tube.

Our stow-away from bay three is back.

"It's trying to get in!" Kathy screams.

Ice covers the tentacles and seems to have partially blinded the robot. The monster manages to orient itself toward our door. It launches itself down the corridor and slams into the hatch. The robot begins prying at the door.

I push back as the metal frame starts creaking. I quickly turn and start working the inner door. No way do I want to be in the lock if that monstrosity manages to break through. I don't even have my mask and gill vest to protect me if we lose our water again.

There is a pop and water starts leaking out. The imminent danger breaks through to Kathy. She springs forward and locks out the controls for the hatch the robot is so anxious to dismantle.

I get the second door open and pull Kathy through with me. At the last second, I spot the satchel floating in the corner. I snatch it up and seal the door just as the robot manages to breach the first hatch. The water in the lock gushes out and instantly freezes all over the thrashing machine. I lock the door and make a mad sprint for the suit locker just down the tube. I get into the suit in record time and seal the helmet just as the mad robot starts pounding on the second door.

"Will that hold it?" Kathy asks. Her voice is shaking with terror.

"No." I open the satchel and find three more grenades. The soldiers sent to guard the Ambassador were idiots. You can't use these things in the close quarters of a spaceship.

The robot screeches its claws against the second hatch.

Then again. Maybe the guards had thought there was a chance they would be fighting a killer bot.

"Get to the next intersection and hold on!" I dive for the hatch and wrap the satchel's strap around the door's big handle. The robot smashes into the hatch again then stares at me through the small window with one of those glowing photoreceptors. I pull all three pins and stuff the grenades into the pouch. I make it to Kathy in record time.

She has seen what I've done. "Are you crazy!"

"Probably." I press my body against Kathy and grab handholds on either side of her. Her face is visible through our fogged faceplates. I give her my best smile. "Hang on!"

The grenades detonate. Their combined force tears a new hole in our hull. Within seconds, the water in our section of the access tubes shoots out into space or freezes solid. My grip holds, and Kathy and I once again find ourselves in vacuum. At least this time I have a suit to protect me.

I poke my head around the corner and cringe at the damage I caused. The lock is now part of a large, missing section of the tubes. I pull myself closer and am glad to see bay four and its passengers are safe. The new damage was contained within the already devastated bay three.

"Do you see it?" Kathy asks tentatively.

I glance around for any sign of the robot. A shining piece of metal catches my eye. It is one of the monster's claws embedded in the wall. I pull it free and show it to Kathy. "Looks like that did it."

"Good. Let's get this tube sealed. We need to pressurize The Tank and get our engines up and running." Before I can say anything, Kathy jumps across the opening.

A metal arm snakes down from outside the ship and wraps around Kathy's waist.

Even as Kathy screams, I take the blade in my hand and slash at the tentacle. It takes two hacks, but I sever the arm. The motion causes what is left of the robot to lose its tenuous grip on our hull. It twists and flails with its remaining limbs as it is flung away from our ship.

Kathy pulls the limp tentacle away and throws it after the diminishing robot. "And stay out!" It takes a few minutes before her breathing returns to normal.

"You okay?" I ask. I check her suit for any leaks. Luckily, the tentacle was missing its claw.

Kathy manages a smile. "Nothing keeps us down, right?"

STAT4783_Location: Unknown.

ALRT9903_88% Damage Sustained.

ALRT9904_Power System Failure Imminent.

MSSN0025_Secondary Mission Failure.

CMMD2090_Transmit Back-Up Unit0089 Activation Code.

ALRT9905_Transmitter Low-Power Reading.

MODE5066_Sending Back-Up Unit Activation Code. Awaiting Acknowledgement…

ALRT9906_System Fai…

"Upper Management" by J.A. Campbell
Alien in the Triassic

Thenna looked around with satisfaction, grasping his forelimbs together to display triumph. He was here and would accomplish the mission, unlike those lazy eggs who said it couldn't be done. The Vema had modern tech, the most advanced habitat suits, and the best ships. The pet shop was such a lucrative success, they couldn't give it up.

Thenna checked the readouts on his suit one last time before pushing through the seal membrane and into the outer airlock. Though he prepared himself mentally for the adjustment from stale, ship air to dank, unprocessed, dirty air, he knew the transition would still be uncomfortable. At least he wouldn't have to actually smell it. Though he usually thought that he could smell the air even though the suit manufacturer swore that was impossible.

Taking a deep, satisfied breath, Thenna checked his readouts one last time, just to be safe, patted his shrinker, and his gathered his specimen containers before hitting the switch to cycle the airlock. The seal membrane was rated for most civilized environments that the Vema encountered, but this untamed and very contaminated environment wasn't something Thenna wanted to expose the membrane too. The solid doors of the inner airlock shut. When the light turned violet, indicating a good seal, Thenna flipped the other switch to open the outer doors.

Where once all he heard was the sound of his breath echoing in his suit and the clicks and quiet breathing of his ship, now the cries of exotic insects barraged his ears.

Wincing, Thenna hoped this trip would go quickly. He needed five specimens. It only took one to make the expedition profitable, but he had cages for five, and the more money he could make, the more likely they'd send someone else next time. Someone better at this sort of thing, cheaper to pay, and far more expendable. He hated this kind of travel, but if his people wouldn't do it, he'd have to do it himself. It was his enterprise after all.

Once his ears adjusted to the raucous cries of the insects, he moved onto his ramp and stared at his surroundings. Color overwhelmed his eyes. He was used to the sterile grays and whites of his ship, relieved only by the deep black of space, the various blinking lights on the readouts, and the occasional colorful space display.

The green dominated his vision for a few minutes, but finally he managed to adjust to the environment and see other colors. Browns of massive tree trunks, vibrant colors of the reproductive parts of the plants. Thenna tried to remember what the scientists who had done the initial surveys called them. Shrugging, Thenna decided it wasn't important. He wasn't collecting them, anyway, though he did wish the creatures he was after lived in the drier, inner parts of the continent, not the coastal areas where plants obscured his vision.

A few clients had tried to put in specific orders, but Thenna knew that he wouldn't be able to track down specific dinosaurs, so he would leave that for other expeditions, with beings trained to track down the beasts the clients wanted.

Thenna looked up at the sky, shivered, and cast his eyes back to the ground. Open sky without the protection of spaceship hull bothered him. He had to focus on the mission, so he went down the ramp and placed his feet on the soft ground. Not used to anything but firm, deck plates, the texture gave him pause. He couldn't bring himself to take another step until he forced himself to remember the mission. He gathered his containers and moved away from his ship. Not far from the burn path the ship had created when it landed, the brush closed over the ground and hid it from view. Thenna shuddered as he moved into the ferns and other plants. They scratched against his protective suit and he had to take a few more, deep breaths, calming his circulation and quieting the alarms in his suit.

He needed to find the creatures and get off this planet. Thenna hoped to get several aquatic specimens and a couple of land-based ones. Per the reports, there were a few, larger predators, but he wasn't worried. Why would a predator bother something that didn't smell like food?

Turning back, Thenna glanced at his ship. A tiny, silver egg compared to the trees that towered above it; the ship seemed fragile, though it could survive the rigors of deep space. Shivering one last time, he called up the map display on his otherwise clear view port and followed the line to the probable location of the first specimen.

The problem with animals, Thenna mused as he walked, was that they didn't stay put unless they were already properly caged. Well, soon, several more animals would be whisked away to designer aquariums, private residences, and fancy collections. Thenna would more than recoup his costs for this expedition and be able to find braver, strong-shelled contractors for the next.

Thenna cursed his way through the thick underbrush, kicking aside rotting vegetation, and getting mud and other things he didn't want to think about all over his nice, clean, environmental suit. At least he was still unsoiled.

Jumping when a branch he stepped on cracked louder than expected, Thenna continued his internal tirade on the weak-shells that had landed him in this mess. He had no idea how they'd even survived hatching with their apparent lack of fortitude.

Another branch snapped, Thenna glanced down at his foot to verify that he hadn't taken an actual step.

He called up his suit's sensors, surprised they hadn't detected anything unusual. They were functioning, as they had been when he left the ship, but the dense foliage had them scrambled, which was odd, since he'd never had issues on any other planet he'd tested the suit on. Maybe it was something in the plant content? They were supposed to alert him to anything approaching.

Shrugging, Thenna glanced around but didn't see anything except more green and didn't hear anything but the roar of insects. Of course, he could barely hear himself breathe over the insects. Stupid insects.

Glancing at his map, he adjusted his course slightly.

Snap.

Thenna sighed and glanced around himself again. This really was getting him nowhere. He still didn't see anything. No small two-legged dinosaurs, no bodies of water to put his traps in for the swimmers, nothing that should be making snapping, cracking sounds. His sensors remained calm. Continuing toward his first destination, Thenna did his best to ignore the occasional, louder, rustle or snapping branch. He had to assume that the trees were weak and breaking. What else could it be? Hopefully a limb didn't fall on him.

Inspired by that fear, he looked up, jerked back, and fell on his rear. Above him perched two, large creatures with membranes between front and hind limbs. Long beaks clacked when he looked up and hooked claws looked like they would make an impression on the suddenly fragile-seeming suit he wore.

They couldn't possibly be interested in him. Primitive species hunted by smell, or so he'd read. Nothing could be appealing about the neutral smell of his suit.

However, they might make interesting additions to his collection, so, still prone, he pulled out his shrinker and adjusted the setting. Catching fliers and creatures in trees was a tricky operation. If they died falling from the heights, they were useless.

He took aim, but the fliers hopped to another branch before he could shoot. Muttering curses, Thenna adjusted his aim, and jumped, firing a random shot as his suit alarm went off.

Now what?

The fliers took to the air, somehow avoiding all of the trees and branches that cluttered the air and were out of range before Thenna could adjust his aim.

Sitting up, he glanced around just as several small, two-legged creatures raced across his legs.

He jumped and almost shot himself in the leg. The bolt sizzled through the underbrush, and plants curled back from the energized air. It would only have stunned him, if that. The suits had some protection against the shrinker's stun energy and it had built-in safeties to prevent the wielder from shrinking one's self. Why the safeties didn't apply to the stun energy, Thenna had no idea. Maybe there was a setting he wasn't familiar with. Oh well, he didn't have to use the things very often anyway. It was typically easier just to let someone else worry about those details.

Scrambling to his feet, he shook out his limbs and verified the integrity of his suit.

Jumping, he cursed when the proximity alarm went off. More of those damn two-legged, tiny dinosaurs. They were already so small he really didn't need to shrink them. He just had to catch one. Switching off the blaring alarm, Thenna turned to look for his specimen cages and frowned. Had something moved out of the corner of his eye?

Sighing, he located his cages and hefted them. He really needed to get these creatures caught so he could get back to his ship and off this forsaken pit of bacteria and decay.

Thenna turned back to his original course and stopped, dropping the cases and, limbs shaking, brought up the shrinker.

In front of him stood a much larger two-legged dinosaur. It's mottled coloring blended in so well with the background, he hadn't seen it until it stepped into the clearing. The most prominent feature was a mouth full of very large, sharp-looking teeth aimed directly at him.

That didn't make any sense, though, Thenna didn't smell like anything editable. He aimed the shrinker, fired, hit the creature and succeeded in... pissing it off.

It roared and charged.

Thenna squeaked and fired again, and again. Why wasn't this thing falling down?

It pounced.

Thenna cried out as his suit lost compression and bacteria and other germs filled his air. A moment later, it occurred to him that the bacteria wasn't the most immediate problem as the dinosaur's razor-filled jaws ripped his suit the rest of the way open, exposing Thenna's feathered body.

It reared back, shaking the ripped pieces of suit and spreading a few stray feathers about. Idly, he noted a few stuck to one of the trees next to him. Some sort of gooey substance. The creature, apparently deciding the suit wasn't tasty, tossed it aside.

Snapping at Thenna, the creature studied its prey, head cocked to one side.

Hoping it would decide the rest of Thenna was as tasteless as the suit, he kept very, very still. The ploy seemed to work until the suit woke up to the damage that had been done to it and gave one, last, gasping squawk of alarm.

This further enraged the dinosaur. It stomped down with one foot, raking backward and shredding the last of the suit and part of one of Thenna's limbs.

The scent of blood filled the air. The dinosaur's nostrils flared. Thenna struggled out of the suit and ran. Or attempted to. He made it one step before the dinosaur pounced again, jaws clamping down on Thenna's back.

The Vema's last thought was that maybe the original expedition hadn't been so weak-shelled after all, before pain overloaded his brain and he passed out.

The dinosaur devoured his meal, spreading feathers and the last of the synthetics in its frenzy.

"Fool's Errand" by Aylâ Larsen
A Clown in the Triassic

BOOM.

I woke with a jolt. My eyes shot wide open and the quick breaths that followed were painful, jagged, and labored. I choked a bit and reflexively swatted my red nose violently off my face, allowing the air to pass through my sinuses freely as I gasped for air. The world rang and vibrated, but after a few seconds grew still. I looked left and right and all around trying to take in as much visual information as possible. From where I was laying on the hard ground, I could see some sort of palm trees and the sun shining mercilessly down. Sweat pooled and darkened areas of my yellow and blue checkerboard suit. Oh my god, I thought. Where am I?

I quickly sat upright and stars pulsed and narrowed my vision, nearly sending me immediately back to the ground. I slammed a white, gloved hand down to steady myself and looked curiously at the dirt as it puffed particles up towards the sky. Dust? I pulled my hand close to my painted face, rubbing the soil between my thumb and index finger, observing it. My brow furrowed and I got to my feet, fiercely turning this way and that, taking in the world around me. No civilization of any kind. More palm-ish trees, overgrown bushes, and tall weed-like structures covered the ground. Large, castle-like rock walls and sheets of gray stone stood diagonally in the distance. A big pond lay about fifty feet from me, grass and more weeds tracing its edges. But no people. No animals. Just a faint hum of insects and my own heavy breathing filled the air.

I swallowed and calmly tried to plan my next move. Okay, what do we know? We know this is fucking crazy, but we'll just put that aside for now since it won't help. We know that it's dry. And hot. So hot. I pulled uncomfortably at my red bow tie and loosened it, tossing it to the ground, since outfit color coordination wasn't the biggest issue at the moment. All right, hot and dry. And tropical, I thought, looking up at the trees. So…not Antarctica? Damn! I should have paid better attention in geography class. Or at least watched Planet Earth one more time. Okay, let's just assume that we're in a remote corner of Asia or Africa. Two continents I ironically have always wanted to visit. But not against my will. And preferably waking-up in a bed. I nervously laughed and immediately regretted it. My lungs could hardly handle breathing, let alone a chuckle. I rubbed my chest and shhh-ed it, making tiny apologies and a mental note not to do that again.

BOOM.

There it was again and this time I heard it, and felt it, clearly – a split second of deafening noise and a bass-filled vibration blew me backward as if I had been punched clean out. The ground shook and the world blurred for a few seconds. A still silence followed and the hum of insects slowly started up again. An earthquake? What parts of Asia and Africa experienced earthquakes? Ugh, probably a lot of them, Riddles. But what earthquake was that instantaneous? Despite how my face was painted, I thought, once again pulling myself to my feet, I was *not* happy about this.

Speaking of face paint, the heat and sweat had melted my multicolored makeup and sent it swimming down my face. I removed my gloves and used them to wipe it away before it came too close to my eyes.

If I really was in a remote location, I had seen enough survival movies to know that I wouldn't last long without water. Just ask Tom Hanks. So, I shuffled my big, red shoes toward the pond, hoping it was clear and safe enough to drink and if not, at least allow me to wash off the rest of this makeup.

Minutes later, I had cleaned my face but thought better of actually swallowing any of the water. It wasn't so much clear as it was clear-ish yellow and without one of those adventure straws (or whatever they're called) or a Brita filter, it was a little too daring for my tastes or stomach. But it *was* cool and I splashed it over my face with relief. As I brought my cupped hands up again, I heard a splash that was definitely not me. Slowly parting my fingers, I peeked through and saw something of a familiar face. Not a friendly one, but one I recognized. A giant, green crocodile had submerged into the pond, his eyes peeking out and staring at me, effortlessly gliding toward me at great speed. I froze for a second before registering the danger and then frantically used all fours to climb up and away from him. I yanked my ankle away just as he snapped his jaw down and immediately tripped in the mud and tall weeds. My rainbow wig toppled off and rolled down to the water's edge. It confused the crocodile and I took the opportunity to escape, lifting myself up out of the tall grass and half-wheezing, half-crying, took off towards the trees. My big red shoes made my steps clunky and plodding but I didn't dare look back in fear that he was following me. I just locked my eyes on the nearest branched tree and, scratching myself terribly, climbed as high as I could. Thinking myself temporarily out of danger, I whipped around and searched for the crocodile. He still sat idly in the pond, my wig wedged between his teeth, gnawing it like bubble gum. I exhaled deeply and winced, gently rubbing my chest with an apology for the second time that day. Okay, I thought looking down at the pond, which countries have freakishly-huge crocodiles?

BOOM.

Hours later, another boom woke me and shook the world again. Forgetting I was up in a tree, I leaned back against nothing and fell. My legs acted like a hinge on the branch I sat on and I swung backwards and smacked the back of my head against a lower branch. Before I had time to react to the pain-

BOOM.

The sound rang shrilly in my ears and the vibrations jostled my legs free of the tree. I yelped and outstretched my arms, falling three feet before I caught the next branch and bit my bottom lip. The branch snapped and I tumbled to the ground, a colorful heap of a person. And he sticks the landing. I maneuvered to a sitting position against the base of the tree and rubbed the back of my head where a bruise had already begun. I instinctively looked back at the pond but saw it was empty. No telling where my crocodile friend had gone. Rolling back my sleeves, I surveyed the scratches and luckily found that they weren't too deep. Between my bruised head, bleeding lip, and sore chest, I had enough problems to deal with. Talk about a sad clown.

As I lay back against the tree, a flock of birds glided overhead. I blocked the sun from my eyes with my hand and squinted up at them. There were six blue birds with long tails. They sailed past me and landed on the banks of the pond. I picked myself up and slowly tiptoed toward them, hoping to get a better look, and perhaps identify their species as a clue to where I was. As I grew closer, their odd shape came clearer into view. About 3 feet long, their wings were thin and narrow, and their tails were pencil-like rods extending far behind them and ending in a small, diamond flap. They stood in the pond, their heads under the water, I assumed, scouring for insects and fish. I crouched down in the weeds, observing and studying their curious shapes. Eventually, one popped her head up out of the water and I stopped breathing. Sitting there atop the neck of the bird, was a scaly and fanged dinosaur head. I blinked hard, praying the image would change before I opened my eyes again. No such luck. The "bird" held a small fish between her upper and bottom rows of needle-sharp teeth, looking like a tiny dragon. She bit into the fish and blood gushed down her neck. She tilted her head up, widened her jaw twice and swallowed it whole. Two more blue "birds" popped their heads up and it couldn't be denied. These were miniature versions of pterodactyls.

Riddles, we're not in Kansas anymore. Oh shit.

I crab crawled bit by bit backwards from the pond and bumped into something that cast a shadow over me. I slowly looked up and saw a red, long-necked dinosaur peer down at me from at least fifty feet up. It paid me no mind, however, and stepped over me, moving towards the pond, each step pounded my heart to a new rhythm. As it sauntered away, a white stegosaurus tiptoed up to the other side of the pond and dipped its head down to drink too.

Without exactly remembering how, I ended up sitting behind a large boulder, sweating furiously, my lungs, of course, still on fire. I wheezed at a high octave, made even higher by pain. The back of my head throbbed and fresh blood dripped down from my now-swollen lip. I sucked on it to make it stop.

The gears in my brain turned like wheels in molasses. Dinosaurs. I'd woken up in a land of dinosaurs. How is this even possible? Was that huge crocodile actually a dinosaur, too? Is this Jurassic Park? Disneyland? I popped my head out from the side of the boulder for a second look. Nope, definitely not animatronics. Where's Sam Neill when I needed him? Then it occurred to me, like a bubble slowly popping up out of the mud: where there are herbivores and…fish-ivores, there are carnivores too. My mind flashed with clips of two children hiding from velociraptors in a metal kitchen. My head dropped to my chest. Checkerboard squares of yellow and blue looked back up at me. While some people were scared of clowns, I doubted a dinosaur would be. I brought my left hand up to massage my smudged temples and then let it drop. My pinky nudged something on the ground that rolled an inch away – my red nose! I grasped it and turned it over in my hands. Some joke, I mused. My index and middle fingers traced the tight slit where the nose opened. I stuck a finger in it and pulled it out, the slit closing firmly once again.

My first week as a clown and I ended up living with dinosaurs. Not what you'd call a great start. The funniest thing about me now was what a pretty picture I must make: a middle-aged, white dude in a white tank, navy boxer shorts, and two, big, red shoes. I'd probably make people laugh more in this getup than with the whole kit and clown caboodle. Some people said I'd never make it, but I don't think this is what they had in mind. I considered 86ing the shoes, but in this terrain, I figured any shoes were better than none. Although, I wouldn't say "no" to a pair of Nikes right now.

I shuffled my shoes along, moving slowly and slinking around trees, being sure to keep out of sight. My plan was to head back to the pond (waterhole) and fill up my red nose like a makeshift canteen. It wasn't the purest water I'd ever seen, but I was as parched as Napoleon

Dynamite from the events of the day and figured if it was good enough for my dinosaur friends, then it was good enough for me. The tiny pterodactyls and brontosaurus-ish creature were still drinking there, but the stegosaurus had disappeared and no carnivores had shown up to the party yet. I reached the point of the forest nearest to the pond where I was still covered. Giant leaves waved in front of my face, shadow and sunlight dancing across it. I took a deep, stinging breath and shot out of the trees like a popgun. My eyes locked on the pond and I sprinted furiously, making a beeline for it. As I neared the pond, the tiny-dactyls parted, running or jumping forward with a small fluff of their wings to a different spot. I stopped at the water's edge. The brontosaur-ish drank heedlessly, paying as much attention to me as if I were an ant. Which to him, I suppose, I probably was. I placed my red nose in the palms of both hands, my thumbs on either side of the slit and stuck it quickly into the water.

BOOM.

The red nose flew out of my hands and pond water doused my face as I landed on my back. I sputtered and tried to reorient myself as the tiny-dactyls took off into the air, wings flapping rapidly and randomly, all shrieking in a cacophony of tones; every man for himself. The brontosaur-ish further contributed to the already-shaking ground, moaning lowly and stomping helter-skelter, trying to get his footing, every foot landed like a mini-earthquake in and of itself. He kicked up a world of dust and I threw the crook of my elbow over my eyes, crawling and scampering away from being squashed like a bug. A foot came down inches from my head and the impact threw me down, my limbs tangling like strangers. I jumbled helplessly across the ground, eventually pulling my knees into my sore chest and my palms over my ears. I put my head down and welded my eyes shut, waiting for the chaos to end. Once the shaking stopped, the sound did too, and I looked up with a stern face. Fear had finally turned to anger.

Enough of this, I thought, as I brushed the dust off myself. Drop a beat, John Williams. I'm about to find out what the hell is going on.

I continued on in my best guess of the general direction of the last boom until I saw what, from a distance, looked like a mound of bubble wrap. As I got closer, I realized it was nothing quite as much fun. A white snake skin, seventy feet long, was coiled up in a pile in the middle of the desert. My jaw dropped open as I paced slowly around it. Ah, I thought, strangely calm. I was wrong. This wasn't Jurassic Park. This was the Chamber of Secrets! As if I didn't have enough to deal with, now I had to be on the look-out for giant snakes? My lips widened into a silly smile reminiscent of the one I had wiped off, and I dove into a fit of laughter. My bottom lip cracked open with fresh blood and I brought my hand up to it and looked at the blood on my fingertips. This pushed me into hysterical, silent giggles and snorts that overpowered my sore lungs, now throbbing with disapproval. What's next? I thought. Aliens? Kaiju? Psycho Killers? Robot Assassins? I doubled over with more laughter, eventually falling to the ground. When the laughs turned into fitful coughs, the humor subsided. My chest and the back of my head acted like speakers connected to my heartbeat, amplifying it throughout my body. Each pulse was painful and it rang in my ears, warning me about my decreasing health meter.

I turned onto my side to take the pressure off my tender head and slipped my bottom arm up over my eyes to shield them from the sun. Regroup, I thought. Since when did giant snakes live at the same time as dinosaurs? That's definitely something I would have remembered learning in school. Or maybe it's *not* a skin. Maybe this is the skeleton of a snake, dried out and bleached by the sun. I took a deep breath as gently as possible. My lungs begrudgingly allowed it. But a skeleton doesn't explain the booms, my mind protested. I doubt "boom" would be the sound effect of a snake shedding its skin, even in a comic book. Think, Riddles. What was it that killed the dinosaurs? I suppose we'll never *really* find out since no humans were around to prove it. But the dominant theory was meteors. Though I was laying down, my stomach dropped to my red-shoed feet. Of course. Meteors. Those would definitely make a boom.

If the meteors were falling, I thought, that means I've woken up on the brink of a mass extinction. And, if it's the one I'm thinking of, it *really* won't end well. Which means when the dinosaurs die…I will too. Could be weeks or days or hours, but one thing seemed certain: I was going to die with the dinosaurs. Wow. I could see the nightly news now: *Earlier this afternoon, scientists dug up the fossils of an ancient clown from the age of dinosaurs.* I smiled again and coughed out a laugh. That'd really jack up their theories.

Such a shame though, I thought casually. Clowning seemed to be in my blood. I'd only been to four classes so far but Clowning Around 101 was going surprisingly well. The teacher, Jumbo, had even called me a natural. I'd always known how to juggle. Unicycling? Easy as the pie I could perfectly throw in my fellow clown's face. Miming, telling jokes – no problem. There was just one subject that gave me trouble. My first clown gig was supposed to be tomorrow, a themed birthday party and I still couldn't master how to-

BOOM. BOOM. BOOM. BOOM.

A wave of dust hit me like a wall and sent me whirling along the ground like a roll of wrapping paper unraveling. My arms formed a sloppy helmet over my head as I spun. Fruitlessly, I pushed my feet down hard, trying to anchor myself to the earth, but clown shoes have about as much traction as a stick of butter and I continued to spin as if I would forever. The echoes of the booms seared my mind, a needle-edged note my ears didn't know how to cope with. I screamed as I tumbled but couldn't hear it, or anything, above the deafening sharp screech. This is it, my mind cried. This is the end!

Next thing I knew, I was lying on my back, both lips now dry and cracked, shaking even after the world had stilled. A groan tried to escape my mouth, but my voice was so shot, a pitiful whimper-wheeze came out instead. My eyes opened. Dust blanketed the world like a dense, tan fog. There was nothing to see, but something to hear.

Clicking noises and huffs of breath whispered at me from the impenetrable fog. At first, the noises seemed to come from my left, then right, then behind me. I turned my head to face each one, my eyes frantically scrounging for answers. I halted my breathing to confirm it wasn't me who was somehow the source. It was not. A few more huffs and silence. I didn't dare breathe. The fog was so thick it seemed like I still had my eyes closed. I blinked hard to make sure they weren't. Slowly, a shape formed a little way off my right shoulder. A wide, scaly, yellow claw. Its heel brushed the ground and three toes settled onto it, each claw tapping one by one onto the soil. Other feet just like it appeared in front of and behind me. Bit by bit, I saw the trace of their bodies – small front arms that dangled down uselessly, hunched-over heads, long, serrated spines and whip-like tails. They were silhouettes against the fog, shadows I could see but who couldn't see me. With their body shapes and claws, I knew they could smell me and despite how much B.O. I was probably sporting at this point, I'm sure I smelled like filet mignon.

I made a map of them in my mind, marking where each of them stood, moving my eyes from one to the next. My best chance was to take advantage of the fog while it lasted and duck out in the space between the dinos at six and nine o' clock. Come on, Riddles, I thought, untying my big, red shoes. One last trick.

Barefoot and bare-hearted, I made a run for it. The dust fog was both a hindrance and a help. It prevented me from seeing where I was going, but it also obscured my location from the dinosaurs who were chasing me. My feet immediately bruised and bloodied as I stumbled over sharp rocks and pebbles, uneven terrain and abrasive weeds that I couldn't see coming. Out of nothing came a large stone which grabbed my left foot and brought me to my knees. I scrambled to my feet and continued to run, limping awkwardly. My chest screamed at me and the back of my head pounded like the drums of Jumanji. My feet weren't too happy with me either, but it was my job to save us all.

Unfortunately, and not, the dust was settling quicker now and clearing everyone's vision. I heard screeches and looked back to see my predators finally catch sight of me. Definitely carnivores – three, yellow carnivores headed right for me, bounding on their two, track-star legs. Limp-running like the weakest of the herd, I was easy prey. I aimed for a glen of trees I could see faintly twenty feet from me.

Suddenly, I heard another screech. Only this time, from a different direction. A fourth yellow carnivore jumped out, right in front of me. I silently screamed and my legs buckled in shock. Clever girl. The carnivore lumbered toward me. I crawled backward each time it took a step nearer. It dipped its head down to me and screeched again. My ear drums rattled like a military snare. Its friends answered, caught up to us and surrounded me. Like birds, their heads moved this way and that, looking at me and each other. End of the line, Riddles. I got to my feet, licked my cracked lips, closed my eyes, and took a final bow.

BOOM.

I woke up back in my own home, lying flat on the floor with a bruised head, a sore chest, chapped lips, and 87 dinosaur balloon animals in green, blue, red, white and yellow – some popped, some not.

"Intimation" by Heather Cowley
An Imaginary Friend in the Triassic

We stand at attention, the five of us who are up for our first missions. There is electric energy in the air, and the giddiness between us is contagious.

"You are true Imaginaries now," says one of the Intimation Council leaders. "This is no longer a game. You have a real case with very physical beings, and the outcome will either have dire consequences or a true conclusion." He looks into each of our faces, but none of us betray fear. We are all eager and ready to go.

"You will guide your being back to where they belong." He hands us each a single sheet of paper with the semantics of each of our individual cases. "Then you will report back with a detailed narrative."

I read my case.

Planet: Earth. Being: Great White Shark
Mission: Your being has accidentally time-hopped to an era long before she was meant to exist. This era, called the "Triassic" era, is full of dangerous creatures that can harm or kill your being.

Guide her away from danger and bring her back to the Earth's year of 2020.

"Once you clear the black hole, you will be dropped beside your being." He looks us over critically. "Your memory may not be clear the moment you wake, but it will come back to you. You will know your being immediately and, of course, it's been drilled into you to keep your being safe. Questions?"

The kid beside me raises his hand. "To get back, we just go through the black hole the way we came?"

"Precisely. Since we are not bound by physical bodies on the other side of the black hole, we can travel even faster than light. Some of you will be at the outer rim of the galaxy, so it might take a few moments more for you to reach your destination. Any other questions?"

No one speaks.

"Good. Get into your pods."

"What'd you get?" Creda asks me.

I unfold my paper and show her.

She sniggers.

"What?"

"Earth is a dump. Sorry you got stuck with that one."

I crumple the paper and shove it into my pocket. "What's yours, then?"

She holds hers out proudly. "M-13 in Andromeda. It's one of the most advanced civilizations out there. Other than ours."

We reach our individual pods and I fold into mine before I can spit an unsavory retort back to her. She is always one-upping the rest of us.

We zip down the single track to the edge of the black hole.

"We just...just jump in?" Creda asks nervously.

I shrug and jump in. The last thing I see is our home as a pin-prick on the horizon.

I open my eyes to find that I am suspended in a body of salt water and there is a white and grey creature beside me.

I can't remember what I'm doing here. Of course, I know that I am a sentient being and that my job is to help misguided creatures of our universe back to where they belong. I just can't remember what exactly the case is that I was given.

This is my first case; I can recall that much. During our training, they said that we might lose some short-term memory during travel, but we will recover it after a time.

A great white shark is suspended in the teal water beside me, and suddenly I remember that she is my mission. I can't remember why, so I reach out to touch her fin, though it isn't so much a physical touch as it is connection of our conscious minds.

She's led an interesting life and a bit of a tragic one. I see her alone in a dirty tank at an aquarium-turned-pet-store, and then abandoned. I feel her hunger when, day after day, an old, human man brings her a cooler full of fish. After several weeks of learning that this man is saving her life, she came to love him.

From this memory, I gather that she belongs on Earth in the 21st century. I glance around and discover that this is Earth, but millions of years before my frightened friend was supposed to exist. How did she get here?

She cowers near a reef and I see that a Thalattoarchon Saurophagis is prowling nearby, probably searching for my companion.

The shark sees me and tries to nudge me, probably to figure out whether or not she can eat me. She can't; I don't have a physical form in this world, and she is the only one who *can* see me.

I look around again and the giant, Triassic predator is still unaware that we are close. How am I supposed to move her forward two-hundred million years? They covered time-travel during training, but it was always a year or two, maybe even five. Not millions.

The Thalattoarchon eventually gets bored and swims away in search of a new meal.

"You don't belong here," I tell her simply.

She begins to swim forward slowly and I remain at her side. My consciousness reaches out for hers again in order to learn more.

She is scared and confused now, knowing that she doesn't belong here. She had followed a human from her era into this one, though all I can see is a bright light and a magical vortex. I surmise this person had a time-travelling device.

I stop and consider the possibility. Humans aren't supposed to have that knowledge and technology for several thousand more years. Maybe I'm wrong about which century she belongs in.

I shake it off. I can figure that part out later. I must experiment with the time travel I was taught, before I try to jump forward more than several years.

I grab her mind again, though this time not for her memories, and the scenery changes but only slightly. The sun is still high in the sky and now there are hundreds of fish surrounding us. Just the daily bustle of Triassic, ocean life.

She opens her mouth wide and I allow her to chomp several of the larger fish. We watch them scatter and hide before I jump us forward five more years.

Everything is still the same, though the fish are swimming in different schools this time.

I try to jump us ten years, then twenty…we manage to go for one hundred. I try for five hundred more, but we end up going seven hundred. I have plenty of room for these kinds of mistakes for now, but I don't want to end up dropping her ahead of her own era.

She swims in circles around me and I reach out to her, curious to know what she's thinking.

She can feel the time jumps and she knows that we are headed to her home. She's excited.

We jump again and again and again, encountering fish and predators alike, and the further we jump, the more they evolve— even within the Triassic era.

She is tired by the time we've jumped half a million years. I don't blame her, but we have to keep moving.

When I touch her consciousness this time, I see her rip into the old man that had kept her alive in the aquarium. She was devastated, but, more than that, she was hungry.

The more we jump through time, the more of her story she shows me. She'd been rescued, too, and freed into the ocean. She'd eaten the men who had rescued her.

I'm starting to feel grateful that I don't have a physical body, because I'm beginning to sense that once I get her back to where she belongs, she might try to eat me, too.

Time is meaningless to a being like me, especially when jumping so far through time, but it really does begin to get tedious.

Every once in a while, I'll actually begin to *feel* one of her memories instead of see it. The grime of the neglected tank she'd been imprisoned in. The relief of the fresh, salt water when she'd been released. The pure fury toward the men who had rescued here mere hours after her care-taker had sacrificed himself to her. I pity her.

She is patient while we time-hop. All of her memories lead me to believe that she is a twenty-first century shark, all of them except the one with the scuba-diver. It must be an anomaly, and I will bring it to my council when I am through with this mission. Our job is to keep the balance in the universe.

Finally, I feel her relief when we enter her era. The creatures are familiar and, for the most part, smaller than her. She feels confident and safe again.

She stares at me with those dark, beady eyes and her wide, sharp-toothed smile. If she could talk, I think she would be thanking me.

I watch for a moment as she swims away to pursue another meal.

Suddenly, just as the council member had promised, I am traveling toward the center of the galaxy and the Earth is nothing but a small, shiny dot behind me.

"A New Home" by Thomas A. Fowler
A Kaiju in the Triassic

She wretched her arms from the volcano's bowels, birthed from fire. The mountain shook from the eruption, and her escape. Moltenia, the monster god of lava, was sent to cleanse the earth. Her skin was blackened rock; blood an orange flame that spat through the crevices of stone. The mountain stood a dwarf in her presence. Her hands moved the clouds. The rage of a lost child would rid the world of joy. She looked down the mountainside. There stood many tiny creatures, scared and fleeing the volcano, and her. Many seemed to be smaller versions of her Kaiju brethren. The dinosaurs were Kaiju children in her eyes.

Moltenia, made of fire, felt warmth she had not known. Within her deep core came a desire to help her new children. Her heart was earnest, and it exploded with concern for the tiny creatures that ran in fear. Along the rift zone, the earth began to crack. Moltenia's care would create an ocean but destroy all life.

"Day 16" by Kimberly Kennedy
Robot Assassin in the Triassic

Day 12: Pangea

He looked out over the landscape, temperate, dry, and vast. The next outcropping of trees was...13.3 miles away. It was a dust bowl land of nothing. He continued on, his scanners running in the background, looking for a live animal.

He hadn't seen much these last few days. Thirteen days to be exact. His batteries were running low. Still, he had time to find his prey.

Day 14: Pangea

A loud shriek was heard coming in from above him, dipping down now to a 45-degree angle right towards his right blaster. His rear scanners zeroed in, it was a large bird of prey, no a therapsid, pterosaur to be exact, with a giant beak of red, along with teeth as large as his fingers.

He raised the blaster, took aim, and BOOM! The bird-like dinosaur was gone, a puff of smoke. He heard a distant chime. Bonus points. It had clearly been an enemy. Unlike the swimming one…

Falling back out of blaster mode, he continued on, scanning the horizon for his prey, Elvis, the king T-Rex. It was nothing personal, he was simply hunting for his mark. He was an assassin, a robot assassin, sent to the Triassic era to find this giant lizard.

Another *bloop* was heard in the back of his operating system. His batteries were down to 20%. Would he find the bird-brained bastard before his batteries died?

Day 16: Pangea… still

5% battery life left. He could feel his less vital functions begin to shut down, perhaps it was time to find a place to rest where he could recharge with his solar panels. Used only in absolute emergencies, it would take him an entire Earth day, 24 hours, to recharge...

Day 16: A suburban basement

"What!!! That's crap! What kind of game is this?!" The video game controller sailed towards the television screen, before bouncing off the thickly carpeted floor at the base of the television. Sam turned towards his brother, Alec, who had covered his face with his hands when the wireless controller had been launched towards the flat screen. Sam, threw his hands up in frustration.

"I don't get it, when I played it at Andy's house the robot was in the Wild West, and it was awesome! He was shooting things left and right, and we got some amazing bounties!"

He continued with his pandering, overdramatic hands, and whiny, high pitched voice. "Why would they make this time period so boring? We've been playing for two hours, which is like a month in game time and all we have seen are those small fricken' insects, the bird thing, and one water creature!" He rolled his eyes as he flopped down on the couch.

Alec finally moved his hands from his face, realizing his brother had not actually gotten them grounded with a controller through the television screen. "It was a pterosaur. And the water creature was a harmless Trematosauris, who only eats plants! Which you shot at and killed. We weren't supposed to kill it, dummy!"

"What do you mean? The bird gave us points!"

"No, the fish dino. It was an innocent animal and you shot it!"

"Well I wanted to shoot something! We are playing a robot assassin! He's supposed to kill things."

Alec jumped up on the couch, which gave a loud groan of protest. "Only the things he was supposed to kill on our list and that is Elvis, the T. Rex. But oh no, you had to go and shoot some big, flippered thing!" A light bulb went off over Alec's head. He pointed in the direction of his brother before wagging his finger at him. "I bet that's why the game got so boring. Because we screwed up!"

"This is worse than that lame game Dad told us he used to play. Washington Road or something. I'd rather die of dysentery than be stuck wandering around some giant hunk of land looking for some stupid, tiny-armed, green lizard!"

"Technically the Tyrannosaurus Rex was a Theropod..."

"Shut up, Alec!" Sam yelled out as he threw a pillow at his younger brother's head.

"You shut up, you big bully." Alec hugged the pillow to his chest, hurt over his brother's foul mood as he jumped up and down on the cushion of the worn, brown couch.

"This is dumb. The Jurassic era is nothing like the movies!"

"Alec! Get down off the furniture." *Uh oh. It was Dad!*

Dad walked the rest of the way into the basement playroom. "Now let that be a lesson to you boys. Pay better attention during history day at school. Should have set your Robot's time machine to the Jurassic era instead of the Triassic era." He chuckled to himself as he began to walk out of the room, avoiding a pile of GI Joes and colored building blocks on the floor. "Oh, and Sam? Oregon Tracks rocked, even when your ox drowned. Where else could you play a game that sounded like a bad country song and learn about history?"

ACKNOWLEDGMENTS

This anthology took a damned village. Big thank you to my writing partner, Melissa Koons, for her meticulous proofreading and formatting on this weird writing experiment. Additional thanks to Jason Evans for the incredible use of his extroverted nature and recruiting many of the authors you see in this anthology.

More thanks to my beautiful wife, Amber, and four kids, Emma, Grace, Holden and Norah for being there and letting me go on this crazy endeavor! One last set of thanks to all the authors (told you it took a damned village!), thank you for your patience as I bit way more off than I could chew with this project. Your patience was phenomenal as I missed my deadlines, your kindness as I had typos in contracts was most welcome, and your willingness to go along for the ride was what made this anthology such a blast to create! It's why I cannot wait to continue this with more installments, reading your stories gives me life!

THE AUTHORS

Scott Beckman

Imaginary Friend in an Apocalyptic Wasteland

Scott Beckman is the author of the high fantasy *Sathakos* series and the stand-alone novel, *Pantheon*. He writes because he likes to imagine far more interesting worlds than our own. Worlds with gods who give their followers superpowers or dragons that build mountain cities, where adventure is always just over the hill and through the dale, and where young heroes explore and discover their fantastic environments for themselves. These are worlds that only exist in imagination, but maybe they could be real, if only we could find them.

Scott lives in Denver, Colorado with his cat, Evie. He enjoys a daily cup of coffee, a weekly exercise regimen, a regular bottle of gin or whiskey, and the occasional trip to far-off places. His biggest influences are Tolkien, Palahniuk, Vonnegut, LeGuin, and McCarthy. He believes there's nothing more awkward in the world than having people look at you while they sing to you, though writing about yourself in the third-person comes close.

J.M. Butler

Clown in the Ocean

J. M. Butler is an adventurer, author, and attorney who never outgrew her love for telling stories and playing in imaginary worlds. Her current publications include tales such as *Identity Revealed* (Tue-Rah Chronicles), *Locked* (A Tue-Rah Story), *Alone* (A Tue-Rah Story), *Mermaid Bride, Through the Paintings Dimly, Why Yes, Bluebeard, I'd Love To*, and more, including the soon-to-be released other stories set within the Tue-Rah world such as *Cursed* and *The Red Fire Dragon*. For the most part, she writes speculative fiction with a heavy focus on multicultural high fantasy and suspenseful adventures. She lives with her husband and law partner, James Fry, in rural Indiana where they are quite happy with their four cats.

J.A. Campbell

Alien in the Triassic

J.A. Campbell: When Julie is not writing she's often out riding horses or working sheep with her dogs. She lives in Colorado with her three cats; Kira and Bran, her border collies; her Traveler-in training Triska; and her Irish Sailor. She is the author of many vampire and ghost-hunting dog stories the *Tales of the Travelers* series, and many other young adult books. She also appears in the best-selling anthology, *Humans Wanted*. She's a member of the Horror Writers Association and the Dog Writers of America Association and the editor for "Story Emporium" fiction magazine. Find out more at WriterJACampbell.com.

Mike Cervantes

Clown in the Human Mind

Mike Cervantes is a graduate of creative writing and communication from The University of Texas at El Paso. He is a humorist, a cartoonist, a steampunk enthusiast, a regular contributor to Denver's many local conventions, and just a swell person. He writes and publishes stories featuring his steampunk hero characters "The Scarlet Derby and Midnight Jay" regularly on his website, TheScarletDerby.com.

Beverly Coutts

Kaiju in an Evil Laboratory

Beverly Coutts lives in the Denver area with her husband and three, unruly dogs. She loves to read and write and has published short stories and poetry. She has her Master's degree in Economics and works as a budget analyst for the State of Colorado when she's not writing. She enjoys her work more than any normal human should.

Heather Cowley

Imaginary Friend in the Triassic

Heather Cowley was born and raised in Northern Colorado where she currently resides with her loving boyfriend and three, adoring fur babies. She discovered her love of writing in Mrs. Girardi's 2nd grade class at Washington Core Knowledge, and from then until high school graduation signed up for every creative writing class offered. In order to break through the inevitable writer's block that plagues all writers, she spends her time reading, crocheting, and boxing. She is currently holed up at a desk in the library working on her novel.

Thomas A. Fowler

Alien in an Apocalyptic Wasteland
Alien in the Ocean
Clown in an Evil Laboratory
Imaginary Friend in the Ocean
Kaiju in the Triassic
Robot Assassin in an Apocalyptic Wasteland
Robot Assassin in a Human Mind

Thomas A. Fowler (Author & *Crash Philosophy* Creator) saw Jurassic Park at the age of 11. It was all nerdy as hell from there. Especially when he stuck around for the end credits and saw "Based on the novel by Michael Crichton." He went straight from the movie theater, walked down the mall to a Walden Books. Since then, he's written movies, plays, short-stories and books. While he sticks primarily to science-fiction, he dabbles elsewhere. He holds an MBA in Marketing from Regis University and was a former Content Creator at a full-service ad agency in Denver, Colorado. Now, he devotes that skill set to a freelance career and to helping authors live their dream of getting published. Somewhere, between writing and advertising, he tries to be a loving husband and responsible father.

E. Godhand

Imaginary Friend in the Human Mind

E. Godhand is a dark fantasy author who lives in Denver, Colorado and runs Black Rat Books. Her office staff include her three rats, Chaos, Order, and Illuminati, and a black cat who bribes her with socks. Read all about ghosts, chaos magick, and surviving death, and ignore the subsequent nightmares. Despite the rumors, Emily does not worship the Elder Gods and is not responsible for the strange bumps in the night. Learn more at EmilyGodhand.com.

C.L. Kagmi

Alien in an Evil Laboratory
Alien in the Human Mind

C. L. Kagmi is an award-winning and bestselling writer of short science fiction. She holds a degree in Neuroscience from the University of Michigan and spent five years working in clinical research before striking out as a full-time freelance editor. She now offers courses and e-books on publishing, science, and worldbuilding for writers at WorldBuildingCoach.com. Her short story *The Drake Equation* was a winner of the Writers of the Future contest and appeared in the bestselling anthology "Writers of the Future Vol. 33" in 2017. Her other short stories have appeared in issues 2 and 5 of "Compelling Science Fiction," the "Event Horizon" anthology of short stories eligible for the Campbell Award, and have been translated for the Vietnamese-language fanzine SFVN.

Carolyn Kay

Kaiju in the Ocean

Carolyn Kay is a scientist by day, and an author, dancer, knitter, and herbalist by night. She's attempting to raise two, fine felines with the help of her husband, illustrator Chaz Kemp. (The results are mixed. *Looking at you, Sif.*) She also occasionally channels a fae changeling named Cinder who posts guest blogs on her website. Her debut novella, *Dien-Vek* is available on Amazon. You can catch up on Carolyn's latest shenanigans at CarolynKayAuthor.com, or on Twitter and Instagram @bewitchinghips.

Kimberly Kennedy

Robot Assassin in the Triassic

Kimberly Kennedy, a romance writer, has always been a creative soul, bouncing back and forth between various crafts and arts. The only one she kept bouncing back to was writing. Being an only child meant creating her own worlds, full of characters that were a combination of people she knew and quirky qualities she thought more of us should have. She now lives in Denver, as a real-life romantic heroine, having a blast vacationing, writing, trying out the amazing culinary and beer-centered landscape that is Colorado, loving the mountains, and motoring around in her little, grey, Barbie car convertible.

Jason Kent

Robot Assassin in the Ocean

Jason Kent is an Air Force veteran, Amazon Best Selling author, and military space expert. From launching rockets to great, new sci-fi, he's got you covered! Combating government bureaucracy and military budgeting cycles, he became an expert at systems engineering, designing space systems, and launching billion-dollar rockets. Along the way, Jason nurtured a passion for exploration beyond Earth's atmosphere and yearned to go where no one has gone before! Unfortunately, the U.S. Space Corps has yet to be formed, leading him to the inevitable conclusion the best way to visit the stars was to write about them. Jason is a licensed professional engineer with experience in diverse mission areas such as reconnaissance, engineering, space and launch vehicle operations, space system acquisition, and missile defense. Each of his assignments broadened his experience in real-world space technology and space business ventures. Jason's books include Kindle #1 Best Seller *New Sky: Eyes of the Watcher*, *New Season: Sparrow's Quest*, *Rifter: Traitors at Teteris*, *Colony Zero: Quarantine Protocol*, and *Far Space*.

A.L. Kessler

Imaginary Friend in an Evil Laboratory
Kaiju in an Apocalyptic Wasteland

A.L. Kessler is an urban fantasy and paranormal romance author best known for her Amazon Best-selling *Here Witchy Witchy* series. She lives in beautiful Colorado Springs with her family and handful of animals. She can be bribed to come out of her office with gifts of chocolate and coffee.

Melissa Koons

Melissa Koons (Proofreader & Formatter) has always had a passion for books and creative writing. It may have started with *Berenstain Bears* by Stan and Jan Berenstain, but it didn't take long for authors like Lucy Culliford Babbit, Tolkien, and Robert Jordan to follow. From a young age, she knew she wanted to share her love for stories with the world. She has written and published one novel, multiple short stories, and poetry. She has a BA in English and Secondary Education from the University of Northern Colorado. A former middle and high school English teacher, she now devotes her career to publishing, editing, writing, and tutoring hoping to inspire and help writers everywhere achieve their goals. When she's not working, she's taking care of her two turtles and catching up on the latest comic book franchise.

Aylâ Larsen

Clown in the Triassic

Aylâ is the creative mind and copywriter behind numerous, award-winning and nationally-recognized advertising campaigns for Colorado-based clients. When she's not being clever with words, she can be found discussing great film and television, singing like an angel, and ranting about mayonnaise. Right now, Aylâ is probably wearing a Disney t-shirt and laughing about a pun she heard two days ago. Learn more at AylaWithaHat.com.

Jennifer Ogden

Kaiju in Human Mind

In September 2017, Jennifer Ogden finally listened to the call to write that had followed her around since she was a little girl. She took a leap of faith and quit her soul-sucking nine-to-five job. Now, she enjoys spending her days crafting words into stories. She believes it takes courage to live life, laughter to bring joy, and love to see hope. Check out her blog at SoManyBooks.info.

M.M. Ralph

Clown in an Apocalyptic Wasteland

M. M. Ralph is an author and all-around creative intuitive living in Denver, Colorado. She is grateful to be a part of *Crash Philosophy*, major thanks to Thomas A. Fowler and thanks you for your interest. She invites you to connect with her on social media for more information on upcoming projects.

T.J. Valour

Robot Assassin in an Evil Laboratory

T.J. Valour's invisible, pet dinosaur landed her in the principal's office in second grade and it has been a rollercoaster of adventure ever since. At work she dances with death and has the honor of recording her client's last chapters of life. When not working, TJ is crafting fantastical urban stories from the safety of her desk. TJ lives in the Rocky Mountains with her wonderful spouse and handsome, but thick-headed, doggo.

COMING SOON

CRASH PHILOSOPHY

SECOND COLLISION

2 NEW CHARACTERS & SETTINGS RESULT IN
24 NEW STORY COMBINATIONS FROM 19 AUTHORS

DINOSAUR   PSYCHO KILLER   SPACE   ALTERNATE
                                                    FUTURE

FEATURING STORIES BY

J.A. CAMPBELL	L.J. HACHMEISTER	JENNIFER OGDEN
MIKE CERVANTES	H.L. HUNER	MARIANNE PAGE
HEATHER COWLEY	KIMBERLY KEANE	M.M. RALPH
JASON EVANS	JASON KENT	SARAH BETH SCHRIVER
THOMAS A. FOWLER	MELISSA KOONS	T.J. VALOUR
E. GODHAND	AYLÂ LARSEN	ROB WALKER
	DAVID MUNSON	

CRASHPHILOSOPHY.COM

Made in the USA
San Bernardino, CA
30 June 2019